The Patron Saint of Pregnant Girls

Also by Ursula Hegi

FICTION

Intrusions

Unearned Pleasures and Other Stories

Floating in My Mother's Palm

Stones from the River

Salt Dancers

The Vision of Emma Blau

Hotel of the Saints: Stories

Sacred Time

The Worst Thing I've Done

Children and Fire

NONFICTION

*Tearing the Silence: On Being
German in America*

CHILDREN'S

Trudi & Pia

The
Patron Saint
of Pregnant Girls

Ursula Hegi

FLATIRON
BOOKS
NEW YORK

THE PATRON SAINT OF PREGNANT GIRLS. Copyright © 2020 by Ursula Hegi. All rights reserved. Printed in the United States of America. For information, address Flatiron Books, 120 Broadway, New York, NY 10271.

www.flatironbooks.com

Designed by Donna Sinisgalli Noetzel

The Library of Congress has cataloged the hardcover edition as follows:

Names: Hegi, Ursula, author.
Title: The patron saint of pregnant girls / Ursula Hegi.
Description: First edition. | New York: Flatiron Books, 2020.
Identifiers: LCCN 2019045244 | ISBN 9781250156822 (hardcover) |
    ISBN 9781250156815 (ebook)
Subjects: LCSH: Domestic fiction.
Classification: LCC PS3558.E4185 P38 2020 | DDC 813/.54—dc23
LC record available at https://lccn.loc.gov/2019045244

ISBN 978-1-250-15683-9 (trade paperback)

Our books may be purchased in bulk for promotional, educational, or business use. Please contact your local bookseller or the Macmillan Corporate and Premium Sales Department at 1-800-221-7945, extension 5442, or by email at MacmillanSpecialMarkets@macmillan.com.

First Flatiron Books Paperback Edition: 2021

10 9 8 7 6 5 4 3 2 1

To my grandchildren A and S—
always and forever in my heart

PART ONE

Summer 1878

A Hundred-Year Wave

With each pregnancy Lotte and the toymaker introduce their unborn to the sea, Lotte with her belly taut, Kalle with his hands on her hips as he guides her in to the peak of her belly. Eyes shut with bliss, with reverie, Lotte feels her baby swim, the wall of her body separating it from the Nordsee. First Hannelore. Then Martin. Then Bärbel. During her fourth pregnancy Lotte gets playful and dives into a handstand, surprises herself and the toymaker who laughs aloud, faced with her feet wiggling above the surface of the sea; but as he reaches down to steady her, one hand on her belly, the other on her buttocks, he's the one who needs steadying because Lotte shoots up, spews water at him, clamps her legs around his middle. Tilts herself to him.

When you grow up by the edge of the Nordsee, you respect it, know it like the rise and fall of your breath. It begins when you learn to swim before you can walk, plunge below a wave and dig your tiny fingers into the silt before a wave can scramble you. Hannelore is daring that way, exuberant in the water like her mother, Lotte, while Martin is cautious. Too early to know with Bärbel who's two that August of 1878 when a freak wave heaves itself at Nordstrand. A hundred-year wave, the Old Women say.

Not that Lotte Jansen miscalculated the tides. Vacationers may drown, foolish enough to walk out too far on the wet sand and get cut off by the surge of incoming tide; if locals die by water, it's in a storm or when a fishing boat capsizes.

This hundred-year wave will enter legend, define Nordstrand as much as the people who tell and retell the story, who consider themselves witnesses—not only those who see Lotte and her children dance and play in the tidal shallows on their way home after the Zirkus performance—but others who'll hear about it later and yet speak of it as if they were with Lotte just before all wind ceases and the sky fades from blue to yellow, blotting the sun. In these stories—memories, the Old Women insist—Lotte carries her fourth baby, Wilhelm, on one hip; her daughters wear smocked dresses and Martin his lederhosen as they chase the retreating tide, laughing, running back ashore and out again, until Lotte offers her free hand to link her children to each other. And to her.

"Free hand?" The Old Women will ask.

"How free can a mother's hand be if she has children hanging from it?"

But you refuse to envision your own children ripped from you. Your grandchildren. Aloud, you wonder why God has punished Lotte and Kalle Jansen without mercy. Because they copulated before marriage? But then you'd all be going under with sin.

"Let's put our feet in the water . . ." Lotte sings to her children, ". . . this is the sun's water."

Who of you hasn't let the sun's water lick your ankles, your calves? You know what that's like. You also know what it's like to go under while you play in the Nordsee as children or swim out far as adults; and you give your memories to Lotte Jansen as you describe how the wave slams into her, fills her mouth and her nose, stings her eyes. And in that one moment all you see and recall and imagine fuses, poised to grow and enter legend.

Legends, the Old Women know, are ancient gossip; yet not all gossip leads to legends. By itself gossip won't last, but legends feed on gossip. The Old Women know if you have a hangnail. If your great-great-grandparents cheated on each other. If you burn your soup. If you carry hate in your dreams.

After the freak wave recedes, people fan across the *Watt* to search for the children—nuns and Zirkus people and toymakers and fishermen and shopkeepers and church people and Old Women and farmers and blacksmiths and big-bellied Girls from the St. Margaret Home for Pregnant Girls—a bizarre crowd hoping to outwit death. Some on Zirkus ponies or horses, water sloshing around the hooves. Some in carriages. Most on foot.

"We'll find them," Kalle vows to Lotte who clutches their youngest against her shoulder.

"We taught them to swim . . ."

"Before they could walk."

Heike from the Zirkus runs toward Lotte, white-blond hair flitting around her face, satin skirt flapping high. Heike, just six years younger than Lotte. Body of a woman, mind of a child.

"Wait, Heike," her mother Sabine calls.

But Heike outruns her, in her fist crepe poppies, gaudy and smelling of barn. When she thrusts the poppies at Lotte, Wilhelm squirms for the red that quivers before him till Heike's mother steps into the red. Blots it.

"Oh, Lotte . . ." Gently, Sabine wipes mud from Lotte's face, tucks wet tangles of hair behind her ears. She's been part of Lotte's summers since Lotte was five and visited Sabine's Zirkus wagon and was allowed to hold her new baby, Heike.

"Flowers for Hannelore," Heike cries.

Lotte draws a sharp breath.

Sabine loops her arms around Lotte. Steadies her and the baby. "I can hold him."

Lotte shakes her head. "No."

"I'll do anything for you."

"Where is Hannelore?" Heike stomps her feet.

Lotte used to think how devastating it must be for Sabine to raise such a child. But now—she shivers.

"We don't know," Sabine tells her daughter. "Not yet."

"Not yet," says Heike.

She loves to play with local children wherever the Ludwig Zirkus sets up for a week, especially on Nordstrand where Hannelore is her best friend. Hannelore adores her. Hannelore can sit so still that she's allowed to watch Heike rehearse her cello with the Zirkus orchestra.

"But where is Hannelore?"

Hannelore. And everyone searching for her and Bärbel and Martin, rushing and returning and setting out again, while Lotte stands rooted in prayer and drenched clothes, Wilhelm locked into her arms. Sun drenches the clouds with crimson that leaks through crevices, fighting the gray. When the incoming tide forces the searchers from the *Watt,* they run for their boats. A few stay in the deep, diving. Kalle leaps into the dory of the beekeeper who lunges for the oars, arms silver with pale hairs, like a god who will go beneath the sea to bring back your children.

❧ 2 ❧

Tilli. Eleven Years Old

Tilli. Eleven years old. Cradling her belly with linked palms, she's out on the tidal flats, among church people who usually shun St. Margaret Girls and how they flaunt their bodies. Church people know to postpone rapture because only then will rapture be theirs in heaven, a rapture far superior to what mortals can feel, and it infuriates them that these Girls have indulged in the act that is sacred after the sacrament of matrimony, but a sin before. A few even manage to snag local men. Yet, the search for the Jansen children makes them allies; they have the sun in their eyes and the sun is hot and slants almost like sun in the morning, that angle, except from the opposite direction; and they shout the names of the children.

They shout: "Bärbel!"

They shout: "Martin!"

They shout: "Hannelore!"

All Tilli wants is to lie down. When she awoke with slow cramps at dawn, she didn't tell Sister Franziska. Later, Tilli thinks, I'll tell Sister later. She was determined to go to the Zirkus, gratis, as promised by the Twenty-Four-Hour Man who appeared three days before. True to his title, the Sisters said, he always appeared twenty-four hours ahead of the Ludwig Zirkus to hire roustabouts and negotiate the fee for setting up in the meadow behind the St. Margaret Home. For weeks the Sisters have prayed for this meadow to dry so the wheels of the Zirkus wagons won't sink.

The Twenty-Four-Hour Man prides himself on knowing how to talk with nuns, but they dicker so craftily—*not proper for nuns, not proper at all*—that he's embarrassed for them. He has no idea they're embarrassed for him because he is ugly and kneads his lumpy chin. They get him to raise his offer, but once he agrees, they demand gratis tickets. As usual he feigns indignation, waits them out by silently counting—to ten to fifty to two hundred—but these nuns are virtuosos of silence who'll outlast him if he were to count to a million.

He sighs, dramatically. "Tickets for all Sisters."

"And for all Girls."

"The Ludwig Zirkus cannot afford that."

"It doesn't have to be the Sunday performance."

"Monday then." He stomps off but halts by the door. Winks.

To announce the Ludwig Zirkus, he ties his painted banners around trees and hires a dozen local men, farmers and merchants and toymakers, who've waited at their regular jobs for months, counting on the wages and free tickets for their families, but even more so on the thrill of being roustabouts for one glorious week. Every August Kalle and his childhood friend Köbi whisper about running off with the Zirkus, even this morning while mucking cages and spreading fresh wood shavings.

For new Girls who haven't been to the Ludwig Zirkus, the Sisters rhapsodize how fabulous the parade will be, eclipsing one another. This is when they are most alike—Sisters and Girls—in their *Vorfreude,* joy of anticipating joy.

"—ornate wagons and horses—"

"—with head plumes and acrobats—"

"—dancing dogs with tutus and hats—"

"—ponies prancing in tight circles—"

"—poppies braided into their manes—"

"—a sad and beautiful clown woman—"

"—red shoes and she paints hearts—"

"—on the foreheads of children—"

And it's all true, the Girls say as they follow the parade through the streets with hundreds of spectators, exhilarated to be part of village life that transpires outside the St. Margaret Home and usually excludes them, except for church where they're confined to narrow pews below the pulpit.

Behind the St. Margaret Home the earth is still so soggy that its scent has become one with the air, thickening your breath. The Ludwigs welcome the roustabouts and remind them that working for their Zirkus means dedication. Perfection.

"Some traveling shows rush to put everything together, causing accidents. None of that with us. We expect you to ensure the safety of our audiences."

Enthusiastically, the roustabouts pull ropes and tarps from the supply wagons; wedge lumber scraps under the wheels; unload animal props and provisions; secure a wide plank that slopes from the first wagon to the ground; bridge additional planks between all wagons. Then Silvio Ludwig unlocks the cages. Spectators in their Sunday clothes cheer and applaud as animals emerge from the first wagon, one after the other down that plank where the priest blesses this extravaganza of creatures living harmoniously, he says, without bars. They smell almost like livestock, Tilli thinks, only more exotic. Livestock makes her think of the barn back home and of her brother who won't be able to find her.

·   ·   ·

During the performance Tilli's cramps escalate—*all worth it, the glory of the performers, the magic*—but now her body is turning itself inside out and she cannot allow herself to collapse because it would be selfish to lie on the ground when everyone's shouting and searching for the toymaker's children. Who are drowning or have already drowned. Tilli screams. Pains slam her to her knees and people surge forward; two church women—*faces like Lent*—are right on her; then Heike from the Zirkus and her mother who checks Tilli's pulse. Lotte runs toward the screaming, certain her children have been found—*any moment now Hannelore will stand up, head above the curved backs of the people who bend over Martin and Bärbel to help them*—but Lotte cannot see who's on the ground until she shoves through the crowd to the center where Sabine and two church women help a screaming high-pregnant Girl who should not be on the *Watt. Should not*—

Heike rubs Tilli's belly. "Do you have a baby in there?"

Tilli says her cramps just started, but the women don't believe her. They get her up, carry her to the St. Margaret Home. My cramps just started, Tilli tells Sister Franziska who slips off her amber rosary and hangs it from the key of the medicine cabinet before she examines Tilli in the infirmary, encircled by murals of gold-plated peacocks big as cattle.

"*Kitsch*," Sister Franziska says to Tilli. "This used to be a mansion, commissioned by a bishop half a century ago. With funds he stole from the church. From the diaspora fund. From the collection basket."

Right out in the open the bishop built his mansion, the Old Women wrote to the archdiocese. Taller than the steeple of the church. Such decadence. Marble stairs that curve to the second and third floors. A conservatory with an aviary where peafowl shriek like wounded children. The Old Women celebrate with *Kaffee und Kuchen* when the bishop is banned to a destitute parish near the Polish border—potato fields and ravens. His peacocks stay on Nordstrand, procreate and survive hunters, except for five killed for food. But the haunting echo of their cries makes it impossible to eat them in a stew or a soup, though some people try: after all, they're used to slaughtering chickens and sheep; still, they feel like cannibals and spit out the stringy meat.

For half a century the bishop's mansion stands empty until a hazy day in 1842, the Old Women recall, when leaves drift toward the ground in yellow currents, and a flock of young Sisters arrives from a faraway village by the Rhein. One carries a cage with orange-beaked finches. In the clearing between church and dike floats an apparition, a dwelling more splendid than the Sisters have seen or contemplated: its edges shimmer in the mist, quiver as if it had metamorphosed untold times. A rush of huge wings. For an instant the Sisters believe the mansion is rising. Cries, then, half-human, half-beast. And three shapes heave themselves into the air.

Sister Franziska and Sister Ida cross themselves.

Sister Konstanze tightens her arms around her birdcage.

But Sister Elinor laughs. "Peacocks!"

The peacocks plop on the roof, talons scraping slate, and ogle the Sisters who ascend the front steps, led by the youngest, Sister Hildegunde, thin hands tucked into opposite sleeves. That day the sisters won't unpack porcelain and cutlery and practical items. No, they only open boxes that hold what matters to them: paints and sheet music and books; a flute and a violin; a weaving loom. Soon, big-bellied Girls arrive, most so young that they giggle and run from the Sisters, play hide-and-seek in the chapel.

The Old Women bring gifts: loaves of bread; canned beans and peaches; applesauce. They have been on Nordstrand for centuries, its chroniclers, its conscience, its judges. They witnessed the flood of 1634 tear the island Strand into four islands, one of them Nordstrand. They fled when the most devastating flood of all obliterated Rungholt in 1362. The Old Women remember Rungholt through their own memories and through what was bestowed upon them over centuries; and they know the urge, the beauty to bestow all this upon the next generations. And with that the urge to pass it on.

Rungholt, so near that when the wind breaks off, you may hear the bells in its church towers beneath the surface of the Nordsee where the sunken island lies intact—people and animals and houses and cisterns and windmills—awaiting the next time it will rise in its entirety. Most claim you cannot reach Rungholt, that it's lost forever, and that you, too, will be lost if you set out for Rungholt. Yet, some believe it rises once every spring just long enough to let you enter.

Before the Age of Knowledge

Out on the tidal flats Lotte Jansen kisses the top of Wilhelm's head and beseeches God to tell her what she's done wrong. "Because if there's a reason you took them, my children, took them, there must be something I can do to get them back from you."

But God, he is silent—as silent as the darkening shapes of the boats on the sea; and when the boats return without her children and her husband steps ashore, it's up to her to barter with God.

She draws the cross where she knows Wilhelm's heart to be, kisses his lips and his belly. Whispers, "Forgive me forgive me" against his damp skin.

He coos. Pats her cheeks—

—*oh*—

—and she—

—howling—

—howling and praying and howling and praying, casts him into the sea. "Take him, God, in return for my other three—"

The crowd pitches forward as if one body, but gives way to Kalle who hauls his lastborn from the sea, reclaims his son who smells of salt and of water, of salt and of earth. When he refuses to hand Wilhelm to his wife, people speculate he'll never forgive her. But the Old Women understand the measure of Lotte's sacrifice, understand the courage it takes to offer your child to God, understand they've witnessed the collapse of her faith. They know what that's like. Not everyone finds the path back to God.

The Old Women have seen many misfortunes, learned to survive the most terrible heartbreaks, and sleep with the fear of forgetting the faces of those they lost. They feel ashamed of their gratitude that their grandchildren and great-grandchildren have been spared. To ward off fate and to honor tradition, they draw close and coordinate what each will cook for the Jansen family in the weeks to come.

"Losing one husband to the sea is not as terrible as losing three children."

"Losing one husband and one son to the war is not as terrible as losing three children."

"Losing one daughter to childbirth . . ."

". . . one son to influenza."

Winning land and losing land again. Losing lives.

Losing—

The Nordsee has a great appetite for sacrifice. Today it seized three lives because the people raised the dikes again to hinder the flooding of *Neuland*—new land. In ditches they trapped the sea, isolated it in long solitary fingers until it could no longer gather force but fizzled out its rage, stagnant while sediment accumulated on the *Meeresboden*—sea floor. They consider it their birthright to defend what they've preserved. But the Nordsee remembers. Retaliates. Swells once again. To keep *Hochwasser*—high water—from invading their houses, people fill burlap sacks with sand and heap them outside their doors where they slump like new kittens.

· · ·

After dark and after the islanders scrub off the gray-black sludge that clogs the wheels of their carriages, the priest holds a Mass for the Jansen children. But their parents are not in church. I nudge Heike into a pew, follow her.

"I want to play with Hannelore," she cries.

Parishioners turn. "Ssshhhh . . ."

Sobbing, the priest is sobbing as he clambers up to the gold and black pulpit to recount the freak wave that launched the children into heaven. "Hannelore Jansen six years old—"

"I want to play—"

I press one finger across my daughter's lips.

The priest's chin quivers. "Bärbel Jansen two years old."

"I want to play with Hannelore's baby."

"Tilli's baby?"

"Ssshhhh . . . Ssshhhh . . ."

"Martin Jansen four years old—"

A child is a child till you are dead. You. Not your child. Especially a child who's not safe in the world. Who doesn't understand why she can't take what she likes; why she's forbidden to sit on the laps of strangers. She'll be up half the night, exuberant with ideas of what she wants to do, and as her voice revs up, I can predict the fall when she's motionless in bed or by the window, barely speaking or eating. Once again I straddle the chasm, feet dug into both rims, to keep myself from going down and up with Heike's moods, help her find the way back to herself. *To me.*

"Three children before the age of knowledge," says the priest. "A sign how precious their lives are to God. That's why He sent the immense wave."

Today I've witnessed how quickly you can lose a child, three children, and I'm terrified more than ever. At least Lotte and Kalle have each other. But Heike only has me. Even if I live to be old, I must find a husband for her, a kind husband to keep her from harm. Since she is without fear, I carry it for both of us, her fear and mine. He, too, didn't know fear, Heike's father.

Or remorse. The Sensational Sebastian was a dazzling man with long arms and an easy laugh, a trapeze artist who was convinced he must keep moving to prevent his body from turning to stone.

"And we have proof," says the priest, "that the wave delivered the Jansen children directly to God. Because once the sun set, the clouds grew darker, but not solid, revealing flashes of heaven that streaked the sky crimson and yellow."

What will become of my daughter if I die tomorrow? Or ten years from now? It's inside your fear where a child who's not safe without you will nest, mistaking it for love. Even I mistake it for love. Heike bounces between impulses, between bliss and desolation. *Himmelhoch jauchzend, zu Tode betrübt.* In her bliss, she gets too affectionate. Men sniff around the big tent, rattled when the Ludwigs and I chase them off. I must be with her every moment, but of course she gets away. One already scraped from her womb before she turned fifteen. Blood, so much blood I feared she was dying. Six months later another pregnancy. When the nurse whispered she could fix Heike, I let her. Because I need my strength for my daughter alone. If Heike had a child, she'd forget to feed it. Forget it's there.

"And purple," adds the priest. "Purple the color of remorse, the color of forgiveness. Purple is in the sky often enough with yellow to make it true for today."

Still in their mud-caked clothes, the children's parents sit in their kitchen where the smell of applesauce is thicker than this morning when Lotte boiled apples with water and cinnamon. Too hot to taste, she warned her children who clamored for a spoonful. After we get home from the Zirkus, she promised.

But they didn't come home.

A promise broken.

Wilhelm's mouth tugs at her breast. Dry, she's gone dry. Her body has forgotten how to keep children alive, the same body that used to make plenty of milk, so much that she needed the nursing as much as her babies. If she waits too long, her breasts swell, harden, a pain so urgent that Kalle has to relieve her. He adores her milk. Once, she pulled him into the church, into the empty confessional, and let him. Lighten her. Push himself inside her as they braced against the latticework.

Wilhelm whimpers against her skin, too tired to scream any longer; and Kalle fetches a saucer with sheep's milk, dips a finger into it. When he slides it between his son's gums, Wilhelm bucks, coughs. Again, Kalle tries.

"Applesauce," Lotte says. "Use applesauce."

Sucking cooled applesauce from his finger, the boy. And swallowing. His eyelids flutter.

Lotte props her elbows on the table. The rim of her clavicle rises. And Kalle knows he has to get away to stop himself from admitting he's brought on their children's deaths with his illusions of leaving his family behind and traveling with the Ludwig Zirkus, adventurous and unencumbered. Wanderlust.

If Lotte finds out, she'll send me away. As children they all played Zirkus. Lotte, too. Strung rope between posts and practiced tightrope walking till they toppled. Inspired by Zirkus animals, they taught dancing to their dogs whose herding instincts bewildered them so that they yapped and whimpered, agitating sheep and cattle. And the sheep did not obey when taught to be ponies and gallop in a wide circle. It took just one to kneel, for the others to stumble into one pile. Lotte was part of all that— except for her it has stayed in childhood. It's like that for girls. They grow into the dreams of women, while boys still wait for the Zirkus and adventure, so close in dreams and yet out of reach. Except for now—

From the table he picks up Hannelore's doll that he and Lotte made together: he carved the trunk and limbs, while Lotte crocheted a yellow dress, embroidered the linen face, attached yarn braids.

Talking, Lotte. She's talking about a horrendous bargain. And how it came to her and how she gave shape to it by promising God—

"What?" Kalle asks, startled. "Promising what?"

Her palms prop up her face, stretch all flesh away from her jawbone and cheeks. "The one in my arms for the other three."

"I would." Kalle tries to pull his finger from his lastborn who only sucks harder, all his life-power concentrated in his mouth. "Even for two. I'd trade this one for two. If we could bring two of the others home in return for Wilhelm, I would." *As long as I don't have to choose.*

But what if I must? Hannelore with the gap between her front teeth, tongue probing where her baby teeth used to be? Martin, sturdy and fast, who can fly from good-natured to sullen in a second? Bärbel who gets dirty so quickly, who loves exuberantly, noisily?

The queasy strength of the boy's suck. Always needing more than his share. Kalle would offer him up for just one. If only Lotte had let go of the lastborn instead—*Lotte grips Hannelore's free hand, makes a circle, saves the three. Or saves two, at least two. Even if the girls can't hold on to Martin, Lotte has her fingers around the girls' wrists, yes, tight, so tight they leave marks. When she carries them home, Kalle tends to his daughters' wrists—don't think about Martin don't—smears lanolin on their chafed skin. Sticky and smelly. Extracted from sheep's wool.*

Hannelore rubs it off. Bärbel drops asleep in his arms, instantly heavy.

"Don't make me lose them again," Lotte whispers.

Dreaming of traveling with the Zirkus is not half as terrible as what you did.

But to say those words aloud will devastate her. He waits for the lastborn to exhale, then yanks his finger from the greedy mouth that's already snapping for more.

4

Invisible

The couple so eager to adopt Tilli's baby rush to the St. Margaret Home but must wait outside the infirmary.

"A very hard labor," Sister Franziska whispers, "because Tilli is still a child herself."

Herr Lämmle groans. "And if she can't?"

"*Kaiserschnitt.*"

"Cut her open?" Frau Lämmle cries.

"It may not be necessary."

"I have to see Tilli," says Frau Lämmle.

Sister Franziska hesitates.

"I won't do anything to upset her," Frau Lämmle promises, and already she's at the door, tiptoes in, crying without a sound.

Sister Franziska follows. "But if I ask, you must leave right away."

Tilli is screaming, throwing herself from side to side.

"Does she have to suffer like this?" asks Frau Lämmle.

Tilli waves her close. "What if it's born without a face?"

"It'll have a beautiful face."

"What if it's born with a harelip?"

"Oh, Tilli—" Sweaty curls stick to Frau Lämmle's temple. "My husband and I will love our baby, no matter what."

The Lämmles used to visit the St. Margaret Home, holding and rocking babies. Wrapping them and unwrapping them. Practicing so they'd be competent once they found the right child. Yet always leaving without one. Until they met Tilli. They're old enough to be her parents, at least thirty, apricot freckles and hair so much like Tilli's that she can picture the child they'd make if they could.

"Yours is one of the lucky babies," they say to Tilli.

"Already chosen before birth because you have good posture."

"And good sense."

It matters to Tilli how much the Lämmles want her baby—no matter how hideous. "What if it's born . . . with just one arm?" she asks Frau Lämmle.

"We already love—"

"I want it to be a boy. I'll name him Alfred. You can change the name. But not right away. Where will you take him?"

"Oh . . . three hours on the train from here. That's why we arrived early. To be here when our baby is born."

"But where do you live?"

"Hush now . . . hush . . ." murmurs Sister Franziska.

"South," says Frau Lämmle.

Tilli wheezes.

"And a bit to the west. I'm not supposed to tell you."

Then the pain again—*a spooked horse into white-blinding ruckus that slams you to the ground*—

"I wish I could suffer this pain for you," Frau Lämmle cries.

That's when Tilli knows the woman is *crazy or lying because no one sane chooses*—

—*to ride your pain that rears up like a spooked horse and lets you crawl into your exhaustion before it rears up with you again and again till a rag on your nose your mouth—nasty nasty—spins you into disgust and fury spins you spins and—*

—in that twilight of retching and spinning one fist one empty fist empty clenches your insides with each heave and the taste as nasty as the smell retching from the empty—

All St. Margaret Girls have been forewarned not to see their newborns, but when Tilli pummels her breasts and howls till she can't breathe, Sister Franziska brings a red-fisted baby wrapped in white—

—when did that happen? when—

"If you promise to calm yourself, I'll let you hold her."

Her— As if the two of us were not enough, Alfred, there has to be a third. A girl—

"You are very brave, Tilli." Sister Franziska wishes she could do so much more for her Girls. First teach them to prevent pregnancy. And then not wound them again by taking their babies away. Still, it would be worse for a baby to be raised by such a young mother. Sister Franziska understands about succumbing to the urgency of her body—to passion and to shame; understands about being banned from her newborn. Forty-one years since—

Tilli gulps and sniffles and lifts her arms to her baby. *To the sweet weight.* Oh— But the generations are all mixed up. *How can my own girl look like the Lämmles?* We will raise your child with love, they've promised. But Tilli knows once she lets go, they'll take her own girl and not return. *If only my baby had a clubfoot. A clubfoot and a harelip! Then the Lämmles won't want her.*

Tilli holds on to her own girl who wiggles her tiny body against her. Roots about. Bumps one cheek into Tilli's collarbone. Tilli pulls her lower, against her breast; but Sister cups the baby's head, gently, guides the rooting mouth away from Tilli.

Girls who give away their babies for adoption right after birth don't get to nurse. Still, their breasts make milk that distends them. Some get blocked milk ducts. Sister Franziska is meticulous when she binds their breasts. Some homes won't bind unmarried Girls, let them suffer for their sins. Like the home in Bonn forty-one years ago. Sister has never spoken of her son, not even in confession; yet, she holds him with every newborn who passes through her hands—*that swirl of hair on the back of his neck, that tiny pucker of lips, eyes ancient and wise imprinting her on his memory*—only to release him anew, with grace. This path toward grace exhilarates Sister Franziska with depths of faith she couldn't have imagined in her prayers when he was taken from her.

She wishes she could imprint this grace on Tilli, temper her wild grief. "Tilli?" She caresses the Girl's shoulder.

But Tilli hides her face against her newborn. *Hide her hide her—*

"Do you believe everything happens according to God's design?"

Hide her where? Tilli grunts.

"If you can believe in God's design for you and your child—"

A flutter of breath against Tilli's throat and her own girl has a face and flawless feet and no clubfoot. Tilli tugs the bedding into a cocoon with space for her own girl to hide and breathe, locks her arms around the cocoon. *You must grip what you cannot bear to lose.*

"—then no one can shame you for having this child." *Shame. The poison of shame.* Sister Franziska shivers and is fourteen again, *still fourteen, and must confess, run away before her parents notice. At the first church beyond her village she stops, anxious to have it over with—confession followed by absolution. That's how it's been every time since she was seven and taught to examine her soul for sins, to be ashamed and ask God's forgiveness. After her first confession: lightness*

where the burden of the sin was before. I could be so fromm. *Pious.*
It's that very lightness she yearns for as she waits on the stone steps for a
priest who'd rather die than reveal her sin. It's like that for every priest,
part of his vows. Some of the martyrs were priests—beheaded or stran-
gled or burned or drowned—because they wouldn't betray a confession.

As Sister strokes Tilli's shoulder, Tilli imagines rising in
the smell of her own girl who is without sin, rising from this
bed—*oh, I can be cunning, can run so fast*—and escaping. She must
not fall asleep. Must stay watchful until she's alone with her
own girl—*oh, we can be cunning, can run so fast*—

—awake, she's awake—*still? again?*—and the infirmary is dark
and keening and she's terrified of the keening and of the empty
where her own girl—

is?—

was?—

how did they get you away from me?—

"Ssshhhh . . . Ssshhhh . . ." Veronika climbs across Tilli,
spoons her.

Tilli keens and the keening *funnels from her baby to her brother*
always curled around one another in the womb in the wicker cradle in
the first bed in the hayloft curled and nothing changes as they inhabit
one another and they never expect it to end and Veronika scoots
her bony knees into the backs of Tilli's knees, rubs the sides of
Tilli's belly while Tilli keens.

Keens.

5

This Odd and Sweet Fusion

Tilli. Breasts swollen, hot with milk her own girl will never drink because the new parents have left with her. To ease the swelling Sister Franziska packs cold, dry cabbage leaves around Tilli's breasts where her chest, just last Christmas, was as flat as her twin brother's when she wrestled him in the hayloft. They've wrestled since before they could walk, in their cradle, their bed, poking and pinching each other, more freckles than white skin all over their bodies, the comfort and familiar shape soothing.

Older by forty-one minutes, Tilli is the stronger twin.

That's what their father says. He likes to tap-tap their noses with his own. "Listen to your sister, Alfred."

Their mother says, "You are the oldest, Tilli. You must look out for him."

Sister Franziska leads Tilli to the house of the toymaker. The instant they enter, the cries of a baby make Tilli's breasts leak. *Like wetting myself, only in the wrong place.*

In the kitchen the priest and toymaker wait. Upstairs the toymaker's wife sits on the bed, clutching a big, furious baby who's straining away from her. Sister catches the baby, swirls him around and toward Tilli who hides the front of her blouse with both hands. Sister asks Tilli to open her arms for the baby. But when she tries to reach across him to unbutton the blouse, Tilli holds the baby like a shield. *Wet and hot on the insides of her thighs dripping from the hollow wet and hot and open* and the baby shrieks and Tilli squeezes her thighs together to keep from spilling herself on the floorboards and the amber beads of Sister's rosary suck the light from the window as she peels back the cabbage leaves. *Slippery—*

As a child, Tilli played with chunks of amber she and her twin gathered along the Baltic Sea. You can tell amber from other stones: it makes sparks when you rub it against your clothes, and it makes the hairs on your arms stand up. At home, they line up their treasures on the windowsills with amber their mother collected as a child, the biggest a quarter-pound. Together, they study each find, fascinated by tiny animals trapped in golden resin from pine trees—a beetle or a worm or a spider still in its web—so lifelike that any moment they may crawl again.

"Relics," Alfred says.

Their mother wears her favorite amber on a ribbon around her neck. To keep it shiny, her mother polishes it with her spit. One edge chipped after it was smoothed by the sea, but inside the green moth levitates, unharmed.

"Insects," she teaches her twins, "are lured by the smell of resin that will trap them, preserve them for millions of years. Since amber is heavier than water, it drifts along the floor of the seas with the currents until a high tide throws it ashore."

In the Stone Age, Tilli and Alfred learn, humans used amber for trade and for ornaments. And for healing. Worn in a pouch near your pain, amber cures toothaches and bellyaches. If you rub *Bernstein* across a snakebite, it nullifies the poison; and if you lay amber on the collarbone of a pregnant woman, she'll confess her secret the moment she wakes up.

.   .   .

"Here now here . . ." Sister tugs at Tilli's nipple.

Tilli flinches.

"For the baby." Sister tugs Tilli's nipple into the baby's mouth.

Thin and sharp and fast like an arrow shot from inside tracking the trajectory of need.

Then a tingling, a stinging as her milk trickles to him, sticky and yellow.

"*Vormilch*," Sister Franziska says. "He won't get much from you this first time. Just a few drops."

Vormilch. Milk that comes before milk. Other Girls had *Vormilch* before Sister Franziska bound their breasts and brewed sage tea. Tilli stifles a sob of release when the baby sucks right away and his shrieks dwindle to sniffles at her nipple that fits him and unfurls his belly. He fills her arms, four times as heavy as her own girl.

She sees her mother lifting the ribbon with her amber moth amulet to Tilli's neck. Saying, "Let me see how this looks on you." But her mother's hands tremble, and Tilli instinctively steps from the circle of ribbon—*why? why then?*—before the amulet can graze her skin. When it slips from the ribbon to the floor, Tilli's mother laughs uneasily, such dread in her eyes, recognizing what Tilli can't begin to understand though she lives on a farm.

From then on wrestling becomes a secret. Still, twice they get caught. Thrashed with the carpet beater. Locked into separate places: cellar and stable.

The morning their father saddles two horses and rides off with Alfred to board him with a farmer two hours away—Work him hard, he demands—their mother takes Tilli to the midwife's house.

In the kitchen she makes Tilli lie on the table and presses one ear against her belly. "Pull her legs apart."

"She can't be pregnant," cries Tilli's mother.

"Wider."

"She's only eleven."

"I had another eleven-year-old," the midwife whispers. "Barely survived. The baby didn't."

Her mother's hand on Tilli's belly. *A fish leaping oh—*

Sister Franziska straightens the mother's legs on the bed. Lowers her head to the pillow. But the mother spins her face toward Tilli. Streaks of silt on her neck and arms. Eyes like cracked glass. "You are a child—"

"She's the only one with milk." Sister Franziska kneels and brings her arms around the mother's shoulders. "Lie down now."

"Don't you have someone older?"

"Veronika. But her milk has almost dried up. I won't make her start over again."

"How old?"

"Sixteen."

"No, no—this child."

"Eleven."

"This is so very wrong."

Tilli kisses the little boy. Too late, the Sisters said. Except now Tilli suspects why they haven't let her nurse her own girl— because of this . . . *this odd and sweet fusion of a baby's mouth with your nipple that sets your body alight, stuns you with foreknowledge— more potent than memory—that he'll be the last child to ever drink from you.*

Think how much stronger this would be with my own.

Too late—

Think of all the children who are never chosen.

.   .   .

"We can tell people the child is mine," her mother whispered. "Raise it as ours—"

"You don't want that," her father whispered.

"Some women raise—"

"If it came from anyone other than Alfred."

"It's family."

"Too much so. What if it has a clubfoot? A harelip? Water on the brain—"

Tilli's mother covers her eyes.

And Tilli becomes invisible. So invisible her parents no longer bother to whisper.

"And what if we raised it—what then? She'll have more bastards . . . maybe one without a face."

Without a face? Tilli can't breathe.

"We never saw that one," says her mother.

"Others saw. And those parents are just cousins. Brother and sister is worse."

"A sin."

Once they name it, sin takes root. Spreads. Blends their voices.

"The worst of all sins."

"They must have known."

"They've seen dogs hump. Horses."

"Held a heifer ready to be mounted."

"Those two cannot stay away from each other."

"It's rather that she won't stay away."

"We don't know that for sure."

"If we send her away he'll take his seed elsewhere."

Sister shifts the baby to Tilli's other breast.

"How old?" Tilli whispers.

"Eight months."

Eight months.

Two hundred forty days.

Two hundred forty times as old as my own girl.

Tilli misses her brother. Misses the habit of knowing he's close by. He doesn't have that either, knowing she's close by. Itching in her palms circles her fingers, circles her palms to the backs of her hands as it does after she eats chicken, even just a few shreds in the soup last night. The baby's pudgy hands pat her breasts.

"I'll pray with you, Frau Jansen." Sister Franziska nudges her rosary at the toymaker's wife who twists her fingers into a knot that won't let the rosary in. Tilli wants to snatch it, hide it, especially when Sister drapes it around the mother's wrists.

I'll steal the rosary, Tilli promises the mother silently. I will.

Downstairs the voices of the priest and the toymaker. The toymaker's voice listless, not exuberant like yesterday at the Zirkus when Tilli saw him with his arm around his wife. *A pretty man. Dangerous to marry a man prettier than you. Every girl knows that.* But the toymaker's wife felt pretty. Tilli could tell by the way she stood so close to her husband with this baby they made together balanced on her hip. For everyone to see. Two girls and a boy tug at them; the girls dark-haired like their father, the boy fair like his mother and baby brother. When the parents smile at each other, Tilli wishes they were hers. Parents like that follow their children to the concession stand, where the father buys little sticks with honeyed nuts for the three oldest, tickling beneath their chins to make them giggle. Parents like that keep their children close by.

"A birthing clinic," Tilli's mother said. "For girls like you."

Her father said, "You leave tomorrow. On the train."

"When can I come home?"

Tilli's mother won't look at her. Her face is gray.

"Two trains and a ferry," says her father.

"He'll travel with you," says her mother.

Dawn. And her mother with her arms down her sides. Stiff arms. Arms too heavy to lift when Tilli embraces her.

"*Mutti*—" she screams. "*Mutti*—"

Her mother motions to the food she's packed.

Hanover to Hamburg: Her father sits across from Tilli, one leg stretched across the aisle so she can't run away.

Hamburg to Husum: His eyes are half-closed, and it comes to her that he's ashamed of her.

Husum to Nordstrand: He won't speak to her until he walks her onto the ferry. "I want to be clear about this. You cannot come home."

"Never?"

"You must never contact us."

"But I'll give it away, the baby. I'll—"

"We cannot trust you with your brother."

"No one needs to know—"

"Nuns will pick you up on the other side." He strides off the ferry, holds up both palms to stop her.

On the dock he waits till the ferry is out too far for her to swim back without drowning.

Nothing out there. Nothing outside my body that is mine. And with that Tilli's insides clench around the baby. *It's all I have.*

Her first night in the long dormitory of the St. Margaret Home the moon keeps her awake; she cries without sound, pretends to sleep while other Girls practice dance steps in their long nightgowns. But they won't let her pretend. Tug her from her bed and into their circle, warn that dancing can get you big. Dancing with men, that is. Two have taken lessons at a *Tanzschule*—dance school—and show Tilli how to waltz and polka. They don't know that the Sisters can hear them dance and are glad for that brief joy. None of the Girls are from Nordstrand. To take a pregnant daughter to a home nearby invites gossip, shame for generations to come. Instead, a daughter is sent away—as far as a family can afford—to shed all evidence of her sin and return home if her parents let her as if nothing happened during this long interruption of her life.

In class the Girls throw blackboard erasers at each other till puffs of chalk swirl and settle on Sisters' habits; but their disobedience stirs Tilli, inspires her. She helps Veronika stitch the ends of sleeves shut and giggles when other Girls' arms get stuck. Lies are not lies, Veronika says, if they have to do with pranks. Then they don't need to be confessed.

6

Some Join the Zirkus When There's Nothing Left

Two days after the wave, Kalle Jansen approaches the Ludwigs about employment.

"Any woodwork. New or repairs."

"The wagon panels," says Silvio Ludwig.

"*Ja,*" his father says, "but—"

"Sick animals . . . I can make them well."

"—but your wife needs you."

"Not anymore."

Some join the Zirkus when there's nothing left, and the toymaker's reasons they understand because they, too, searched for his children and have seen him and Lotte comb the edge of the sea, heading in opposite directions.

"I'm good with sick animals," he says quietly.

Silvio Ludwig lays both hands on Kalle's shoulders. "We know you're a skilled worker."

"Skilled and strong," Herr Ludwig agrees. "If you still want to work for us next year, you can."

But the following day the toymaker is back, and the Ludwigs can see he's determined to get away from Nordstrand.

"If not with us, then with another Zirkus."

"We can't afford to miss out."

They shake hands with him, Herr Ludwig squeezing hard to prove his strength because he is weakening. Some nights he startles himself awake, terrified he'll cry if he closes his eyes. But when he must cry, he does so quietly, afraid of waking his son. Most of all, Herr Ludwig is afraid of being afraid.

Friday morning Kalle wraps his carving tools into layers of flannel. In the kitchen Lotte sews an antler button back on Martin's cardigan. She's been like that for days: washing and mending the clothes of their children.

"I can't stay," he whispers.

"When will you be back?"

"I— I don't know."

She yanks the needle through a hole in the button, through the knitting, yanks the needle up through the other hole, across the antler button, down into the first hole. It's dim in the kitchen where the windows face the slope of the dike.

"The Ludwigs hired me to travel with them."

She slips off her thimble. Bites off the thread.

He winces. "Bad for your teeth. You know that it can do more damage than cracking a walnut."

She jabs the needle into the pincushion. "Coward." Her voice is eerily calm.

But he feels her screaming inside and wishes she would scream at him, strike and kick him though they've never inflicted pain on each other. "It may be easier for you if I'm gone."

"Easier for me? Don't you lie to me."

"I'm not lying."

She folds Martin's cardigan. Flattens the wool with her fingertips. Unfolds the cardigan.

Kalle needs to get away from her. But won't it be rude to turn his back?

"It's a lie to say you're doing this for me. You coward."

He takes one long step backward and it's like trying to reach ground from the third rung of a ladder. Another step. And another. Until he feels the door behind him.

"Be gone then," she whispers.

Outside the farmhouse, his dogs lie curled around each other, twitching in their sleep. He gages the mood of the Nordsee: chalky like laundry water; sky steel-gray. Mist swishes across the flats, a thousand tiny feet, curves up the dike making him feel he's walking on unsteady land that can betray him.

From that mist a black sail emerges, coasts along the crest of the dike: Sister Elinor on the convent bicycle. Chasing after her is *Verrückter Hund*. Crazy Dog. That's what the Sisters yell after him with much affection, "*Verrückter Hund!*" Long legs on a short frame. Fur that matches the Sisters' habits and wimple: black except for white on the throat and forehead.

Sister Elinor is the oldest of the Sisters, but her body is the most agile. She relishes the strength in her thighs, the exquisite pressure of the seat.

When she waves to the toymaker, the bicycle wobbles, and he drops his bundle, sprints up the dike. *Wolf-like with his powerful legs and ice-blue eyes. Like the eyes of the Alaskan wolf on her holy card of the Alaskan saint who journeyed up and down the biggest river in Alaska—the name, what is the name of that river?* The toymaker grips Sister's bicycle, one hand on the frame, one against the back of the saddle, braces her with his body. Heat bolts from her toes through her knees and up, barely contained by the folds of her habit, a heat that makes her hem ripple. *If people knew what bliss nuns can feel, they'd find us less mystifying.*

"Would you like to rest, Sister?"

She remembers the name of the river. "Yukon."

"Yukon?" He looks a bit *gewöhnlich*—common—with his fleshy lips and beard stubble.

"Your children inhabit my prayers."

He stares at the ground. Tries to swallow. "Thank you, Sister."

"I used to be a ballerina. As a girl. As a young woman." She tries to stop talking but her voice gets faster. "I danced on four different stages. I'm sorry, I don't mean to be prideful, but I was adored, admired. I was born New Year's Eve of the past century. Seventeen ninety-nine. If only it had been four hours later, during the first hours of the new century . . ."

The toymaker raises his black eyebrows, one unbroken line.

"I have been staring at you," she says. "I must get home."

"Would you like me to walk with you?"

That damn heat throughout her body again. "Oh no." Sister Elinor climbs on the bicycle and pedals away from him, past the thatched roof of the beekeeper, past three other farms, past the church, and the Zirkus wagons in the meadow of the St. Margaret Home, pedals hard, reminding herself to pray. Pray for the toymaker's wife. Pray for the big-bellied Girls. Pray for those who believe they can tame the sea. *Such hubris.* They only provoke retribution; must relinquish more than they seized. Not only with the sea but with all that makes them grasp for more.

Including lust.

Including God.

Past the sheep and the stench of sheep Sister Elinor pedals. Fur and grass and shit—something satisfying about that smell. Two old sheep kneel on their bent front legs, muzzles to the earth, ripping and chewing and worshipping while the Holy Spirit breathes into all that exists. You don't see the Spirit, only His handiwork: these lines of trees bent forever to one side; these sheep on their knees; these geese flying low above the Nordsee.

.   .   .

The toymaker arrives while we're packing to leave Nordstrand. Smudges of gray beneath his eyes. Right away he helps load and secure our wagons—we don't have to tell him. He notices what needs to be done.

When he rips the front of his shirt, I offer to mend it for him.

"No, thank you." He smells of new wood and new sweat.

I can tell he's accustomed to being settled because he carries displacement in the slope of his shoulders. "I repair clothes for everyone here." In my wagon I slip a needle from my pincushion. Lightly, I touch his shirt. *Heat through my fingertips.*

"My wife would be embarrassed . . . to send me off like that."

"Did she have a choice?"

He blinks, startled.

I cut the thread—

"Good," he says. "My wife bites the thread. I worry she'll ruin her teeth."

"How considerate you are." I push the thread through the eye of the needle.

"Bees." He tilts his head. "In your walls. I hear bees in your walls."

"We don't have bees."

I could tell him that bees have chosen to build their hive in the ceiling of our Annunciation wagon, but I don't. I don't want to. Heike adores our bees. Too respectful to sting us, they prove their gratitude with honey that trickles from above so we can set out bowls and feast on the freshest honey without getting out of bed. Our skin has turned golden as honey, and our bodies move like silk to their humming. My daughter and I grow light-headed at the scent of honey, swoon. It was good until a month ago when the balance of bees and humans shifted: we'd awaken with honey in our hair, honey on our sheets, and when we'd arise, our feet would stick to the stenciled floor.

"Should I take off my shirt?" Kalle blushes.

"All you need to do is stand still." My needle pricks his skin.

A sharp breath. He doesn't complain.

I don't say I'm sorry. Because I'm not.

"My neighbor is a beekeeper."

"I know. He was just a boy when I first met Lotte."

"She trades him marmalade for honey. Our children don't get ill because we eat honey that comes from blossoms in our neighborhood."

Our children. He has forgotten, I think. For one merciful moment he has forgotten the freak wave, the horses' strong-muscled movements. But I'm forever running across the flats to search for his children while bellies of clouds grow weighty and heavens turn crimson laden with gray. One woman says the colors in the sky are a sign the children are alive. Or proof of their deaths, another says. Red sky at night sailor's delight, a man says and then cries because there's nothing delightful about this sky.

"But you—were there." Tears in Kalle's eyes.

I nod.

"My children—"

"We all searched, you and the beekeeper by boat."

He picks up the satin bodice I've pinned for Luzia The Clown. Sniffs it. "Honey—even here."

"Careful with the pins."

"Sticky." He taps his index finger against his thumb. "When we get to Nordstrand I'll ask the beekeeper to take your bees away."

"We don't have bees." I prick him again. Because I'm furious how easy it is for men like him and The Sensational Sebastian to run away from their women and children, afraid they'll turn to stone if they stay too long.

Lotte closes her shutters against the rumble of the Zirkus wagons. Within an hour, neighbors enter her house to comfort her with food and commiseration.

"Your husband will be back," they say, voices prim with dis-
approval.

"He and you have such deep love—"

"Bottomless love, I mean. Oh—"

Flustered, they're flustered. Agree that Kalle is devoted
to her.

"He is devoted to you, Lotte."

But he ran away—

"He will be back."

Lotte holds herself tall—drawing on rage and guilt—until
Sister Elinor and Sister Ida pull up in the carriage to take her and
Wilhelm to the St. Margaret Home. When they lead her into a
chamber on the second floor where the Sisters live, Lotte col-
lapses on the narrow bed.

"Wilhelm—" she cries.

"We have him in the Little Nursery with the other children
and the Girl who nurses him."

"Just for now. Until you are strong again," says Sister Elinor.

Lotte sleeps. For twelve hours she sleeps. Is roused by Sister
Ida who feeds her soup. Sleeps again.

The St. Margaret Girls adore Wilhelm, and he adores them
right back, most of all Tilli whose smile glows when she carries him or nurses him or washes his hands cupped within hers.
Wilhelm. Who became hers when her own girl was taken from
her. *Destined. Seamless. Wilhelm.* Sometimes she locks her eyes
with him, wills him to always remember her. Always. Even if
she starts out sad, he takes her into bliss. Sometimes, alone in
the dormitory, that bliss gets to be so much that she's afire and
must press her bare breasts against the window, let the cold glass
mirror her to herself, and she is glorious.

Sister Franziska says, "Two other Girls have milk now."

Tilli bounces Wilhelm on her hip.

Sister Franziska says, "Any time the nursing gets too much for you, I'll ask—"

"It's not— It's not too much."

"—the other Girls."

"Wilhelm won't drink from anyone else."

"That's a good reason to try."

Tilli says no. "Please no," she says.

Wilhelm's eyes move from her to Sister Franziska and back. His lower lip quivers as if he understood every word.

Still, Sister Franziska arranges for two other Girls to nurse Wilhelm, and he fights the unfamiliar smells and breasts. Tilli feels vindicated when Sister Franziska returns him to her. He nuzzles his face into the dip between Tilli's neck and shoulder, but she's careful not to show how much she loves him because Sister will pry him off, gently, and send Tilli to help with bigger children, the four- and five-year-olds.

7

For Medicinal Reasons Only

The Old Women share meals and medical advice but compete with one another to become the Oldest Person. Knee-bends and toe-touches and jumping jacks. Two can still do a hand-stand and one practices ancient Chinese eye exercises she got from a visiting missionary for a donation.

They didn't become Old Women during the same decade or century: it's rather that their circle replenishes itself as girls become women and women become Old Women who pass through lives, generations, floods.

They drown in great floods.

They survive great floods.

They birth fifteen children.

They are barren.

They steal a neighbor's husband.

They help neighbors who are poor.

They are impatient with those who believe they can ward off *Hochwasser* with gifts: paintings of powerful waves with ti-ger claws; porcelain bowls decorated with roses floating on a glass sea; carvings of shipwrecks on the backs of whales. *Kitsch*. When there is so much you can do instead: dry out the *Neuland;*

separate it from the sea with dikes that you stabilize by planting grass; herd your sheep to graze and fertilize the earth; dig long ditches into land that lies below sea level and must be protected; build windmills to pump seawater from those ditches.

The Old Women know how to relieve a hacking cough and reduce the swelling in your ankles and cure that dryness deep inside your down-there. They find out from Frau Bauer who cures her dryness when she asks the nurse, Sister Konstanze, for advice.

In the infirmary, Sister shows her how to release her own wetness. "You rub this little pearl-sized bump." She guides Frau Bauer's hand. "Right here."

Joy like a hiccup, then. And Frau Bauer blushes high-red.

"For medicinal reasons only," warns Sister Konstanze.

"But then Sister winked at me," Frau Bauer reports to the Old Women, "and said I must be vigilant . . . not take too much pleasure."

"At what moment will this rubbing turn into sin?"

"I trust Sister."

"Oh, I'm not surprised."

"She knows about women."

"She knows about medicinal issues."

"And she has practically given us permission to attend to our health."

"Oh, you!"

"Our own health . . . take it in hand." Maria laughs and covers her jaw.

But not enough to hide the new bruise. Custom is: You avert your eyes. Pretend not to see. Avoid questions when someone is injured or distressed. Prop up dignity with your silence. But as you get older, you're no longer afraid to ask.

"What happened to you, Maria?"

"You know you can come to my house—"

"—any time of night or day."

Two Old Women stroke her hands, whisper to her.

"He is a good *Doktor*," Maria says.

The Old Women nod. "True."

"He respects his patients."

"But he harms you."

Silence, then, until Maria laughs. "What did I do all those years without Sister Konstanze's permission?"

The others are quick to fill in. Normality.

"I thought I invented that little pearl when I was a girl."

"You did."

"We all did."

"I didn't."

"Stop it, or I'm going to wet myself."

Laughing hard. Teasing.

"Who gets to say what's too much pleasure?"

"Sister did not say that we must not take pleasure."

"Like absolution . . . only in advance."

"You all knew about the little bump?"

"I didn't," says Frau Lindmann.

"Ha!"

"Really now?"

No one believes Frau Lindmann anymore. She's been lying about her age, adding years—five or seven—so she'll earn the honor of becoming The Oldest Person of Nordstrand. Whenever the Old Women press to see her birth certificate, Frau Lindmann claims she lost it when she immigrated as a child from Jutland with her parents and grandparents.

"People from Jutland are rugged."

"It's the cold that hardens their bones."

"People from Jutland should not be counted."

By then Frau Lindmann is shunned even more than as a child when she immigrated in dirty embroidered boots.

. . .

Every summer solstice, Nordstrand honors its Oldest Person with a *Fackelparade*—parade of lanterns. Church bells echo in recognition of the one who has succeeded in living the longest. First communion children braid a crown from *Kornblümchen und Klee*—cornflowers and clover, fasten it to the hair of the Oldest Person or, if no hair is left, to the top of the head with a chin strap. Only four men have earned this honor during the past century. There almost was a fifth, but when he went out in his fishing boat and was lost in 1876 the day before the *Fackelparade,* the next Oldest Person stepped forward in an embroidered silk dress no one had seen on her before. A dress like that would take weeks to sew and embroider.

How convenient, people gossiped.

How convenient that her rival vanished in the Nordsee.

To offset their unease, people joked, speculated.

"Did he bend over too far to haul in his catch?"

"Was she in the boat with him?"

"Was he helped to a stumble?"

Dangerous, they agreed, to be a very old man on Nordstrand.

Tradition has it that the Oldest Person teaches a class in *Heimatkunde*—local history, of value to the children, but also to the old because it keeps them alert and spry to consider their favorite topic and assemble details. Generations have learned from Oldest Persons about history and nature and events of Nordstrand. Some lessons teeter between fabrications and facts, more enchanting than what teachers are allowed to teach.

Oh, to be crowned, to be celebrated—a recognition that validates your life, your endurance—

PART TWO

1842–1845

8

Sisters and Girls Thrive
in the Salt-Drenched Air

Sisters and Girls thrive in the salt-drenched air. At dawn they waken to the screams of peafowl scratching in the yard; and they convene in the chapel. A few Sisters become more devout and crave the structure of religion to validate that they haven't taken a wrong turn. In the chapel one Sister will lead, recite a prayer, while the voices of the others collect in the responsorial and offer intercessions for the Girls, especially those who dive from their beds frog-style and land on their bellies to shake out the baby.

"We understand your wish to be free of all this again," they tell the Girls.

"We can also understand God's wish for your child to come into the world."

"They don't act like real nuns," the Girls whisper to each other.

"They don't even punish us."

"Maybe they're not real nuns."

The Sisters educate all Girls, not only those younger than four-teen and still of school age. Each Sister teaches the art form she's passionate about, plus one scholarly subject: Sister Konstanze tapestry and biology; Sister Hildegunde painting and mathe-matics; Sister Ida theater and physics; Sister Elinor music and history; Sister Franziska poetry and health.

Of course, there is prayer, too. Along with poetry. And weaving. And ballet taught by Sister Elinor. So what if the Pregnant Girls look clumsy while dancing? Their laughter, even if it comes from embarrassment, sets something free in them—humming and light—that distracts them from their dread of childbirth. In their hometowns, many graves have headstones with the names of dead mothers and their dead babies, and the Girls know death may chase them to the St. Margaret Home. Even if they cannot imagine the dying. Even if some are con-fused about how babies get inside you and how they will get out. But they've been to funerals of Girls who split open when their babies got out of them.

Nights, when they're frightened of the dark, the Girls huddle and dance and wait for dawn when they'll help the Sisters laun-der and iron piles of musty damask sheets and tablecloths; scrub through layers of scum on walls and floors; peel moss from the wide stone steps; prune the dense growth between mansion and dike; hold still while Sister Konstanze cleans their blisters and cuts, slathering them with lanolin salve extracted from sheep's wool.

Mesmerized by the finch couple, the Girls take turns spread-ing a frayed altar cloth across the cage so the birds will sleep. Afterward, Sister Konstanze steps outside to offer prayers of gratitude beneath the stars. She has done all the asking she'll ever need to do: God has granted her the one she loves, and their lives are suffused with His blessing. At dawn she's the first to rise. Without waking Sister Ida, she slips from their cell and walks down the stairs to visit her finches, lifts the altar cloth.

Orange beaks poke from the grass cocoon she has woven for them.

Once a week all Sisters meet to discuss the Girls' health and achievements and fears. Together, they figure out how to help the Girls, encourage them to become friends, to have confidantes their age, especially if they're cast out by their families. They know what the people of Nordstrand say about them: that they don't act like real nuns, that they float in a floaty world with art as their God; that they are dreamers.

"They say we're too generous with the Girls."

"And that we are not strict enough."

"Oh, but we are strict. About kindness."

"If one can talk about kindness that way, yes."

"Strict about separating Pregnant Girls from Birthing Girls."

"Because it would terrify them. For good reason."

"Dangerous, to give birth."

"Even more so for the youngest Girls whose bodies are narrow."

"And tight."

The Sisters know that one of five Girls will die from complications during birth or from childbed fever, a deceptive killer that lets them recover for a day or two before claiming them. Infants die so frequently—one of three—that some mothers won't name them before they leave them behind at the St. Margaret Home. Many families are superstitious about naming and wait till their children's first birthdays. Until then, they believe, they've given birth to a little death that may solidify into life and celebration. Only then.

The Girl who traveled the greatest distance is from Burgdorf where neighbors recommended the St. Margaret Home to her parents. A mansion by the Nordsee, they said. Where daughters can give birth and give away babies. Just a day's train journey away. And so discreet. These neighbors vouch for the St. Margaret Home because their daughter is its founder. When Sister Hildegunde was just eighteen, she asked her parents to relinquish what would have been her dowry so she could leave the Mother House in Burgdorf—where her passion for art was considered frivolous, rebellious—and establish her own community of Sisters.

"You know we'll do anything for you, Waltraud," her father said, "but not for the church."

"Sister Hildegunde," Waltraud reminded her father.

That name! It made her mother want to chant in her loudest voice: Waltraud Waltraud Waltraud Waltraud Waltraud . . . Such a humorless child when she was growing up. *Fromm und verwöhnt.* Pious and spoiled. And much loved.

"The church takes everything a nun or priest owns."

Waltraud snorted. A childhood mannerism that still disgusted her father.

"It matters to me," he said.

"Because it's about money."

"Because—" He studied the barges that strained against the current, the same view of the Rhein as from their villa half a kilometer upriver. "Because the church has already snatched our only child."

"Surviving child," her mother whispered.

"I'm sorry."

"I'm sorry too," Waltraud said. "I get so focused on one plan that I don't consider how it affects you."

"Thank you," her mother said.

"I'll pray to be more aware of that. Four of our Sisters want to leave Burgdorf with me."

"Renegades?"

"Artists. We believe it's a calling to bring forth the talent you're born with, that the talent will destroy you if you do not bring it forth."

Or mock you if you do bring it forth. Of course Waltraud's mother couldn't say that aloud. She'd never seen a talent for painting in her Waltraud—only the fierce belief that she had a talent. She felt her husband's eyes on her. Embarrassed by Waltraud's gaudy paintings, they took them off the walls and stored them in the wine cellar, wrapped in two layers of linen.

"I envision a convent with a school for young girls who get pregnant and must leave home."

Her father blushed. "I didn't know you were interested in that . . ."

"Sister Franziska trained as a midwife. I thought of an art school, but Sister Franziska says we can have both. We're committed to help those girls and their—"

"Why is that?" her mother asked.

"To change what'll happen to them. To give them a safe place where they can wait for their babies, surrounded by art. Of course they'll also get an academic education."

"So where do you envision this school?" asked her father.

"I've been thinking of our vacations up north . . . of clouds and rain."

"Easy on your skin." Her mother smiled. "You loved the Nordsee."

Waltraud's eyes drifted toward each other and she trained them toward the outer corners, willed them to settle as her *Opa* taught her, the only other albino in her ancestry. "That abandoned mansion by the dike . . ."

"I wonder if anyone lives there now," said her father.

"It's too big for you," said her mother.

"Other Sisters will join us."

"When?"

"Eventually . . . Soon . . . And there'll be the students."

Her father nodded. "We can find out, Waltraud."

"We'll have an infirmary. A nurse, too. Well—almost a nurse. Sister Konstanze didn't have time to finish nursing school before she entered the convent."

"We must set up a trust to protect the property," her mother said.

"Why?"

"To block the church from taking possession."

"Just please make sure the trust reads: Sister Hildegunde."

9

St. Margaret and the Dragon

When the Sisters agree to name the mansion St. Margaret Home, after the patron saint of pregnant women, Sister Hildegunde prays for enlightenment. She slides her bone-white hands out of her sleeves, builds a wooden frame, stretches canvas across it, and sets up her easel in the dimmest alcove of the chapel. There, inspired, she paints St. Margaret, a martyr who defied the devil when he attacked her disguised as a dragon.

She hangs her painting in the dining room, astonished the Girls are scared of the dragon.

"St. Margaret isn't even in the painting."

"Yes, she is."

"Where?"

Sister Hildegunde points to the dragon's wide open teeth. "He swallowed her. Don't you see her hands holding the crucifix that sticks from his jaws?"

"How do I know it's her?"

"I'm the one who put her there."

"Did you paint her face inside him?"

"No, but—"

"I hear her scream."

"Her eyes are scared."

"Is she dead, Sister Hildegunde?"

"No, no. It is the dragon who will die."

"But she is the one stuck inside him."

The Girls shudder, try to laugh.

In her alcove, Sister Hildegunde approaches the painting again. She considers the cross in the patron saint's hands, a cross big enough to club a rabbit, say, or a chicken; but not a dragon. She enlarges it. Twice. To prove the dragon's internal bleeding from this cross, she dabs crimson to the dragon's jaw and chest before she summons the Girls.

"You don't need to be afraid. St. Margaret's cross has sharp edges that will destroy the dragon's guts."

"But the cross is on the outside."

She sighs. "Once he swallows a little bit more of St. Margaret, the cross will be inside and cut him. He'll start heaving till he vomits her out."

"I vomited for three months," says one Girl.

"I vomited for five months," says another. "It began with a discomfort in my throat . . ."

"That dragon already killed the saint dead."

". . . a discomfort that's more tenderness than irritation, a tenderness in the upper front part of my throat . . . just below my jaw that began as soon as I found out that I was no longer not-pregnant . . ."

The other Girls roll their eyes as she drones on. Even her prayers are endless inventories of what she's done wrong in thought and in action, and what she could have done better in thought and in action.

"That saint won't come out."

"Except in bloody lumps."

They shiver.

"This cross I painted," Sister Hildegunde says, "will save St. Margaret's life. I made sure of that. See how the shape of her body bulges from the dragon's front? That means she is about to emerge unharmed to defeat the dragon."

But the Girls cannot picture their patron saint inside the dragon. Hands with a cross are not enough.

"That bulge can be anything."

Palms stroking bellies.

"A baby dragon."

They giggle. "Or his tail."

The Sisters whisper about Sister Hildegunde as they have ever since she singled them out to teach at her art school: that she's too young to lead them; that she's haughty. They question if she truly has a calling or became a nun because light stings her bone-white skin. Habit and wimple may shield her, but she still has to turn from the sun.

Her art is so bizarre that they must be tactful in their responses. Usually an approving nod will do without involving the sin of lying. Anything to do with praise, they can say aloud to her: how awed they are by her power to get this mansion for them; how grateful that she's chosen them to relocate to this timeless snippet of land in 1842.

But this dragon needs intervention.

Sister Elinor: "She needs to know that the Girls don't want to go into the dining room."

Sister Konstanze: "If our Girls don't eat, they'll get sick, and that'll harm the babies, too."

Sister Franziska: "True."

The Other Sisters: (nodding, although, sometimes, they don't appreciate her directness and irreverence) "So true."

Sister Franziska: "Let's vote for one of us to talk to her."

Sister Konstanze: "Not me."

Sister Ida: (in her scratchy whisper) "She can kick us out."

Sister Elinor: "She never has."

Sister Ida: "She'll call us ungrateful."

Sister Franziska: "She's spoiled."

The Other Sisters: "Of course Sister Hildegunde is spoiled. And not one of us dares say it aloud."

Sister Konstanze: "Then how do we tell her the painting is grotesque?"

Sister Ida: "Let's leave her an anonymous note."

Sister Konstanze: (leans against Sister Ida) "You don't mean that."

Sister Ida: "A short and polite note that her painting is leading to the starvation of our patients. It's only practical."

Sister Franziska: "Practical is not always the most compelling approach."

Sister Ida: "Compelling? What about truthful."

Sister Konstanze: "You can be so . . . sneaky."

Sister Ida: "You promised not to say that anymore."

Sister Elinor: "I suggest we vote."

Four sets of eyes on her.

Sister Elinor: "Oh no. No."

Four hands up. Quickly, the Sisters nominate Sister Elinor to be the messenger. The one most enlightened, they say, the only one of them born in the previous century.

But the intervention is a catastrophe. Sister Hildegunde stumbles back from Sister Elinor's words, seized by such nausea that she cannot go near her easel. It gets so bad that she won't enter the chapel for Mass or for vespers.

"The dragon terrifies the Girls," she confesses to the priest. "Some of the Sisters, too."

"May I see it?"

She hesitates.

He knows her by her confessions. Knows all the Sisters by their confessions: Sister Ida is secretive; Sister Elinor takes pride in her body; Sister Konstanze prefers birds to humans; Sister Franziska is greedy; Sister Hildegunde is brilliant but not arrogant as others see her.

"I cannot go back into the chapel," Sister Hildegunde says.

He curves his fingers around her elbow. Gently. "I'll stay with you."

As he studies the dragon blood and the dragon teeth and the dragon gore, he thinks what tragedy it is when the desire to create is stronger than the talent. "Such tragedy . . ."

Sister Hildegunde holds her breath.

"Such . . . a depiction of tragedy."

"Thank you."

He reaches inside his cassock, brings out an ironed handkerchief and unwraps two *Makronen,* keeps one for himself. "Someone left them for me in the confessional."

Sister Hildegunde takes a nibble. "They see the dragon. We see the saint."

As a young priest he cleansed her soul, traveled every weekend from Husum to Nordstrand—on foot and by ferry—to hold Mass and hear confessions of Sisters and Girls and parishioners. Troubled by the opulence of the St. Margaret Home, he asked the young Sisters not to spoil him with lavish meals and lodging. In his own calling he strived for humility and was proud when he achieved it. Yet, he felt slighted by the plain food and the spartan room in the carriage house where he could reach every wall with his arms extended. Here, the young priest prayed for God's guidance: if the Sisters were to serve him one lavish meal—*just one, dear God*—that was not in keeping with his humble lifestyle, he would submit to God's will and consume this lavish meal so that it wouldn't be wasted.

"Do you ever ask for what you like best?" asks Sister Hildegunde, a fleck of coconut on her upper lip.

"I can't think of anything." *Schokoladenplätzchen und Marzipan und Lebkuchen und Linzer Torte und Spekulatius* . . .

"But if . . . what would you ask for?" Her skin the palest of all skins, luminous—

—and his pulse a drum, a kettledrum. He points to the dragon and St. Margaret. "A powerful work of art . . ."

"Thank you."

". . . but perhaps—"

"Tell me."

"—too powerful? For these young souls already traumatized? They see the dragon. We see the saint."

Sister Hildegunde is swamped with pity for these young souls. "I can make St. Margaret more welcoming."

"Welcoming . . . ?" The priest is seized by coughing and covers his mouth.

She whacks his back between his shoulder blades. Whacks again. And again. *And the fire of her hands throughout his flesh a celestial union this is where I live where I truly live—*

She opens her lips for another nibble. "If only the Girls could see what you see."

Sister Hildegunde Confronts
Her Dragon

A week before the anniversary of the Sisters' arrival, the priest invites the parishioners to the first annual recital and exhibit. "A momentous day for all of us at the St. Margaret Home, the culmination of our mission to educate our students in the arts—"

Whispering from the center church pews. Scoffing.

"In addition, of course," the priest adds quickly, "in religion and scholarly subjects. One week from today, at seven, we welcome you to celebrate the achievements of our faculty and our students. Theater and dance and music. Paintings and tapestries. We'll serve refreshments."

More scoffing and whispering.

The Girls are sweating.

The priest is sweating. "Such scrumptious refreshments," he says.

Sister Ida turns in her pew and glares at the scoffers and the whisperers. Raises her index finger to her lips and gathers herself for a fierce soprano that comes out as a hoarse whistle. "Ssshhhh . . . ssshhhh . . . ssshhhh . . ."

"Ssshhhh . . ." Sister Elinor adds her voice. A deep contralto. "Ssshhhh . . . ssshhhh . . ."

Silence from the center pews. But the Girls are giddy with adoration for Sister Elinor and Sister Ida who've taught them the range of the singing voice, let them play with extremes— screech and growl. For months the Sisters have rehearsed with them, studied and discussed, encouraged each Girl to choose her own area of performance.

Long before the curtain opens, the Girls take position onstage. During their rehearsals they've performed music and theater and poetry with joy, confidence, absorbing every new Girl into the recital. Everyone has a part. But now they hope the people of Nordstrand have forgotten about the recital. Hope the curtain will stay closed. The faint hum of an audience, and Sister Ida tugs at the curtain—

—*opening it? already?*—

No, finding the middle so she can peek through the gap. "We need a little more time."

Sister Hildegunde rushes backstage, talks to the Sisters, then approaches the Girls. "My parents are excited about your recital. They've traveled a long way." She nods to Sister Elinor.

Sister Elinor cringes. "Good news . . . we have a small audience tonight."

"Such a relief." Sister Ida laughs, but her eyes are angry. "That means fewer palpitations for all of us."

The Sisters step away, and when the curtain opens, they already sit in the front row with other Sisters, the priest, and two old people the Girls don't know, applauding and applauding, though nothing has happened yet. The Girls are ashamed, something the Sisters forgot to consider, ashamed to display their bodies onstage for outsiders to judge. Applause again when the recital ends, mild applause that matches their accomplishment.

But it's not the end of the evening yet. The Sisters pack the uneaten refreshments into baskets and all set out with blankets and with lanterns for a feast on the dike. One Girl starts singing, then others. Two recite poetry. What has been excruciating onstage becomes playful, fluid. Lights and laughter bob toward the moon on their ascent.

Infants are born and Girls leave and new Girls and finches reproduce. Only a few Girls take their babies home with them, and the Sisters try to find families who'll adopt the rest of the babies. Sadly, there are always more babies than families. When the nursery gets too crowded, the Sisters separate it into two: Little Nursery on the ground floor and Big Nursery on the second floor.

It's not that easy to accommodate all the finches. The Sisters house them in the peacocks' aviary; however, the gaps between the bars are too wide, and the Sisters visit the toy factory with drawings of cages, some small, others wide enough for several finches. In Sister Konstanze's tapestry class, Girls braid long grasses into cocoons for inside the cages, and the Sisters trade finches with the people of Nordstrand for sourdough starter and geraniums, honey and eggs.

Storks build nests on steeples and chimneys while Sister Hildegunde confronts her dragon, mixing earth colors on her board— umber and sienna and ocher—layering and covering until her painting looks so muddy that it can be mistaken for an ancient canvas stashed for centuries in a bell tower. Or in a potato cellar, Sister Hildegunde thinks, and decides to stop painting.

She still teaches art but without passion. Her students believe it's because they've offended Sister's dragon and are cautious with her, shield her from seeing how bored they are with her art theories. Her confessions, too, are without passion—no spite or doubts—causing others to fear she's fading altogether.

When the priest asks Sister Elinor for advice, she assures him the Sisters are watching closely.

"Her skin is paler than ever."

"I know. And she is too thin."

"She won't look me in the eye."

"She is not interested in you."

His head snaps up.

"Or in me," she says.

"Oh."

"She is not interested in herself."

It's the priest's idea to engage Sister Hildegunde in training St. Margaret Girls to become *Kindermädchen*—nursemaids.

"Once they leave here, there isn't much for them. But if we qualify them as *Kindermädchen* it will guarantee good work for them," he tells her.

She trains her pale eyes on his left shoulder. "More of a chance."

"True. They're learning important skills here. They already know how to care for babies. But think of their advantage, Sister Hildegunde—how many mothers-to-be get to practice on so many babies?"

"It is a unique situation. But there is risk in exposing our Girls to so many infants. What if they become enamored with them? What if they want to keep their own?"

"We must be more aware of that."

"Work together to prevent it."

He blushes. "We'll draw up guidelines for a *Praktikum*. List everything the Girls already do—feeding children and bathing children and keeping children safe—"

"And learning . . ." Sister folds her hands in prayer. "As part of the *Praktikum*."

He leans toward her. Smells incense and turpentine and

something else he can't name. "You mean instruct children in basic learning?"

"And in the arts. Music and painting and weaving. We'll issue a certificate that qualifies each to take care of an entire family." She fingers his sleeve just above his wrist.

He tries to exhale.

"I'll write each a letter of recommendation," she says eagerly.

"Brilliant!"

"On fancy parchment."

"Embossed."

"Too much to do for any Girl," the Sisters say when Sister Hildegunde presents the plan.

"True," she agrees. "That's why our certificate will list what they've learned to do. Not what they do every day."

"What certificate?"

"A certificate to make them more employable. After they complete a *Praktikum*."

Three months later the priest writes to priests in other parishes to recommend the new *Kindermädchen*. "They are qualified to bathe children, feed children, swaddle children, protect children, instruct children in early learning and music and painting. Their skills will benefit the entire family, including cooking, canning, baking, cleaning, washing, ironing, and sewing. They have successfully completed our classes and *Praktikum* and have earned their certificate as *Kindermädchen*."

For the Sisters the youngest Girls evoke their own girlhood. Awkward with new girth, they knock over candlesticks, say, or jugs of water. In the wide corridors they jump rope. When the Sisters forbid it, the Girls jump rope in the cellar of the church.

It's for them the Sisters pray extra rosaries. Because their bodies are not grown enough to push a child into life.

One Tuesday at vespers, it comes to Sister Hildegunde that St. Margaret deserves more than one painting. A series, she thinks. Like Christ's fourteen stations of the *Kreuzweg* that manifest his torment and death on the path to crucifixion and resurrection. St. Margaret certainly won't need fourteen stations, just a few so that those Girls—children actually—will be motivated by the saint's courage.

She stretches another canvas, smears the first layer of oils with her palette knife, and paints through the night with loose strokes, hands and mind flying till the violet blue before dawn reveals St. Margaret—pristine and tranquil—standing next to the dead dragon, gown spotless, one translucent foot on the scaly hide, not one gash, bite, wound, cut, slash, tear, or bruise on her.

When she sets the panels side by side, she decides there must be a transition between St. Margaret inside the live dragon and St. Margaret outside the dead dragon. The following night she works on the dragon vomiting up St. Margaret. But it's all wrong. Too meticulous. Too fussy. By showing everything, she is limiting herself. Why paint each dragon toe and toenail when it is more compelling to suggest the talon? With her palette knife, Sister flies at the dragon—strains, punches, retreats, charges—and in scraping off what confines her, uncovers passion.

Of course the Sisters notice.

How can they not?

Something has come unstuck in Sister Hildegunde, turned luminous. Some say it happened overnight, others that it changed over decades. But they agree that Sister Hildegunde's strokes have become translucent, raw canvas showing through the colors. With broad sweeps she captures the essence of the bishop's mansion that must have been ready to claim her from the first day she walked toward it, levitating above the meadow in all its beauty and vulgarity; and she is still walking toward it—from every angle—humbled by how it gives itself to her, afloat on layers of mist, its windows shaped like peacock feathers, iridescent blues and purples, the feather-eye.

That glowing window becomes her signature: it may fill her canvas, appear as a tiny window high in a tree, or at the horizon.

Bishops fly up and settle on the roof. Inspired by half-human cries of peacocks, Sister Hildegunde applies the heads of bishops to the bodies of peacocks.

Poppies the size of pear trees grow around the mansion, giving shade to the Sisters who stroll beneath them while a bone-white little girl carries a baby up the front steps.

Frau Bauer says the red poppy trees remind her of the Black Forest.

"Everything reminds you of the Black Forest," Sister Hildegunde says.

"Would you trade the painting?"

"For what?"

"For some three-legged milking stools. My son Köbi makes them from a design our ancestors brought from the Black Forest when they came here for a wedding and didn't leave and—"

"We don't need milking stools."

"But they can be used for other activities, like . . . like weaving and painting and maybe even gardening if you like to sit while pulling weeds and they don't wobble like most stools if you sit off-balance even if you are drunk—"

"That"—Sister's pupils drift toward the bridge of her nose— "is not a problem for us." She closes her pale eyelids and—with an expression of utmost concentration—directs her pupils to reverse their direction.

"I'm sorry, Sister Hildegunde. I didn't mean you get drunk and I'm sorry if I tired you out—"

"How many milking stools?" Sister opens her eyes and the pupils are in the center again.

"Three?"

"Ten."

"Oh—"

"For our older children. Even if they fidget, the stools won't tip over."

The next painting to sell is that of the bishops on the roof. Several people want it, but the blacksmith is the first to arrive with money. The other buyers ask Sister Hildegunde to make more paintings like that.

"A painting of the bishops hiding behind a chimney."

"Or of the peacocks shoving the bishops off the roof."

But Sister will not take assignments. Sister is in a hot rush to capture what comes to her in story-dreams so consuming that she can't tell if she's painting in her chapel alcove or in her imagination. Only when finished will she let others see her paintings, and when they tell her how magnificent they are, how transforming, it doesn't matter to her because she's already in a swift current toward another story-dream, and it's the beauty of it that drives her, the not-knowing. To give rise to images that were not there before—she teaches her students— that's what we must do. Not a serene process, it can't be, she tells her students, and inspires each Girl to dare enter the swift current of not-knowing toward a vision of her own.

PART THREE

Fall 1878

11

Translucent Moons

At the St. Margaret Home for Pregnant Girls, Lotte Jansen sleeps while Girls play with Wilhelm in the Little Nursery, rock him atop their bellies. He's too big already to remind them of the babies that will come out of them.

But not yet not yet not—

Or maybe not at all if it's true that storks pull babies from the sea, pull them out dripping, and fly them to you and bite you in the leg till you scream. Leave a brown circle on your leg, a Mutterfleck. *Mother's spot.*

They whisper to Wilhelm he's lucky he has a mother who can take him home with her.

But for now Lotte sleeps. Ten hours. Eight. Punctuated by short spans of being awake when she can trust her despair to be waiting for her; can trust that despair to paralyze her when Sister Franziska brings Wilhelm to visit her; can trust it to render her silent when her cousin, Nils, rides across the tidal flats from Südfall to sit with her.

Nils slides the chair next to her bed.

"Lotte may not answer you," Sister Ida has cautioned him. "She is in the deepest of all sorrows. Just talk to her."

Nils tells Lotte stories from before: before the wave; before the children; before Kalle. Stories from when they were children and she'd sit on his horse behind him, arms around his waist. Flying. *Forever flying. Forever ten years old.* To attend school on Nordstrand, Nils rides his horse across the *Watt.* His parents lease the only house on Südfall; depending on tides and winds, he stays with Lotte during the week and returns home after school on Saturday.

"You got so happy," Nils says, "when you were allowed to ride with me to Südfall and stay till Monday morning with us."

One May when Lotte stayed on Südfall, high tide and a full moon swept away the eggs of nesting birds. Not a story for her, Nils decides. Not now. Maybe never. Even though the birds started over, enough time for them to have young ones. Another story he won't remind her of: climbing the steps to the attic with Lotte and hiding in the rowboat his family keeps there. When *Hochwasser* rises around the house, they can ease the dory through the hatch. Nils wishes he had memories without the Nordsee for Lotte; but he cannot separate the Nordsee from their lives: its roar; its whisper; its changing surface; its salty taste on your skin; its force when it tumbles you.

In the Little Nursery Tilli trims Wilhelm's fingernails and saves the translucent moons in her handkerchief box. She can see herself in his house, trimming his fingernails every week.

"Soon," she tells him, "soon I'll move in with you and your *Mutti.* Just the three of us."

She is getting used to him being so big. His legs dangle from her arms. One morning she yanks him from her breast because he kindles such hunger *for her own girl—how then did they get you away from me while we slept cocooned?* That's when she remembers—

—remembers the jab of a needle—
—a gentle voice here here hands peeling—
—my arms open peeling your skin from my skin—

She squeezes her eyes shut and summons her own girl at her breast and lets Wilhelm's mouth back against her to relieve the hunger of her own girl because her body makes what her girl needs and is there for Wilhelm and therefore her girl cannot be so far away.

Nils brings his sketch of a starling to the St. Margaret Home and reminds Lotte how Sister Sieglinde taught them about starlings and their migration in third grade. As Lotte holds his sketch—black speckled feathers, straight bill—she finds her own sketch of a starling tacked to the wall of their classroom. Finds the wetlands where she and Nils and Kalle wait with their teacher just as schoolchildren over centuries have waited for the *Schwarze Sonne* of spring.

"Where are the starlings?"

"*Ja,* where?"

They scan the sky, shield their eyes against the last glow of day. At first just swarms of mosquitoes and the stink of soggy earth, ancient and moldering layers of death and decay; and yet growth feeding off that rot.

"Now tell me, what do you think of when you see starlings?" Sister Sieglinde asks.

"Starling soup."

"My *Mutti* bakes starling pies."

"My *Opa* taught a starling to sing," says Köbi.

"My uncle shoots them."

"Where do they go in the winter?" Kalle asks.

"South," says Sister Sieglinde. "France and Belgium. Who remembers the Latin name for the European starling?"

Raised hands.

"*Sturnus vulgaris.*"

"Good. Now who can tell me its two goals?"

"Sleep."

"And they don't want to get eaten."

"Good. Now what happens when their need to sleep gets bigger than their fear of being eaten?" Sister Sieglinde has thought about choices like that, prayed over choices like that.

"They wait for the best moment to fly down into the grasses."

"Before it gets dark."

"In the last twenty minutes of light."

"Real fast—"

"—like stones falling from the sky."

"At sixty kilometers, that's how fast."

A few children elbow one another.

"Faster," Lotte cries.

"Twenty times."

Elbows flying. Jabbing. Children laughing.

Sister Sieglinde tells them to stop, but one of her eyebrows lifts, enough to slow down their elbows, to reduce jabbing to bumping to rubbing. "The starlings," she continues, "have three different means of communicating. They constantly look around. They listen. And they make signs with their wings. *What is my neighbor doing? I'll do the same. We want to go down into that marsh in this formation, now. There has to be water* . . . But as soon as they go down, *Raubvögel*—birds of prey—snatch up starlings, and the flock closes around the gap, shifts direction to escape. That's how you can tell what type of attack is going on."

She doesn't have to tell her students that the magnificent dance of the starlings is a massacre. They know. And yet they can relish the beauty of the dance and not be shocked by the massacre because they're used to eating chickens and sheep and pigs whose slaughter they've watched or assisted. Perhaps to them killing has its own beauty, while Sister Sieglinde still feels like the squeamish child who hides under *Oma*'s bed whenever

Mutti pins down a chicken on the tree stump and swings her hatchet. *Streaks of dried blood on the rings of the stump—*

"Why didn't you warn us?" Lotte asks when her cousin visits again.

"No one knew."

"If you'd been here you could have warned us, pulled my children from the wave."

Nils understands the *Watt* better than most. Like his father, he boosts his fishing income with *Wattführungen,* guides tourists on hikes, fourteen kilometers across the *Watt* between Nordstrand and Südfall, then his mother's *Kaffee und Kuchen* and a little profit from that, before the return to Nordstrand. From Nils the tourists learn about nature and history, about the difference between an island like Nordstrand and a *Hallig* like Südfall that floods nearly thirty times each year. A *Hallig* exists in balance with the tides, Nils tells them. It does not have dikes, but *Warften,* meter-high hills erected by people where they build their houses and barns. During floods, they herd all livestock to the *Warft.* Nils will caution tourists against the danger of hiking on the *Watt* without a guide. Easy to miscalculate where you are and how soon the tide will come in. You may get trapped by water rising around you, cutting off your way to the shore. Soon—but Nils is not about to tell this to Lotte—he will include a warning about a freak wave that killed three children in his family.

The Sisters negotiate a lease of the Jansens' farmland with the sexton who's known to be reputable when it comes to work and church, but deceitful about his age. He sends a *Knecht*—hired man—to work the land and supply Lotte with eggs, milk, and fair payment.

Although the sexton is nearing seventy, his face is pink and unlined, his hair full, and he claims to be two decades younger than the old men who know they sat on the school bench with him. They suspect he's getting himself injected with the piss of goats.

"From a veterinarian in Hamburg."

"Pregnant goats, I heard at the barbershop."

"To keep himself young."

"I think the goats are in Bremerhaven."

"Maybe from Bremerhaven and from Hamburg."

"He's away on the train often enough."

"How expensive do you think?"

"We could ask him . . ."

"*Ja,* also how it's done."

But the sexton, galled by their audacity to ask, claims he doesn't know anything about pregnant goats.

12

Belly Dancers and Apostles

Remember when we found treasures on the *Watt*?" Nils asks.

Lotte stares toward the window.

He shifts his body into the path of her gaze. "When we were in third grade . . . that spring the Nordsee carried off muck and sediments above Rungholt. Remember?"

Outlines of cisterns and of cellars.

"Tell me what you remember," Nils whispers.

Posts and plow tracks. You can hide in those memories. Vanish.

"There was talk of treasures," he says. "You and Kalle and I were eight. We hiked out at low tide with hooks and pails and shovels. Entire families were out there, digging. You and I found the handle of a plow."

Three shards of clay.

"Two shards of clay," Nils says.

Three.

"You were good at finding treasures for the school museum."

He reminds her how proud they were when they brought a treasure to their teacher. And though Lotte doesn't answer, it feels like a conversation because he senses that she, too, sees the shards of clay, the handle of the plow, images that he's seen and that move them both forward into other images: the shelves and glass cases that displayed maps and diaries; fragments from ceramic bowls and whetting stones; stiff garments and kitchen utensils from ancestors; jewelry that people willed to the museum.

Every find is worthy of investigation. An ancient inkwell. Half a spinning wheel. A copper teapot. Brilliant shards of ceramic that date back to foreign sailors who traded on Rungholt. Generations of students have practiced their handwriting on cards that document each artifact by name, century, location, and finder.

Tintenfaß | 14. Jahrhundert | Bennersiel | Dietrich Maier | Kupfer Teekanne | 17. Jahrhundert | Herrendeich | Rosemarie Link |

Over centuries, the museum has grown, curated by the current teacher, who has a desk in the museum. After hours, the teacher is allowed to use the museum as a parlor, sit in the embroidered armchair or lie on the sofa, eat at the fourteenth-century marble table, surrounded by seascapes and framed documents. Unless the teacher is a Sister and must be back at the St. Margaret Home before dark.

From the stillness of her bed in the St. Margaret Home, Lotte maps the route of the Ludwig Zirkus through her longing, into towns and villages along the Nordsee, up the coast through Germany, into Denmark, and then back through Germany into Holland.

Next August he'll have to come back because the Ludwig Zirkus will set up on Nordstrand once again. You cannot be sure of the exact week. Something unforeseen may happen along the way—sick animals or broken wheels—that'll push all performances back or ahead. But once you hear that the Zirkus is performing in Husum, you know Nordstrand is next. Will he come to the house? Or will he avoid her? Hide out in one of the wagons? Keep his door locked if she were to come to him?

Maybe she'll be the one to hide with Wilhelm in the house. Let Kalle be the one to come to her. But what if he doesn't? She understands why he left, but she can't understand why he doesn't write to her. And why he stays away. She thinks of Sabine Florian with her strong, willowy body. Sabine, free and fearless, who should use her body to anchor her daughter to earth—not tempt another woman's husband young enough to be her son.

If Lotte could, she'd stop her longing—kill it throttle it burn it. It sucks you in, seduces you into hope unless you withdraw instantly. Because there are two sides to longing, hope and the danger of letting hope devour you. Longing trips you. Tricks you. And yet gives you brief respite from your despair while beyond your window the seasons stage their extravagant transformation: winds sweep across yellow rapeseed fields where countless blossoms sway as if one surface, and clouds ripple like wetlands after the tide retreats, dappled valleys and ridges as if the earth had turned itself upside down.

Longing. But not grieving. Not for Kalle.

To grieve him and her children together would be disloyal to her children.

When the Ludwigs meet with Kalle about restoring the wagon panels, both want magic and passion; but where the father envisions additional Bible scenes, the son wants to replace every panel with scenes from *Arabische Nächte—Arabian Nights*.

"Too expensive," Herr Ludwig says.

"We need something more exciting than virgins and apostles," Silvio says.

Kalle listens carefully to figure out how to get along with both. "It may be dramatic to merge your story lines—"

"That's impractical," Silvio Ludwig says.

"Impractical," his father echoes.

"It would keep your costs low," Kalle says.

The Ludwigs glance at each other. Then at Kalle. Wait.

"I won't do unnecessary work. I'll keep what I can of the Biblical panels."

He begins with the kitchen wagon, removes the rotting half of The Last Supper and splices in veiled belly dancers who gyrate toward the leftover apostles. As a toymaker he's created intricate features, but with the Zirkus he's learning to work on an expansive scale. By afternoon he's exhausted but can't sleep at night because he dreads waking up and remembering he'll never hold his children again.

The memory of body—impossible to overcome. The memory of how they latched on to Lotte: *Hannelore wanting to do it all for herself as soon as she could, both hands pulling Lotte's breast toward her mouth; Martin always curious, turning his head to follow whatever was happening nearby, stretching Lotte's nipple; Bärbel with her fervent appetite and will, clamping onto Lotte—lips, gums, tongue, teeth—*

Once again he barricades his soul, takes refuge in feeding the animals and shoveling their droppings till he's drowsy, only letting himself think of what needs doing that moment and what needs doing the moment after that moment until he's calmed, gladdened even, by their nearness and smell, by his hope that he's good with them. He doesn't do his other work. Tells himself that he is the veterinarian, at least closer to being a veterinarian than anyone in the Zirkus. He cooks gravy for the sick animals, just as he used to at home. While he browns a bit of meat and simmers it, adding water, the animals sniff the air, press closer, and he calls them his little cannibals, talks to them till he calms himself and the meat is in shreds and has turned into gravy that tastes like meat; and when he pours it over feed they've already refused, he gets even the most reluctant animals to eat, gets life to flare in their eyes again, ignoring the advice of anyone who's told him that grazing animals don't eat gravy because that would be cannibalism.

At first both Ludwigs are enthusiastic about Kalle's work; but one evening in the kitchen wagon, Herr Ludwig is agitated. For a while they eat silently.

"Yesterday you liked the belly dancers," Silvio says.

His father shakes his head.

"We agreed, *Vater.*"

"Did not."

"We agreed. On everything. You forgot."

"Did not."

Silvio points to his father's uneaten food.

"Don't want to."

"You're letting yourself get too thin."

"No belly dancers on my wagon!"

"Don't you get sick."

"Oh . . ." His father picks up a wedge of boiled potato, bites into it cautiously, fingers against his lips, hands like claws.

"You hear me?"

"No belly dancers! Your mother would be outraged."

"We can keep our wagon silver and black. Let's wait till we see what Kalle does with other wagons."

"He's not doing his work."

"Sabine says it's sadness about his children."

13

The Old Women Ride Their Bicycles to the Cemetery

Even when it rains, the Old Women ride their bicycles to the cemetery, one hand holding an open umbrella, the other steering. On their handlebars sway watering cans, sisal nets with gardening tools and flower pots. After they cross the bridge across the moat, they get off their bicycles. Maria is limping. Nothing, she says when they ask what happened. No, she says when they offer to carry her supplies up the steep path.

They scrape flecks of moss from gravestones, clear family plots from weeds. They know one another's stories and the stories of the buried ones, recognize the moment before everything shifts—into sorrow or bliss or rage—and calibrate those moments even if half a century has passed. Like when Maria—the day of her wedding to the lanky fisherman she's loved since she was sixteen—brought the new *Doktor* to the bed of her mother.

Better if her mother had not tried to make her wear her old-fashioned veil and climbed on a chair to reach the top of her wardrobe. Better if her mother had not broken her femur when the chair tipped. Better if the Herr Doktor had not presented himself at his best—skillful with clean hands and new shoes. Better if Maria had not jilted her fisherman who still waits for her after nearly half a century. Better if Maria had not married the Herr Doktor and moved into his fancy villa with the two verandas. Because he beats her, the Herr Doktor, beats their five daughters. You'd think a family of women could stop one bow-legged man. Poison him. Bludgeon him. Drown him. Suffocate him. The Old Women fantasize.

For now Maria walks at night. Her jilted bridegroom only had to wait one year before she sought him out. She gets her deepest sleep in the morning hours. When her children were young, they'd find her asleep when they'd climb from their beds. The older girls would get the little girls dressed and fed.

Whenever Maria's husband prescribes another sleeping tincture, Maria pretends to swallow. "My grandmother had the same sleep pattern," she'll lie. "Awake in the dark and sleeping into the morning hours."

Most nights Maria and her jilted bridegroom are on his fishing boat between midnight and predawn, find one another in passion and in tenderness.

He has offered to kill her husband. "Why do you stay with him?" he'll cry.

"I promised in marriage."

"You did not promise to let him beat you and our daughters."

Our daughters.

Three of Maria's five daughters are his, their appearance no giveaway because both men are blond and bow-legged. Her daughters only know him as the generous fisherman who sells them his freshest fish for the lowest price. All five believe the Herr Doktor is their father, a man they fear and despise.

"I wish they were all mine," the fisherman will say.

"You'd be a good father."

"Once I kill him, we can tell our daughters they're mine."

"When they visit you in prison? When you get out, we'll be

ancient, and people will whisper at our wedding how bizarre it must be to caress each other when we're so very old."

He laughs. ". . . And that we probably don't want this anymore."

"This . . ." Maria reaches for him.

Although the cemetery is on a hill with a moat around it to drain away groundwater, the earth is spongy, and if you set a plant into the ground, water seeps in from below and the sides. Worse, of course, if you take shovels to a new grave. A coffin will displace that water with a gurgling sigh you don't want to think about at night. The most merciless burials are for drowned children whose parents have to give them back to water.

"At least the Jansens were spared that."

The Old Women fret about the Jansen children as they have every day since the drowning, face-down in the Nordsee, though no one saw them like that. No bodies. No graves.

"Lotte still has Wilhelm to live for."

"That child worries me, so gloomy—"

"He bangs his head."

"I've been bringing her cream."

"Sister Elinor says Lotte craves red cabbage."

"I fixed the latch on her door."

"My sons will repair the roof of her barn."

"I'm baking bread for her."

"Cheese and buttermilk."

The second most merciless burials are for mothers who die in childbirth and are buried with their infants—born dead, or alive for just a few hours.

14

Silvio Climbs into His
Father's Bed

Long before dawn, crying from Herr Ludwig's wagon and Silvio runs to him, rubs his shoulders, dries tears and snot from his face; but his father is inconsolable, rolls his head. Mottled skull beneath sparse hair. Silvio is taken by a crazed pity. *When did you get so old?*

"Why are you crying?" he asks.

His father smiles through tears. "It always gets better."

"That's what you like to tell all of us."

"That's what your mother always told me." And he is crying again, harder.

"Do you remember why you are crying?" Silvio asks and—since he doesn't know how to comfort his father—climbs into his father's bed. First then, that awkwardness of touch. The dry skin. But the crying lessens, and his father settles himself with his bony head on Silvio's shoulder. Drops one flaccid arm across Silvio's chest, arms that used to lift Silvio when he was a boy, lift him to reach for things high up. *Wir zwei.* The two of us. Or to hide a flask where his mother cannot find it. *Wir zwei.* Silvio's mother doesn't allow his father to drink, says it's indecent, and the not allowing spills into shrieking, spills into lies.

Some nights Silvio finds his father roaming, searching for his wife, and leads him back to his silver and red wagon.

"How can I stop him?" he asks Hans-Jürgen.

"We cannot tie him down."

Cannot gives way to can. Not tying him down, though, they agree. But anchoring him, a kitchen towel loose around each ankle, fastened to the end of the bed. Still, the old man gets his hands on the floor, squirms on his elbows till his sweaty feet slip from the dish towels.

"He is agile," Hans-Jürgen says with admiration.

"That he is," says Silvio who fears he is not doing enough for his father. But when he offers to move back in, his father won't accept.

"Why not?" Silvio asks.

"Because—" His father opens his palms as if talking to someone particularly dense. "—Hans-Jürgen is your family now."

"You are my family."

"My dear boy . . . You don't need to make up stories for me."

Kalle—

    —*thinking he is awake*—

    —*thinking he feels children nearby*—

    —*or is he just dreaming about children? He doesn't recognize them. Misplaces them again.*

But he knows he is their father. A negligent father. Rootless. Despair fills his soul. Over days and weeks, that despair swells, presses Kalle's organs aside until it becomes too cumbersome to walk, to leave his bed. He worries about his farm. What needs to be done. Repaired. Come winter, the roof of the barn may buckle beneath too much snow.

I storm into Kalle's wagon, yank the covers off him. "You and I are taking a walk."

He snatches at the covers to hide himself.

"You're not working. You're not coming to meals."

"Tomorrow . . ."

Again, I yank the covers away.

"I need to wash up."

"First the walk."

"I stink."

"You do."

He closes his eyes.

"You can walk while you stink." I tug at his arm till he has to sit up.

But he lets his body go limp and slumps back.

"I can't do this." I raise both palms. "I'm already raising one grown-up child and it's unfair—no, selfish—to expect me to do that for you."

"I'm not expecting—"

"I cannot watch your endless needing—"

"I am not a child."

"You ricochet from one extreme to the other."

"I don't understand—"

"Of course you don't because that's all part of it too . . . assuming I'll do it for you, understand it for you, and lay it out for you to understand, but I can't do one more thing for one more person because I'm already raising a child who is twenty years old—" Soaring within me: fury and injustice and love and fear that'll choke me if I don't let them out. "—and I'll keep doing that for another twenty years, for Heike yes, but not for you."

Ranting, I know I'm ranting but can't stop, though it has little to do with Kalle Jansen other than that he is a man who has left his wife and child. "All you men counting on women to stay while you keep leaving so you won't turn into statues—"

He shrinks back as if I'd doubled in size.

"—while we don't even think of leaving and when Heike shakes her head it's like she's shaking water from her hair and that may be endearing for a decade until it becomes disgusting and all the pretending that she's brilliant and endearing—"

"What right do you have—" He is trembling.

"—and you know what else is disgusting? You sitting in your own filth feeling wounded while your wife—"

"What right—" He starts again. "What right to make your loss greater than mine?"

I stiffen, arms by my sides, and he steps into my storm, tries to calm me; but I flip my arms to my shoulders scissor-like, hurl him off.

"It's about Heike?" he whispers.

"No," I say. "Not entirely."

"Of course not entirely," he says and meets me there. Lets me burst through his listlessness, his torment. That day.

And in the days to follow. Lets me yank him from his bed until he can on his own. Lets me make him wash himself and make him walk and make him work on the wagon panels.

On my wagon, he preserves the *Jungfrau* Maria but whittles down the archangel Gabriel and replaces him with Ali Baba's cave, so that the *Jungfrau* stands forever waiting—not for that archangel, I believe, but for Ali Baba to creep from his cave, tempt her with jewels and gold stolen by his forty thieves.

15

Foundling

On *Allerheiligentag*—All Saints Day—the first day of November 1878, a dwarf baby is abandoned inside a church in Emmerich, the last German town before the Dutch border. *Allerheiligentag* gathers all martyrs—the nameless and the famous—into one feast day to ensure none is ignored. In ancient times each martyred saint was honored on the anniversary of martyrdom; but the Romans killed so many more that it became impossible to document all martyrs' fates and names.

When the Ludwig Zirkus arrives in Emmerich that afternoon for winter training, a priest carries the foundling to the Rhein meadow where our crew is setting up.

"The girl will fit in with you," the priest tells us.

Silvio tilts his head. "Why is that?"

"She'll be more . . . accepted if she lives with her own."

"Her own . . ." Silvio nods. "But I'm not a dwarf."

The giant Nowack pushes past him and claims the tiny baby with the big head from the priest—*eighteen years of marriage and five miscarriages*—and in an instant his wife, Luzia, is by his side, one palm on the baby's belly.

"She's half-starved," Kalle says.

"We cannot take a baby on the road," says Silvio, known for his attention to safety for everyone, animals and humans, especially his father. And this baby is even more vulnerable than his father.

"We've taken a baby on the road before." Luzia motions to my daughter who caresses the baby's hands.

"That was twenty years ago," Silvio says, "and we're all much older."

"Does she have a name?" I ask the priest.

"I don't know."

"With foundlings there's often a note pinned to the blanket."

"Not with this one."

"But did you check inside the blanket?" I insist.

He glares at me. "I said there is no note." And starts an endless story about an endless journey across a bridge that's sometimes flooded and he's not sure if he has to stay overnight to hold the wedding Mass for his brother's ninth daughter and that he could not take a baby with him. "Will you keep her for just one day?"

Luzia and the giant Nowack huddle around the baby as if that could hide her from Silvio who's grumbling. "One day. She can stay one day."

"She's half-starved," Kalle says again.

Luzia carries her when we crowd into The Last Supper and the smell of yesterday's lentil soup. Her husband dips his little finger into a pot of mashed potatoes, then into the mouth of the baby who gulps so quickly that her throat inflates and shrinks.

"Like a boa constrictor," says my daughter.

"Not so fast," the giant Nowack murmurs to the baby. "We have plenty for you. Always."

But the mouth is already open, searching.

"A boa constrictor with teeth," my daughter says.

"I thought I felt something sharp." Luzia sticks a finger into the mashed potatoes and feeds the baby. "Isn't she too young for teeth?"

"She's almost a year," Kalle says.

"But she's so tiny."

For someone so new in the world, the foundling has an abundance of blue-black curls, uncommon for the coast with its fair-haired people.

"Her mother must be a local girl," the cook says, "her father some foreigner from down south."

"Spain, maybe. With that olive skin." Her husband drops his arm around her.

"Why local?" I ask.

"Because it happened in a local church," says Luzia The Clown.

Luzia's dainty wrists make Kalle yearn for Lotte's strong wrists. He and Lotte started loving each other as children. In fourth grade they promised to marry. Such clarity of knowing had to be a sign they were destined to be together. At sixteen, he was ready to court her but too embarrassed by warts on his fingers. He visited the beekeeper, known for a wart potion he blended in his workroom. After he rubbed it into Kalle's hands, he wrapped them with gauze, told him to leave it on for thirty-seven hours. That's how long it took for gauze to absorb the warts. But to keep the warts from finding him again, Kalle had to bury the gauze behind the St. Margaret Home. That's what he did, though he was up to his shins in cold muck that smelled of something dead. Fish, he assured himself. Not bodies of battle-dead from the German-Danish War a few years before.

He snuck back on the path between the church and the St. Margaret Home where candles flickered behind a stained peacock window. When his warts didn't reappear, he proposed to Lotte on the tidal flats at sunset—as was tradition—when the tide was out. They married the following October when Lotte turned sixteen. Eventually, they had children and lost children and he left her. Not right away, though. He did try to stay. For days he tried to find his way back to Lotte in their grieving while Wilhelm shrieked.

"The father could be from Italy," Silvio says.

Herr Ludwig nods vigorously. "Venice. Where your mother grew up, Silvio." *Memories like fireflies alighting briefly . . . here and here again finding . . . not just impermanence . . . but richness, an everlasting glow that exhilarates him.* "Our marriage was bliss and harmony."

The Twenty-Four-Hour Man rolls his eyes, and I elbow him.

". . . more than I ever dared dream. Silvio remembers . . ."

But Silvio pretends not to hear.

"Quite a few dark-haired people live in Holland," Kalle says. "Like my great-grandparents."

"Venice," Herr Ludwig insists. "I knew five dwarfs in Venice."

"Is she a dwarf?" Heike asks me.

"A beautiful little dwarf."

The baby flails her short arms and legs.

"Let me," Kalle says, and when Luzia hands him the baby, it's like holding a bundle of bubbles—

—*a bundle of bubbles*—

—*his Bärbel all over again*—

—*belly down on his knees*—

—and he lays the foundling across his knees, gently, with her belly down and kneads her back with his thumbs till the gas bubbles pass and he, too, is crying and plummeting into the sorrow he's fled since the day of the freak wave. He used to remember everything. So why can't he remember who was next to Lotte when the wave came at them? She has told him. Or has she? What if he imagined she told him? Imagined that the day of the wave he knew but didn't want to know? The not knowing has blotted the knowing—and all he has left is this uncertainty. Herr Ludwig has told him it was like that for him after his wife Pia fell to her death, and that he thought it would be like that from then on; but his memory came back after a year, sharp as always.

As Kalle lifts the dwarf girl against his chest, the longing for his own children wells up a hundredfold, makes his jaw ache. He hums to her, strokes her wide face. *From now on I am part of your story . . . and you of mine.*

Too dim in The Last Supper for others to see his tears, but he hears them say how good he is with babies. And he's grateful they can recognize that.

The giant Nowack and Luzia line a basket with a blanket. Just for one day, they promise Silvio Ludwig. And keep the dwarf child from one day to the next until it becomes forever. But Luzia's bliss erases her beauty so that she looks too wholesome, content. Tragedy has abandoned her and she has to paint it—the downturn of lips and eyes—for each performance.

Kalle transforms God's burning bush on their wagon into Aladdin's magic lamp. They love his plan to whittle down God, then overlay a harem and carve a little Red Sea between the harem and Moses who is about to part the waters.

"God," says the giant Nowack, "must be whittled down once in a while."

"You—" Kalle starts laughing. "And here I thought you were serious."

"No, you didn't." The giant Nowack nudges him with his elbow.

Silvio pretends to be startled whenever he notices the found-ling. "You're still here?"

He carries her to see the dancing dogs. Teaches her to ap-plaud.

"Are they giving you enough to eat?" He shakes his head till a *Zwieback* falls from it.

Though the child lives with Luzia and the giant Nowack, they all raise her. It's only natural that they name her after Pia Ludwig, the dazzling high-wire artist.

It so pleases Herr Ludwig. Animates him. "Pia . . ." he mur-murs to the baby and kisses her toes, her fingers. "Fireflies . . ."

Hans-Jürgen Nowack bends toward him. An ease in that, a generosity. "Tell me about the fireflies, Herr Ludwig."

The Whirling Nowack Twins arrived at the Ludwig Zirkus just days after me. One Twin is a giant; the other a runt. They audi-tion with the runt on his back, knees bent, and when he raises his bare feet, the giant comes from a running leap to stand on the soles of the runt, who propels him into a headstand, then a dozen somersaults. Graceful and strong, they fly apart and—in less than a heartbeat—land on their knees, side by side, arms spread.

"Excellent," Herr Ludwig says.

I applaud.

"Usually we start with me juggling him," the giant explains, "and work up to the more difficult acts. Like this."

"Our audiences won't believe Twins," says Herr Ludwig.

"We've never had a problem with that," declares the runt.

"Once they find a reason to doubt you, they'll doubt every-thing our Zirkus does."

"Not with us," says the runt.

"Not with the Ludwig Zirkus." Silvio takes a step toward him.

The two glare at each other like roosters about to strike.

"But—" the runt starts.

Silvio slices one hand through the air. "You'll find another Zirkus."

"Cousins, then?" The giant's voice, mellow. A shelf of eyebrows as if chiseled from wood and not yet finished.

"And are you?" asks Herr Ludwig. "Cousins?"

"Yes," the runt says without blinking.

"We can do cousins," says the giant.

"And we can juggle anything."

"Dogs and torches."

"Furniture."

"I'm Oliver," says the giant.

"I'm Hans-Jürgen."

Silvio chews on his lip. Glances at his father. Both nod.

"Cousins, then," says Herr Ludwig. "The Whirling Nowack Cousins."

16

Going Maternal

Usually Girls leave the St. Margaret Home within months or even weeks of giving birth; most return to their families, but Tilli invents reasons to stay, readies herself for the Sisters' requests before they can voice them. She welcomes frightened new Girls who've heard about this far-away mansion where they can learn to play the harp, to paint and embroider. But first they must learn how to take care of the children already there. In the Big Nursery on the second floor she introduces them to the older children, shows them how to coax them out of sadness before it can close around them. How, the Girls ask, and Tilli says by just loving them, by singing to them and making shadow animals against the wall with their hands and hers. In the Little Nursery she shows them how to bathe infants so that even the fussiest ones stop crying. She warns them about people who want to adopt babies. "They'll be all nice to you, but once they have your baby, they don't want you. Some lie about where they live so you can't find your baby again."

She coaches the Girls in fainting—collapse gracefully or lurch toward the ground. "Fainting gets you out of church, you and at least two Girls who get to carry you out."

"I don't want to get out of church," says the newest Girl, Marlene.

But the others practice fainting. A game who can faint the fastest, lie still the longest without moving her eyelids.

Marlene has prayed to give birth in church, proof of immaculate conception. Since she doesn't know how this baby got inside her—just as it happened to the *Jungfrau* Maria—she vows to raise it just like the *Jungfrau* Maria raised her Baby Jesus. And if that means lamenting at the foot of his cross when he's a man, Marlene will make that sacrifice, too. Soused by religion, she is a bad influence on other Girls, especially Hedda who sleeps on the narrow bed across from her and becomes Marlene's best friend because both are determined to keep their babies. The Sisters worry they'll sway other Girls who have signed adoption papers. Keeping a baby can be romanticized by Girls if they don't get separated right away.

One Sunday the wife of the blacksmith stays after Mass and surprises Hedda and Marlene with a generous offer: they and their babies can live in the room above the smithy in return for housework and letting the wife of the blacksmith help with their babies. She has the sad and hidden gaze of barren women who forever yearn for babies. Her husband doesn't believe in adoption, she says, but has agreed to her plan.

Whenever Tilli takes Wilhelm out in the *Kinderwagen*—baby buggy—she wants to keep walking, take him to a place far away. As her outings with him get longer, the Sisters suspect she's going maternal on them. They've seen this happen with other Girls and it devastates them.

"Not good for Tilli."

"Or for Wilhelm."

"Trying to replace her own baby."

"It prolongs her heartache."

"Poor girl."

"Wilhelm also gives her joy."

"I've written to the parents. Twice," Sister Hildegunde says. "They won't take her back."

"Tilli won't understand."

"They say Tilli is immoral."

"Oh, please!"

"That she seduced her younger brother."

"Younger? She only has one brother and he's her twin."

"They say she'll do it again."

"The only ones immoral are those parents. They chose the boy over her."

"And she's such a considerate girl."

"Warm-hearted."

"A good worker."

"What if we sent her upstairs to work with the older children?"

"Older than her own child. Older than Wilhelm."

"She has been Wilhelm's wet nurse. Think of the bonding."

"It could have been any other Girl."

"But it wasn't. I tried to get Wilhelm used to other Girls, but he refused to nurse."

"But to separate her altogether from Wilhelm . . . it's not right."

"Not altogether. She'll still see him."

"Whatever we do, we must preserve Tilli's dignity."

"Her dignity, *ja*."

"Just less time with Wilhelm."

Concerned about Tilli's attachment to the boy, Sister Franziska carries him upstairs for more frequent visits with Lotte.

"I need your help in the nursery," she tells Lotte one afternoon.

"I can't."

"At least your presence." She situates Wilhelm in his mother's arms.

"Tilli likes taking care of him."

"Tilli is too devoted to him."

"She loves him."

"Some Sisters worry she's gone maternal!"

Sisters can be so naive, Lotte thinks. It has to do with being virgins. Soul this and soul that—and what of the body?

"She's still a child . . ."

"Who gave birth to a child."

"I don't know how to be near children."

"I have seen you with your children and—"

"—and they died."

Sister Franziska holds her gaze, fearless of Lotte's pain, though a pain like that can blind you, lay bare your own pains raw and sudden. "I've known you all your life—as a child, a woman, a mother—and you were always loving and patient."

She coaxes Lotte into helping her.

"Just one hour tomorrow. This once."

And then again.

"Two hours."

Soon, half days.

"We can pay you."

"You're giving me so much already."

As Lotte assists Sister Franziska and tends to newborns in the Little Nursery, she feels a generation older than the pregnant Girls, though she's just twenty-five. Sister teaches her all she knows about keeping their Girls alive during and after birth: bleedings; cold compresses; enemas mixed from linseed tea and new milk and laudanum.

"Each child we help into the world," Sister Franziska tells her, "makes our losses more bearable."

Your losses too? But Lotte doesn't know how to ask.

Easier to talk with Sister Franziska about what needs to be done. Like how to bind their breasts after delivery. "Above all we must be merciful," Sister says. "We must not do it too soon. We must not wrap the bandages too tightly."

As Lotte digs herself into training, Wilhelm stays in the Little Nursery where Tilli watches over him. Other Girls want to play with him too, but they have to ask Tilli first. She allows them to play house with Wilhelm and her, but she gets to say how. The Girls take turns being Wilhelm's *Mutti* and *Vati;* they laugh when they get him to crawl after a ball they roll from one wall of the nursery to another; they like to dress him up with clothing from the bin that's stocked with knitting and sewing projects the Old Women do for the St. Margaret children.

When Sister Franziska decides it's time for Wilhelm to stay with his mother every night, Lotte doesn't object. Doesn't object when he leans against her, little breath warm. Guilt is no longer her only lens. Joy manages to claim a few minutes of her days. Wilhelm sleeping next to her lifts her hours from limbo. Soon she looks for him during the day, ventures to the nursery; it surprises her how content Wilhelm is with the other children: he reaches for them, laughs. Instant siblings—*don't think that don't*—

One afternoon she finds him with Tilli on their hands and knees, imitating the Sisters' black dog, *Verrückter Hund.* Crazy Dog.

Tilli stands up. "I'm just visiting for a few minutes."

Wilhelm coos when *Verrückter Hund* rolls over, folds those absurdly long legs against his belly, makes himself a small bundle.

Lotte crouches, pats the white fur on the dog's sturdy neck. "When did you learn to crawl so fast, Wilhelm?"

Everyone wants a bit of Wilhelm, Tilli thinks. Other children, Pregnant Girls, the old Sisters. *And now his mother.* Who rubs the dog's pink belly. Pink. Wilhelm crawls around the dog. Hits his head against a chair and screams. His mother scoops him up, kisses his head, whispers to him, but he's inconsolable, stretches his arms toward Tilli, only stops crying when Tilli bends toward him.

At first Lotte is relieved. *But why then do I feel resentful?*

And from Tilli a small triumph. *Lotte needs me.*

17

Marlene and Hedda

One Sunday morning Marlene's prayers are validated. As the contractions rip through her, rip her open, she curses the baby, curses God, curses her best friend, Hedda, who is on the floor cradling Marlene's head to protect it from crashing against the bottoms of the pews. Marlene's blasphemy paralyzes the priest in his pulpit who suddenly can no longer distinguish between St. Margaret Girls four decades ago and all St. Margaret Girls since, including Girls in the pews below him. *New faces young faces and yet the same.* But the Sisters are distinctive, young when he was young, old now that he is old. One of them he has loved. Loves still. He has given Sister Hildegunde no indication; but she understands he's devoted to her and that he'll hear her confession any time, night or day. Not that he has occasion to be alone with her at night. Sister Hildegunde only comes to his confessional in the mornings after Mass, arrives with two Sisters who genuflect and file into a pew to wait for each other while one whispers sins to him.

.   .   .

"Let's get you down from the pulpit." A hand around the priest's wrist.

Instinctively he covers it with his hand—*finally oh*—covers *Sister Hildegunde's slender hand and the black hem of her sleeve worn at the edge, the vow of poverty, of austerity. Sister Hildegunde tugs him from the pulpit, one step two steps down to the next plank before descending to the lower plank.*

"Careful now," Sister Hildegunde whispers.

"Thank you," he whispers back.

"One step two steps down."

Sister Hildegunde is old. He is old. Except she looks young because the wimple conceals her neck. Nuns have that advantage. While his neck betrays his aging. Creases and folds. But that's changing because he's discovered how to intermix youthfulness and penance. At home, after morning prayers, he remains on his knees, tilts his head back as far as he can, and opens his mouth wide to stretch the skin on his throat; he holds that pose until it's torture and then enhances his suffering by stretching his lower lip across his upper lip in the direction of his nostrils.

"Now we are both old, Sister Hildegunde."

"I'm Sister Elinor."

"No!"

"Yes."

Dizzy, he is dizzy. Oh— "You are not Sister Hildegunde?"

"I'm not." Sister Elinor steadies him. "It's too late to move Marlene to the infirmary. She waited too long."

"Marlene cannot do that here," he objects.

But Marlene does. Such disruption—curses and tears and hiccups and a whirlpool of Sisters who hustle Girls and parishioners from the chapel—*out now out*—but not enough Sisters to shield the priest who has never seen a crotch, a bloody crotch, a bloody baby. Whenever he administers last rites to dying mothers, he protects his modesty and sits by the head of the bed.

This Girl isn't even on a bed. This Girl sprawls on the floor of the church with her legs spread and proclaims: "My son's name is Jesus." Then crosses herself.

Sacrilege. The priest has never heard of a person named Jesus. And this Jesus is so scrawny and gray-skinned that the priest must christen him right away—naked as he's born.

Sister Franziska grabs Baby Jesus from the priest, holds him upside down by his feet, and whacks his rump.

"Don't hurt him," Marlene wails.

When Sister slaps him again it comes to Marlene that her true calling is to be a nun. "Such an offering to God," she cries, elated. "Such an offering to all you Sisters—"

Sister Franziska lays Baby Jesus on the altar and opens her wide mouth across his face to find a gossamer thread of breath.

Marlene's teeth shatter and she tries to sit up, but Sister Hildegunde guides her back down.

"My Baby Jesus and I will live with you at the St. Margaret Home."

Sister Hildegunde and another Sister spread cold wet sheets around Marlene. "She is burning up."

"You—" Marlene wails, "you would reject the *Heilige Jungfrau* if she stood here with Baby Jesus in her arms."

"We're trying to save both of you."

In the dark dormitory the girls huddle around Hedda and wail with her. But then one steps away. Another. They stomp their bare feet, hard, pound their soles into the floor, and howl as they dance sideways in a circle. When Hedda tries to join in, she teeters and they all link arms to steady her. Faster now, their dance. Like a drum beat in the chapel below, where the Sisters pray over the bodies of Marlene and Baby Jesus. *Nothing has changed. Everything has changed.* When the Sisters arrived on Nordstrand they were young. Now they are old, while the girls remain young, forever replaced by new girls who play pranks and die and dance and squabble over who is the best nun. Some adore Sister Franziska, compassionate and accomplished; others swear Sister Elinor is the best, light-hearted and generous.

First dawn and Sister Ida shakes Lotte awake.

"What? What is it?"

"It's Hedda! Sister Franziska says for you to deliver the baby."

"I'm not ready."

"Hedda is ready. Hurry—"

"Hedda isn't due yet."

"Well, she is ready."

"But I've never done this alone."

"Sister Franziska says you know how." Sister Ida starts crying. "She's in the chapel praying over Marlene and her baby."

"Oh God— Both of them?" Now Lotte is crying.

"Yes. Both—" Sister Ida's voice gives out, and she taps her throat with two fingers. She motions to the bed where Wilhelm lies asleep on his stomach. "I'll stay with . . ."

Hands sweaty on the banister, Lotte hastens down the marble stairs.

But in the delivery room something odd happens: her hands become knowledgeable, and her heart grows steady. There's nothing beyond this sacred work, no fear, no sorrow. *Only Hedda. Now.* Sacred to be the first to touch Hedda's newborn, sooner than Lotte touched her own newborns because a midwife held them first. *But now Lotte's hands.* Now. And though the streaks on Hedda's daughter—white and pink—are the same as on Lotte's newborns, this bringing into life does not tilt her into her own loss as she feared, but calms her, allows her to give something she didn't know she had.

I can do this?

I can do this again.

"Don't forget," Hedda says. "I'm keeping her."

"I won't forget." Lotte lays the infant against Hedda's breast.
"Is Marlene dead?"

Lotte strokes the Girl's damp hair. "Yes."

"Promise you won't let anyone take my baby."

"I promise."

Hedda shivers. "They'll try to adopt her. Tilli said to Marlene that people will be all nice to you, but once they have your baby, they don't want you."

"No one can take her."

"Tilli said to Marlene that some come from far away with false names and lie about where they live so you can't find your baby again."

"Tilli doesn't know everything. Look at me, Hedda. You did not sign adoption papers. The Sisters and I won't let anyone take your daughter. We know your decision. We also know you make good plans."

After confession on Saturdays the Old Women gather for *Kaffeeklatsch*—coffee *und* gossip—in each other's kitchens to compare penances the priest has assigned.

"He usually is fair."

"Fair enough."

"A bit pompous."

"And vain."

"He does those neck stretches he learned from the sexton."

"Two vain men."

"With sagging necks."

"Sagging everything."

The Old Women laugh.

"Still, he is generous and will sit with you through your grief, even your rage."

"He wants to be a good priest."

"And a good man."

"But he's more like a boy."

"Well-meaning."

"And naïve. He thinks he knows more about the Sisters than they know about one another."

"He doesn't even know that Sister Konstanze and Sister Ida lie with each other at night."

"Then why do we know?"

"Because we know how to know."

"So philosophical."

"Do you think he's truthful with his own confessor?"

"Not about coveting the bride of Christ."

"Hoping to break the sixth commandment."

"I don't think so. For him it's more exciting to follow Sister Hildegunde around."

"Lusting from a distance."

"Distance because Sister Hildegunde knows how to get away from him."

"Or send him off with a list of duties."

"Don't underestimate chaste obsession. It outlasts other obsessions."

"Like Maria's fisherman."

"You can tell by the purity in his eyes."

"He never had another woman after Maria jilted him."

"Some pursued him. Some in this very room."

The Old Women count on one another to keep confidences. But one may get reckless and take gossip outside their circle, gossip she has no right to. "I thought you'd want to know . . ." She may even spin stories. Intoxicated by the curiosity of her listeners, she won't notice when the Old Women exclude her from matters of confidence. This is instinctive, does not need discussion. Easy enough to wish the reckless one a good morning; to share a recipe or news of a grandchild to be born; to sit together embroidering initials on handkerchiefs and knitting mittens linked with crocheted rope, impossible to lose; to construct huge *Schultüten*—school cones from stiff paper, paint them in bright colors, trim them with ribbons and pictures that reflect each child's interests; to visit merchants who are glad to contribute gifts for the six-year-olds starting school. To sweeten their first day, the Old Women present each child with a colorful *Schultüte* as tall as a six-year-old, each different in decor, each filled with hazelnuts and a blackboard; dried apple slices and marbles; raisin bread and a ruler; chalk and initialed handkerchiefs and alphabet blocks. They tell the children how a *Schultüte* eased their first day of school.

"I still have mine."

"I still have my grandfather's *Schultüte*."

Frost Sketches Flowers on the Windows

Frost sketches flowers on the windows of the St. Margaret Home the morning Lotte prepares to leave. After breakfast the Sisters embrace her and Wilhelm.

"I'm so grateful to you," she tells them.

"And we are proud of you."

"I'll be here for work every day," she promises.

As she carries Wilhelm home, fog rises from the ground, shrouds people and animals, houses. Her front door sticks and she presses the length of her back against it, rocks until it gives. Inside, the smell of absence, damp and stale as if no one had lived here for years—not months. Here, too, frost flowers on the windows, but already melting, growing luminous.

Late into that night Lotte is startled awake. Knocking at her door. A steady and relentless knocking.

Tilli. In a panic and without a coat. "I'm strong I can work for you—"

"You can't be out there without a coat." Lotte pulls her inside, leads her to the chair by the stove.

"I can work for you in your house and in the fields. I can help with Wilhelm."

Lotte tucks a blanket around her. "For now—" She keeps her voice as gentle as she can. "—I need to live in my house alone."

"But you're not alone. You have Wilhelm."

"Alone with Wilhelm, then."

"Please, let me stay." Tilli's chin trembles. But she manages to thrust it out and say, "For now."

Lotte rubs the Girl's shoulders. "Oh, Tilli—" If she could just hire her, she would; but to let her live here means more, means she cannot turn her out, means making Tilli her family. If only Tilli were not so pushy.

"I can cook and I can darn and I can wash windows and floors and—"

"I need to learn how to live alone with my son."

"Where is Wilhelm?"

"Upstairs asleep. You'll see him tomorrow."

She lets Tilli stay the night, sleep by the stove, and in the morning they walk to the St. Margaret Home with Wilhelm.

One day when Lotte doesn't get to the St. Margaret Home at dawn, Tilli arrives and insists she take care of Lotte who is feverish, weak. Wilhelm is screaming, full diaper and empty belly. After Tilli cleans him up, she brings Lotte a tin cup with cool water. Lays a damp washcloth across her forehead.

Wilhelm paws at Tilli's breast. He knows how to open buttons. Is determined.

His mother is watching Tilli who suddenly feels cautious.

"Should I?" she asks. "He's hungry."

Lotte nods but it irks her seeing her son at Tilli's breast. He loves Tilli better than her and it can't be good for him if this continues. *Or for me.*

Spit bubbles, Wilhelm blows spit bubbles and Tilli lifts him high. They giggle and he scrambles his little legs in the air to get back to Tilli.

He doesn't look at me like that. Still, Lotte is glad he has another person who loves him. And that's true. She should be glad. Also true: Tilli is taking him away from Lotte. My last child.

"He wants to come to you," Tilli lies, afraid Lotte resents her for Wilhelm's love. *But Wilhelm has been mine till now.*

Lotte holds up her arms and Tilli nestles Wilhelm on the bed.

He pats his mother's face, plants birdie kisses on her nose.

She says, *"Mein lieber, lieber Junge."* My dear, dear boy.

His pats get harder.

"That's enough." Tilli tries to catch his hands in hers.

His face darkens. He slaps his mother.

But Lotte doesn't flinch. "It's because he remembers me tossing him into the sea."

"He is too young to remember."

"Oh, he knows, Tilli."

PART FOUR

1859–1866

Men Who Turn to Stone

What seizes my heart the first time I see The Sensational Sebastian is how he fastens his eyes on me, only me, as he lets go of the trapeze and catapults himself through the air in his emerald suit. *A man built for flying.*

I'm sure he hasn't performed with the Ludwig Zirkus because I went to the show every September when the Zirkus arrived in Rodenäs, my village near the German-Danish border where I went to school and served my apprenticeship at the Becker Mode Atelier. I came for the stories the ringmaster staged. Herr Ludwig had such high regard for his monkeys that he assigned them roles in his Biblical stories, elevating them to saints and angels. Affectionate and clever, they brought him whatever he wanted for his stories—banners or candles, a stuffed parrot or Moses's stone tablets. Although his stories began with scenes from the Bible, he roused his audience to change the outcome with their imagination and memories. As ringmaster, he tapped into your hunger for magic because he understood you hadn't come to see a performance. No. You'd come so that he could show you what you wanted, something fantastic, so uniquely yours that later—when you talked about the Ludwig Zirkus—you'd mention details others won't recall, the white dog's blue eyelids, say, or that Luzia The Clown reminded you of your *Erbtante*—inheritance aunt.

Outside the big tent, The Sensational Sebastian stands in his shimmering suit and extends one hand as if to bless me. He lays two fingers between my eyebrows.

"I have not seen you before," I manage to say, intimidated by his elegance and confidence.

"It's my first year with the Ludwigs."

Instead of going home, I let him lead me toward a wagon decorated with panels of life-sized angels and saints. The entrance is in the center of a carved panel with the Annunciation scene. As he folds down his front stoop, the door swings open, and I have to laugh because here I stand in front of the *Jungfrau* Maria while the Archangel Gabriel informs her she'll carry the son of God inside her womb.

"Why are you laughing?" The Sensational Sebastian asks.

I motion toward the panel. "Plenty of warning for any woman who has her doubts about immaculate conception."

"Ah. So you would like to come inside."

"I would like to stay outside," I say, intent on hiding my awkwardness.

"Should I believe you?"

Quickly, I sit down on the front stoop. Hide my hands in the pleats of my skirt, hands chapped from fine stitching and from lace. "I'm a seamstress. Wedding and evening; silk and satin; lace and beads—"

"Does the seamstress have a name, or must I invent one for her?"

"Sabine Florian," I say, wishing I'd let him invent a fashionable name for me.

The Sensational Sebastian lowers himself next to me on the stoop, one elbow braced against the Archangel Gabriel's wooden knee. His thighs stretch the emerald fabric. Those eyes of his—burning my skin.

I want to touch the dip of his throat. *No*—

"Don't let some archangel scare you away." His smile. No woman in the world for him but me.

I know I can't tell my mother about meeting him. She's so proper and strict that she won't see his beauty. Just his danger. *As if I didn't know.* I turn from him, point at the pink-gray sky where geese pull their arrows toward the Nordsee—large arrows and smaller arrows—their harsh calls dwindling the farther out they fly.

But he won't let me distract him. "All those Bible scenarios bring us customers. Even the preachy ones justify buying Zirkus tickets. The Ludwigs aren't even like that."

"Like what?"

"Church-fearing." He tells me about growing up in a Zirkus family. "Once I was two I trained daily, bending and leaping and hanging."

"That's awfully young."

"With children you have to start early."

"Not that early."

"I walked on my hands before I turned three." He sounds proud. "I earned my own money before I could count it."

He doesn't have the propriety to spare me from his gaze as most people will when your face is afire, and I long to brush against his thigh, undo the braided closures on his emerald jacket. The fabric is worn shiny, but the design is fashionable, sculpting his chest and waist and shoulders.

I can learn to copy this design once I sew his clothes . . .

.   .   .

Though my mother has warned me about the fragile worth of a young woman's reputation, I follow The Sensational Sebastian into his Annunciation wagon.

"I've never been with a woman who wants sex as much as a man," he tells me when I wake to sun through the curtain and the shadow of a wash line against the wall.

The heat of his breath races from my ear to my down-there. I feel luscious. Greedy.

"Women," he says, "endure men's lust without pleasure."

"I can't believe I'm the only woman who—"

"Oh . . . but you are, Sabine." He studies my face, closely. Is he shocked by my appetites? Intrigued? Trying to prove to himself—and to me—that I'm not like other women?

I'm embarrassed, push back. "How many women?"

He makes a fist, counts his fingers as he lets them pop up, makes another fist, and continues counting. "Eight. That includes you."

"Hardly enough for your assumption about women."

He laughs. "You'll make me reconsider."

"About those women before me . . ."

He presses himself against me, traces my jaw from one ear lobe to the other.

". . . those women merely endured you?"

He yanks an invisible blade from his chest. "How about you and men?"

"Nine," I lie, tripling my sins to be ahead of him.

"Did you count me?"

I try for a mysterious smile.

"Did you, Sabine?"

"Not yet." I swing myself across his thighs, flick my thumbs across his nipples, then rake my fingers toward his navel—*who am I? what am I doing?*—and down through his pubic hair without touching him, there, not yet, though he bucks to get himself into my hand.

.   .   .

The Sensational Sebastian and I live three wagons from the kitchen wagon called The Last Supper. I've missed my chance of returning home the night of the show. Missed it again the following morning. And now that I've missed that chance for eleven days, it's too late to go home. *Too soon.* I earn my wages: mend costumes, match old designs, help The Sensational Sebastian brew an elixir that he claims will make mortals live forever. Though skeptical, I make sure he swallows a spoonful at breakfast, because every time he performs I'm terrified he'll tumble into death: his hand will sweat and slip from the trapeze or he won't catch the trapeze as he flies toward its arc. I cannot imagine being without him.

At the concession stand, before and after each show, I sell his elixir in clay pots with calligraphed labels, *Für Immer*—Forever. Next to me our cook sells *Würstchen*—sausages, and *Brötchen mit Fisch*—rolls with fish. Her face is lovely except for the lower half, sunken as if her features were patched from different lifetimes.

"If you are ever ill," she tells me, "I'll make your favorite food for you, but I need to know what it is. Now. You may not be able to tell me if you ever get deadly ill."

"*Kuchen. Apfelkuchen.*"

Customers wait in line for our Venetian candy, a golden confection of nuts and honey, so unlike the cheap candies other Zirkusse sell. Our recipe comes from Herr Ludwig's dead wife, Pia, who grew up in Venice where she sold her confections from a wooden display strapped to her waist.

"And your second favorite?"

"Some other *Kuchen.*"

She nudges me. "Confess."

"*Erdbeertorte.*"

"A sweet lining to your stomach, then, Danish Woman!"

"Why do you call me that?"

"Because you're from the Danish border and are fluent in German and Danish."

Everyone at the Ludwig Zirkus speaks and dreams in several languages, evidence of where we've lived and worked, plenty to serve us as we cross the borders. Dutch, German, and Italian for both Ludwigs. French and German for The Sensational Sebastian. Russian and German for Luzia The Clown. Half a dozen languages for Marliss The Cook and her husband.

Back home in Rodenäs, I recalled my dreams upon waking, but being with The Sensational Sebastian erases those flicker images of night, draws me beyond my skin, toward him.

We travel north, cross the border into Denmark to perform in Tønder and Boderslev. No matter where we stop, we barter Zirkus tickets for food: vegetables and fruit in season or canned; wrinkled apples and pears and carrots from the root cellars of farmers; fish and sometimes meat.

In the towns where we set up the big tent, The Sensational Sebastian points out statues in parks and cemeteries. "Men who turned to stone because they settled in one place."

"Those statues have never been anything but stone."

"Ach, Sabine . . . Sabinchen." He cups his long hands around my face. Kisses me. And again.

"Chiseled from stone to resemble humans," I whisper into his mouth.

"I love you so much." Tears in his eyes. He blinks them away. "You're so lucky it's me you found."

"Before you turn to stone?"

"No no." His laugh lines deepen.

"I miss my dreams."

"I mean lucky you didn't get seduced by one of those fellows who have a new woman every season. Some women will follow a Zirkus for months."

"And now I'm one of them?"

"Not like you. Last spring a woman from Oberkassel followed us. She was after the Twenty-Four-Hour Man. As usual."

"Every night I used to dream."

"Audiences think Zirkus people are amoral. That's why they
expect behavior they won't tolerate in their towns. I still don't
see why the Twenty-Four-Hour Man. He's so ugly."

"So ugly he's handsome."

"Is that what you think?"

"It's what Cook says."

"What else does she have to say about her husband?"

"It's . . . confidential."

"Tell me." He plants flutter kisses all over my neck.

I laugh. "He isn't just called the Twenty-Four-Hour Man for
arriving twenty-four hours ahead of the Zirkus."

"Too fast, then?"

"Stamina."

The Ludwigs barter a young lion from a big Zirkus that won't
keep crippled animals. His left hind leg turns inward—a gen-
uflection, a curtsy—so that he stumbles over himself; but he
doesn't look clumsy.

"He looks majestic," says Luzia.

"Like a Sphinx," Herr Ludwig says.

"Good temperament," Silvio says.

"Let's name him Egypt."

Egypt becomes ours for two ponies and forty hours of tent
repair by The Whirling Nowacks—Icarianists—not only quick
and talented at foot juggling one another, but also at patch-
ing and mending canvas, using pliers to yank long needles with
twine through the stiff fabric.

At the Ludwig Zirkus, the lion Egypt does not have to brace
the head of the ringmaster between his jaws.

He does not have to leap through burning rings.

He does not have to feign fury.

He is Egypt now, the leading actor in Herr Ludwig's scenario: *The Seven Plagues of Egypt*. Egypt is content to amble around our arena, led by Luzia The Clown. I design a saddle for him, silver and cognac damask, and one matching stocking that we pull up high on his injured leg and anchor to his saddle where seven monkeys teeter and clutch one another.

Every performance is unique. What remains the same is Herr Ludwig's dignity when he strides into the ring, tuxedo and top hat, giving all of you magic and exhilaration that make the intake of your breaths more vibrant.

20

Young Widows with Infants

Once I'm with child, I stop correcting The Sensational Sebastian about staying in motion to prevent his body from turning to stone. It's a story he needs to believe—just as I need to believe that with me he'll be different. Stay. Forever the playful lover who turns to me, only me, after he's dazzled every female in the audience.

But he grows restless. Smokes more. Can't fall asleep in the quiet. We winter on farmland by the Rhein in Emmerich, the last German town before the Dutch border, where local children come to spy on our training sessions.

I nest. Sew blue curtains and line them with muslin. Stencil the wooden floor of the Annunciation wagon with clouds.

The Sensational Sebastian likes my decorating.

Then The Sensational Sebastian does not like my decorating.

"Too much like a woman's place."

"Herr Ludwig likes it."

"That man is unnatural. Just watch him with those monkeys."

"What are you saying?"

"You know why he is famous as a monkey trainer?"

"Because he is very good at it."

"Because he has . . . unnaturally close relationships with monkeys. That's why he looks like a monkey."

"He does not!"

"Crossing over. A territorial thing. I heard one of his monkeys mauled him."

"Heard from whom?"

"From him—I heard it from him. So proud of being understood by monkeys. Accepted by them. Not a word about the danger."

"I don't believe you."

"He thinks he is so remarkable. Courting monkeys."

"That's nasty. You get like that when you're bored."

He stretches out on our bed. "Come here, Sabine."

I shake my head. "Don't talk nasty about him."

"Just look at his ears."

The second week of February 1859, it gets so cold that The Sensational Sebastian and I don't want to get out of bed. Snow pelts the river at a slant as if drawn with chalk, but inside our Annunciation wagon we keep each other warm.

"I think Luzia likes the giant Nowack," I say.

"What did you find out?"

"Nothing for sure. Just intuition."

"She's a great performer."

"So is he."

"But that huge forehead!" The Sensational Sebastian leaps up, pounds the window.

I rise to my knees, brace my belly. "What is it?"

"Stop it, you!"

A cluster of farm boys, hooting and throwing snowballs at two dogs frozen together while mating. As the dogs yowl and try to scramble in opposite directions, the boys throw more snowballs.

"Stop it, you!" The Sensational Sebastian pounds the window.

The boys shriek. Clap.

In a frenzy now, the dogs bite the air. Struggle to pull apart.

Stark naked and yelling, The Sensational Sebastian leaps from our wagon, shakes his fists at the boys; a thick stripe of brown hair crawls up his back and neck; tufts of hair sprout on his shoulders. *Like a bear, a savage beast.* The boys scatter.

As he kneels in the deep snow and steadies the dogs, rubbing their throats and muzzles, I think what a tender father he will be after all. I had no idea he could be that gentle, that patient. Tears in my eyes, I watch him slide his hands low beneath the dogs' bellies, stroking and talking and warming them till he can guide them apart.

The Sensational Sebastian loves me for as long as he can see the exit. As I grow wider around our child, I block the light. Still, he gets past me. Joins another Zirkus that's traveling inland. Proves himself a visionary. And me a dreamer.

"There are men like that . . ." Herr Ludwig tells me. "Always on the way to somewhere else."

"Was he more restless than others?"

"He was terrified."

"Of me?"

"Of living in any one place and forgetting the road. Many of them are. I hope you'll stay with us."

I thank him. Because how can I go back home to the shame of being with child but without husband? "At least here no one knows me."

Silvio Ludwig yells for the runt. Testy with one another, they haul the Annunciation wagon next to the Ludwigs' as if the Zirkus had been expecting me all along.

"Now that we're neighbors," Silvio tells me, "I hope you won't hear my father's snoring."

"I'm far enough away."

"His snoring wakes me up several times a night."

"I usually fall asleep early."

"It's been getting worse. I'm tired all the time."

I don't tell him that, by three in the morning, I'm awake, mouth dry with fear of what's going to happen next. To keep that fear at bay, I recite a list of my sewing plans till I doze off.

> *new outfits for dancing dogs*
> *iron Luzia's cape*
> *take in seams on Herr Ludwig's tuxedo + remind him to*
>   *eat more*
> *mend costumes for Whirling Nowacks*
> *buy fabric for Egypt's stocking and saddle blanket*
> *blankets and clothes for the baby*

I promise myself to stop believing anything The Sensational Sebastian tells me, including the powers of his elixir *Für Immer*. No more flimflam guarantees. No more concocting Forever. Silvio Ludwig shows me how to concoct his mother's Venetian candy, sticky and sweet.

My dreams come back to me.

The child of The Sensational Sebastian begins her break from me six weeks and three days after he's made his break. Pains take me while our caravan travels along bumpy roads through flat terrain, far from any town. Silvio Ludwig saddles a horse and rides off in search of a midwife.

His father stays with me. "It always gets better," he says when I scream.

The iron smell of blood so strong it's like a taste.

I curse The Sensational Sebastian. "What's his true name?"

"Didn't he tell you?"

"He said The Sensational Sebastian."

"Fritz."

"Fritz?"

"He was born Fritz Fuchs."

Laughing pulls my belly against its own rising, crushes the layers of myself. I heave.

"Would you like me to get one of the women?"

"I came to many of your shows before I met him. I—"

"*Tief atmen,* Sabine." Breathe deeply.

"You are the best storyteller."

"This story is for real."

"I looked forward to your stories in the ring all year long."

"Let me get Luzia."

I'm taken by an abrupt longing for my mother. Want my mother with me. Now.

"Luzia said to get her if you need her."

"She'll keep talking and talking, not listening, just talking."

"I can ask Cook."

"She'll want to stuff food into me." I feel nauseous, as if I've eaten too much.

"She gets like that. With all of us." He smiles. "Tell me about your mother."

"How do you know I'm thinking about her?"

"Tell me your mother's name."

"Heike."

"Tell me about how it was between you . . . before you came to us."

"My mother has secrets. My mother—" I moan.

"Go on, Sabinchen."

"—only eats half of the communion host. My mother says—"

"Go on."

"—one must never use up all of the Lord."

Herr Ludwig cups the crest of my belly with his hands, leans in to listen. His hair falls away from the ear that faces me, a nubble, a chewed-up nubble that he usually hides well under his hair or hat.

I don't feel disgust. Just a strange tenderness for him.

He raises his head, shows me how to draw with my fingertips, circles small and large that reach along the sides of my belly. "Like this, Sabinchen."

I whisper, "You have secrets too."

"Many secrets."

My belly rises and hardens. "Secrets about . . . the monkey."

"What monkey?"

"The one that mauled you."

"Circles. Make circles . . . Circles."

I concentrate on those circles, make them come together around the peak of my belly button, then widen along my ribs, my waist.

"Very good."

His praise brings me to tears. "Thank you." Crying and gasping for air.

"*Tief atmen,* Sabinchen," he reminds me.

I suck in all the air in the wagon. All the air in the world. Push it out.

"I was arrogant," he says. "Assumed a human code of behavior from animals. Gratitude and ethics—"

"My mother—"

"*Tief atmen.*" He guides my hands around my belly. Hums to me.

"My mother walks with the whole length of her body lean-
ing forward—"

"So do you, Sabine."

"My mother makes . . . lace."

Screaming, then.

"—lace . . . the most . . . expensive lace in Rodenäs."

Screaming I'm the one screaming, while Herr Ludwig keeps
humming and saying, "It always gets better. It always—"

Hands limber and sturdy tug the child from me. "A girl," he
announces in his ringmaster's voice just as she wails and flings
out her arms as if startled by her own voice. "What a little performer."

I reach for her.

"Already she wants applause." Gently, he lowers her onto my
belly.

Slippery, she is. Slippery with whitish streaks and with blood.
No air between her and me, that's how close, except now she
is outside me and already rooting about. I didn't know it was
possible to love like this, and with this love comes the shock
that my mother must have loved me like this. How I must have
devastated her by leaving without word. To lose my daughter
is too much to fathom. I hold on to her. Give her my mother's
name. *Heike.*

"Young widows with infants," Herr Ludwig says, "can count
on the mercy of their neighbors."

"Everyone knows I'm not a widow."

"Your child doesn't."

"How about old widows?" I laugh though I'm stretched sore.
"What separates us young widows from old widows?"

"Youth and—"

"—and evidence," I claim, feeling reckless, giddy.

"Evidence?"

I caress my baby's sticky belly. "Evidence of *fögeln*—" I cover my mouth. But I've only shocked myself.

Herr Ludwig chuckles. "How very . . . astute."

"I never talk like this."

He kisses the baby's feet. Kisses every one of her toes.

"I'll name her Heike."

"After your mother."

"But what do I tell people about her father?"

"You may give him my wife's death." Tears in his voice. "Pia loved the high-wire."

As he tells me the story of her last performance—so dazzling, so audacious—*I see Pia Ludwig spin, not the rapid fall he witnessed as a young husband, but the forever-spinning toward the arena, and as the sawdust rises around Pia's sequined bodice and settles on her throat, her lips, I feel the tearing of my heart that I didn't allow when The Sensational Sebastian became lost to me.*

"Wait here." Herr Ludwig hurries for the door.

"Where would I go?"

Within minutes he's back with something bundled in linen. "Think of it as a gift from my beloved Pia." He folds back the linen and shakes out a huge shawl—deep blues and purples so close in color that the strands shift as he drapes it around us.

The baby and I flicker in and out of sleep nursing and sniffing each other—drowsy and moist and warm—and when I open my eyes Luzia is swaddling the baby, then cleaning me while the baby tugs at my nipple with tiny piglet slurps, tugs me toward a sweet-swampy pond of sleep till a smell hauls us to the surface, vanilla, and Luzia dribbles *Vanillepudding* between my lips while we flicker out again in the midst of swallowing, fusing.

✎ 21 ✎

I Kill The Sensational Sebastian

I wrap Pia's shawl around Heike and carry her to The Last Supper wagon where Cook has baked my favorites: *Apfelkuchen und Erdbeertorte.*

"Today," she says, "we must eat *Kuchen* first. Then stew."

Silvio fingers the edge of the shawl and nods. "I'm glad it's yours now."

"Thank you."

"We've been planning to give it to you."

"Did your mother weave it?"

"When she was pregnant with me."

Luzia The Clown kisses my baby's lips and smiles. "God, how I want one of those."

She never smiles during performances and gets our audiences to laugh at her melancholy as she plods through the sawdust on floppy shoes that are longer than her legs. As a child, she was a good gymnast. At fifteen, she attached herself to the Ludwig Zirkus with visions of being an acrobat. For years she kept herself reed-thin, held herself in, then figured out she wanted acrobatics, not famine. That's when she reinvented herself and became Luzia The Clown, zany and graceful and round. Beautiful as long as she personified melancholy. But when she smiles, she looks wholesome. Ordinary.

"*Gut?*" asks Cook from the end of the wagon, where she's rattling pans on the iron stove. The bed is at the opposite end, curtained off, built into the width of their wagon.

Her husband dabs whipped cream from his lumpy chin. "Divine." He kisses his fingertips, opens them toward Cook, a pale beauty as long as she covers her mouth with her wrist when she speaks, to hide her worn teeth.

"So . . . I heard of a trapeze artist at a Zirkus near Bremen who calls himself—"

"Sabine may not want to know that," Herr Ludwig interrupts.

"—The Fantastic Ferdinand."

I lay down my fork, queasy with old lust.

They're watching me, worried.

I let the silence sit until I can trust myself to speak. "Why not The Wonderful Waldemar?"

Nervous laughs.

"Close enough."

"How about The Cowardly Cornelius!"

"I'm sorry I started this."

"Cheating," I say.

"Cheating what?"

"I like The Cheating Cornelius."

"The man or his name?"

"Sabine likes the name—not that man."

"Not *that* man."

"I got a name that fits him just right. The Thoughtless Theodor!"

"The Lying Leonard!"

I laugh aloud.

"The Lying Leonard will sell you his lies as miracles in a jar with—"

"*Meine Damen und Herren . . .*" Silvio Ludwig leaps on the table and crosses his heart. Ladies and gentlemen. "It gives me inexhaustible pride and unfounded delight to introduce to you The Lying and Cheating and Cowardly Cornelius . . ."

At the long table, my tiny daughter travels from one nest of arms to the next, while we outdo one another with bogus names for her father, making this funny and scandalous. And we're doing it, we're succeeding. I laugh aloud. Everyone wants to hold Heike, and my body feels cold where before she was warm against me.

I borrow the death of Pia Ludwig and make it fit The Sensational Sebastian, the sort of death I dreaded while I loved him and couldn't imagine a life without him. I embroider his fall from the trapeze, make sawdust rise around him and then drift down. Yellow flecks land in the luscious dip of his throat. Or on his eyelashes.

And yet. And yet, some nights I evoke The Sensational Sebastian: the tops of his feet pressing up hard against my soles, his palms flat against the top of my head, containing me within the borders of his body as only a tall man can.

Heike sleeping.

Heike laughing.

Heike eating.

Whatever she feels, I feel.

Even when I'm sewing or ironing, I'm aware of her every breath.

The Ludwig Zirkus becomes our family. Luzia cuts and paints paper butterflies that she hangs from our ceiling to entertain Heike who lies on her back, kicking and reaching for the colors and shapes. The runt Nowack buys her a frog puppet, green felt.

The giant Nowack knits a blanket for her. The Twenty-Four-Hour Man brings a wooden duck with wheels. Herr Ludwig buys her a wicker baby carriage and a soft brush. She falls asleep in his arms whenever he brushes her hair.

I write a letter to my parents: Your granddaughter is strong-willed and lovely and funny. Tear the letter apart. Write another. And tear that apart too. Whatever I write is not enough.

"Once I sew a good mourning dress," I tell Luzia, "I'll take Heike and visit my parents."

"An elegant mourning dress," Luzia suggests.

She comes over a lot more since Heike's birth, holds her and sings to her; we've become closer this month than the entire year I've been here. In trunks with fabric remnants we find pieces of silk in yellow and in green. When we boil black dye and soak them, they don't match. I'm disappointed.

But Luzia is excited. "You can do something stylish and daring with two shades of black."

"I don't feel daring."

While she covers twenty-four tiny buttons with the lighter black silk, I design a dress similar to one I made at the Becker Mode Atelier.

"Stunning," Luzia says when I model the dress for her.

I've been away for nearly a year when I visit Rodenäs, Heike in my arms. I'm elegant in black, a young widow grieving. So much compassion and joy from my parents who welcome Heike and me with a celebration dinner; former classmates are envious of my freedom; and men gape at me with a frank hunger never aimed at me before.

My mother takes me aside. "Men think once you've done it, you want it all the time. Blessed fruit of your womb and so on and so on."

I stare at my pious and proper mother who perhaps was not

all that pious and proper, and we both clasp our palms across our mouths so that others won't hear us giggle.

For all of them, I let The Sensational Sebastian live just long enough to breathe his undying devotion to me. What remains the same in all versions is how my *Krämpfe*—cramps—begin while I kneel by my dying husband in the arena, and how, that very night, I birth our child. Again and again I kill The Sensational Sebastian. A shy pleasure, some days. But mostly the need to prune the offshoots of that love.

Herr Ludwig lends me a green leather book, *Arabische Nächte*. "It belonged to my Pia. She read these stories to Silvio. Every night. I listened too." His face transforms—tender and sad. "Stories that Scheherazade told King Schariar to save her sister and herself and countless other virgins from his massacre. Eventually, Scheherazade taught him to be compassionate."

From Silvio I know how turbulent his parents' marriage was. Accusations and promises. Elaborate drama every day of Silvio's childhood.

Herr Ludwig traces the embossed design on the book's cover. "You may borrow it, Sabine. It's the best thing I own."

Is he so fascinated by Scheherazade because, unlike his wife, she lived on?

"The one story I don't believe," he says, "is the central one that makes all other stories possible. How a woman so courageous and resourceful can marry such a beast." He gives me a meaningful glance. "I want stability for Heike."

"So do I."

"Stability for Heike and you . . . and for my son."

So worldly he is, understands that his son likes men. Yet, is hoping for a cure? Me?

"Silvio is amazing with Heike," he reminds me at least once a week. "Have you noticed?"

To Silvio he says, "You'll make a great father."

"You two go out and dance," he tells Silvio and me. "Dance is the poetry your feet make. That's what the poet John Dryden said two centuries ago. I'll stay with Heike."

Silvio and I are both twenty-four, and we like to dance and eat and talk about men. Some nights he leaves a pub with some stranger. But he never brings him home. *How terrible it must be to hide who you are.*

22

Luzia The Clown and the Whirling Nowack Cousins

Our audiences love the Nowacks who amaze you by top-pling your expectations. One Nowack is much taller, wider in the chest; the short one barely weighs half as much but has the strongest little legs. Their size difference is extreme, and when they run into the arena on bare feet, you point and shout. No matter how often you've seen the performance, you still expect the giant to juggle the runt. The act starts as usual: the short Nowack walks to the center of the arena, lowers himself onto a wide carpet pillow that makes him look even smaller, and lies back, knees bent; except this time he does not raise his legs but lets his knees drop open, turns his face toward Silvio who stands near the curtain, fastens his eyes on Silvio who crosses his arms across his chest, recrosses them, face crimson.

Herr Ludwig flicks his ringmaster whip into the air, twice, before the short Nowack snaps his knees shut and raises his legs, flexes his bare feet so that his soles are parallel to the ground. When the tall Nowack runs toward him, the short Nowack catches him with his soles and launches him into the air, whirls him head to toe, then side to side, a blizzard of motion while the short Nowack lies without motion, except for his soles.

"You keep your eyes on your partner," Herr Ludwig admonishes him after the performance. "To not do that is dangerous. For him and everyone."

Late one evening Silvio and I meet at a rathskeller with Luzia The Clown and The Whirling Nowack Cousins. When Luzia orders *Bratkartoffeln mit Speck*—fried potatoes with bacon—the waiter says it's too late to prepare warm food.

She scowls. "Nothing will come between me and my *Bratkartoffeln*."

"I'll get you whatever you desire." The runt winks at her and slips the waiter a ticket. "I used to work for a famous Zirkus, very prestigious—"

"You are embarrassing yourself," says the giant cousin, voice low as if it came from his toes.

"—and I got them whatever they desired . . . Not some mud show like this."

"Tell me more about your prestigious Zirkus." Silvio leans toward him. Sets his hook. He has an instinct for *ausfragen*—asking—until nothing is left.

"I have a fiancée," the waiter hints.

"Congratulations." The runt sighs and tosses him another ticket, plants his elbows on the table, stretches his jaw forward till his flushed face is a hand's width from Silvio's. "This prestigious Zirkus had a dozen big cats and a dozen teams of horses and a dozen—"

"I'm sure those dozens and dozens are more prestigious than our animals."

"You want any? I'm good at bartering. They have so many animals . . . I can go to them."

"What for?"

"For you. Barter." The runt's voice turns lazy. "If that's what you want."

Silvio shakes his head, dazed. Usually he's good at spotting an upcoming crisis, takes it out of its wild spin, freezes it, till he can resolve it. But not now. "Barter what for what?"

"For what you want to . . . offer."

As Silvio blushes a deeper crimson, I see the heat between those two that I've mistaken for hostility.

"Labor," the runt says. "I'm talking about physical labor."

Luzia and I glance at each other, and I bite my lip to keep from laughing. She coughs into her fist.

"Whose labor?" Silvio demands.

"Not mine," says Luzia The Clown.

"*Macht Platz!*" The waiter yells at us to clear space as he advances with Luzia's *Bratkartoffeln mit Speck.*

"Admit it," I say to Silvio.

He flinches. "Admit what?"

I let him wait. "That you two enjoy fighting."

"Only about *Bratkartoffeln*," the runt explains. "Silvio is mad I didn't get him any."

Luzia perches her delicate hand on the giant's broad wrist, and it's then that her sadness merges with the giant's sadness, igniting more bliss than two people can possibly generate. He closes his long eyelids because what he sees is for him alone: *Luzia on her bed in his arms, toes just up to his thighs, lips against his throat. A low rumble of his laugh. "You are a beautiful man," Luzia murmurs, and it doesn't matter if her voice comes from his longings or from their future.*

You are a beautiful man. It's in the giant's step when he walks with her from the restaurant; it's in the way he extends his elbow in case Luzia wants to walk arm in arm. But before she can, the runt slows in front of her so that she has to bump into him.

"I didn't mean to push you," she tells the runt.

"Yes, you did. The imprint of your bosom is on my back."

"Don't be an *Idiot*." Silvio Ludwig butts his shoulder against the runt's.

Luzia laughs. "I hope that imprint lasts you a lifetime. Because that's all you'll get."

A lifetime. That's what Luzia and the giant Nowack promise one another—a lifetime of joy and of sadness and of trust, shared. I sew the wedding garments: Luzia wants a gown she can dye and wear as a costume in the arena; the giant Nowack asks for a blue tuxedo. "Midnight-blue."

"My father's snoring is getting worse," Silvio Ludwig mentions the morning after their wedding at breakfast.

"I didn't sleep all night," Silvio Ludwig mentions the following day at dinner.

"I'm exhausted," Silvio Ludwig mentions during rehearsal.

"I don't want to keep you awake," his father says.

"You don't snore on purpose, *Vater.*"

Every day Silvio bemoans his lack of sleep, the circles around his eyes his proof. But Luzia has a different diagnosis. "Lovesickness." For weeks, Silvio goes on like this, until his father asks why he doesn't use the empty bed in The Whirling Nowacks' wagon. We still call it that though the giant Nowack lives in Luzia's wagon.

"I haven't thought of that," Silvio says.

When I wink at him, he blushes. A terrible liar.

Hans-Jürgen pretends indifference. Shrugs. "No one uses Oliver's bed."

"Then Silvio should move in with you," Herr Ludwig says.

"It's your Zirkus . . ."

"Would you mind if Silvio—"

"Your Zirkus."

"Oliver's bed is bumpy," Silvio will complain to his father, to anyone who'll listen, even Heike.

Luzia and I are sure he doesn't sleep in Oliver's bed but is building evidence if his father were to ask.

"Too much evidence," Luzia warns him.

"You can stack your dishonor against mine," I tell him. "A lover you can keep a secret; a child you can't."

23

Tell Me the Story of
How My Vati Could Fly

I marvel at my daughter's strong little body.

Marvel at her first step.

Her first word: *Mutti*.

When she laughs her belly quivers; and when she gets upset she bawls like a lost calf. I brace myself. Try to hold the middle. While I stitch, she sits on the floor by my sewing box, plays with the shiniest buttons, pushes them toward stripes of sun that lie on the floor. Heike moves with the sun.

From Herr Ludwig she learns to count by lining up her buttons and clapping her chubby hands: *Eins zwei drei vier eins zwei drei vier . . .* She is learning so quickly. Faster and faster she gets to twelve. Where she stops. And starts with one again.

A fidgety sleeper, she'll shrug off her covers. Always warm where I'm chilly. Just before dawn she'll burrow into bottomless sleep and fight awakening. Every morning a new battle with the light; eventually, I let her sleep. No matter what time she climbs out of bed, she's groggy.

.   .   .

Over the next years I learn how time and facts can be manipulated; whenever Heike asks about her father, I concoct tales to shield her from the truth that he abandoned us. Her favorite tale is of him flying.

"Tell me the story of how my *Vati* could fly."

"When your father flew through the air, every woman in the audience believed he was looking at her alone."

"But then he fell."

"True."

"And then he died."

"Now he's in a beautiful cemetery."

"On a hill."

"True."

"With statues."

"Big statues, *ja*."

"Apple trees."

"True." I beam at her.

"I saw how he fell."

"You weren't born yet, Heike."

"I saw him."

It unnerves me how she absorbs my lies as memories of her own—his fall, his death, yellow sawdust on his face.

Along the way I befriend women. If you want friends, Luzia has told me, you cannot wait because soon you'll be on the road again. "You have to charm them with your frankness, your humor, your praise of whatever you can genuinely praise about them."

"I already have you."

"You do. But you need more friends."

"Sometimes I shock people," I tell Luzia, hoping she'll say I don't shock her.

But she nods.

"I was shy as a girl until I found I'm not afraid to say what I think. You think I shock people?"

"*Ja.*"

"Do I have to be more careful?"

"You like to shock people."

I have to laugh. "Yes."

"Why give that up? We're never anywhere long enough for you to offend anyone."

"I don't want to push you away."

"No chance."

For the third time in a week, Heike wants the story about the frozen-together dogs.

"One cold day my *Vati* saved two dogs."

"True."

"It was very, very cold."

"*Ja.* He ran from our wagon into the deep . . ." I wait for her to finish my sentence.

". . . snow and he chased the boys away because they . . . because—"

"Snowballs," I prompt.

"Because the boys threw snowballs at the dogs."

"Your father helped the dogs get apart."

"Was I born yet, *Mutti*?"

"You were still waiting to born."

She pats my belly.

"Inside our wagon I kept us warm . . ."

"With me in your belly."

No stories of storks and babies for my daughter.

I kiss the top of her head. "Then I heaped all our scarves and all our blankets on the bed."

Of course I don't tell her how I heated her father's chilled body with mine, fingers roving over him, pulling the most fro-

zen part of him into myself, and how I was overcome by an odd
and ancient power that reached for me through centuries. And
after all I don't tell Heike, I take her to play in Luzia's wagon
while I rush back and lock the door so that I can lie with my
hands on myself until they become his.

You braid your daughter's hair.

 Remind her to wash her hands.

 Demonstrate for the hundredth time how to tie her shoes.

 How to boil two eggs.

 To count beyond twelve.

 The again and again.

 And no forward.

 *When she doesn't want to hear or see you, she shakes her head and
makes her hair fly till she's dizzy, then opens her arms to steady herself.*

 Or fly away?

The winter she's seven, I send her to school in Emmerich;
but she runs away from school, new scratches on her knees and
elbows.

"It pains me," her teacher tells me, "to tell you that your
daughter is quite . . . slow. That's why other children push and
tease—"

"You must not let them do that to her."

"That's what I try." She nods, a small-boned woman with
a friendly mouth. It's clearly hard for her to say this: "Heike's
mind cannot—"

I must not allow her to finish. "I read to my daughter every
evening."

She folds her hands as if in prayer, tips her fingers against her
jaw.

"My Heike has always been a good learner. She remembers
the stories I tell her, and she tells them back to me."

"She has some . . . basic knowledge."

"Good, then."

"But it pains me to tell you—"

Keep your pain to yourself, I want to shout.

"—that Heike's mind cannot hold on to more advanced learning."

There it is—what I've been trying to figure out for many months—why Heike is no longer making progress with numbers and the alphabet and linking letters into words.

"Heike gets in her own way if she doesn't want to do something," says the teacher. "She'll put the side of her face on the desk, slide it back and forth, avoids eye contact."

"I've never seen her do that," I lie.

"Heike puts a lot of effort—"

I lean toward the teacher.

"—into not learning."

"I promise to work harder. I'll practice letters with her, words . . . and I'll read her stories till she falls asleep and—"

"*Sehr gut.*" Heike's teacher sounds pleased. Very good.

"—and someone else in our family . . . her grandfather will teach her more about numbers."

"That's exactly what we recommend for children like Heike."

Children like Heike?

But maybe I should be encouraged. I imagine all of us helping Heike to move forward, including this teacher who smiles although her friendly mouth quivers.

"We recommend that the family teaches the child."

"I already have some plans how we—"

"At home."

It's only then that I understand in my bones: my instinct to keep Heike safe can never be enough, no matter how many people teach her about words and numbers and stars, about nature and legends, and I love her fiercely—a thousand times more than I already do.

. . .

Herr Ludwig counts and writes down numbers with Heike; Luzia shows her how to weave long grasses across a forked branch;
I teach her how to form the easiest letters, beginning with: *o* . . .
c . . . *v* . . . This is better for her, we reason, than school, where
she'll learn to compare herself to other children, get hurt by
words and fists.

She loves the learning, loves our attention, takes into her
mind as much as a seven-year-old will. And forgets the rest.
People can't tell, not yet—she's still like other seven-year-olds.
Fast and agile. Running, skipping, somersaults. Fascinated by
the trapeze. *Too dangerous.* The Ludwigs and I conspire to distract her. Herr Ludwig hires her to help with his act, to follow
him into the arena with the Zirkus Bible, watchful about the
order of Bible stories he directs. I nudge her into the orchestra
conducted by Herr Ludwig, who procures a wooden box with a
child-size cello. Heike whispers to her cello. Listens to it. With
music there's nothing she has to learn or remember; it already
lives inside her, ready for the hum and vibration of her cello.
Music threads itself through her body, through her arms and
fingers and chin and thighs.

In the audiences I notice other women's daughters dressed up
for the occasion, daughters who will grow into women. Eventually, I come to pity their mothers. My daughter will always
be my girl.

People click their tongues. "That one . . ."

Let her be! Let her be a child, then. Mine—

I teach her as much as she can take in, choose tasks we can
do together. I make new costumes, and she loves the silken and
diaphanous fabrics, wraps herself into the brilliant colors that
contrast this barren landscape. When I mend rips and holes, she

does the basting, long uneven stitches, while I do the fine hemming and seaming; and all along I praise her—I have to, praise every tiny effort, every tiny fragment of every tiny damn effort, every—

She cups my cheek.

I flinch from her hand.

"Mutti?"

I smile. Make my lips go wide. Turn them up at the ends.

"Are you angry with me, *Mutti*?"

"No. No no no. No—"

"You're making your scary smile."

Have I mentioned my delight in my daughter? She likes flying insects. Strawberries. Pretty buttons. Whenever she sees one she likes, I buy it for us—one at a time—and design costumes to go with those buttons, reinforcing seams to withstand vigorous acts. Old costumes I restore—apostles and angels—concealing worn fabric and puckered seams with trim and embroidery. I know the difference between expensive fabric and cheap, and the Ludwigs let me buy the best they can afford. I teach Heike what I've known since childhood watching my mother sew: even cheap fabric will look expensive if you add quality buttons.

She is the most enchanting girl I know. When she plays the cello, she is resilient, intuitive, this girl who cannot count past twelve, accomplished with the cello in a way no one can understand. As she grows, the cellos grow too. She laughs and weeps easily, says whatever she thinks.

"Music is your magic," Herr Ludwig tells her, "your very own magic. We're all magicians in a way, divining what lies beneath the surface of the ordinary and the extraordinary. And the amazing."

PART FIVE

Winter 1878–1879

24

A Quicksilver Murmur

The Old Women lean from their front windows for hours. Pillows between bosoms and windowsills, they let gossip ferment. Across the space between their windows they comment on everyone who passes; click their tongues at couples who walk hand in hand in public; applaud when children play hopscotch or do cartwheels—just as prior Old Women applauded them when they were little girls—and in that become children again, living all moments of their lives at once—*child, woman, Old Woman.*

Now that Lotte Jansen is back in her house, the Old Women help as much as she lets them. They feel an added meaning to their days because Lotte makes them more compassionate. Measured against her misfortune, they've been spared the worst, and they take comfort in their luck, in their competence. They fret about Wilhelm.

"I saw her carry him across the dike to where the others drowned."

"That poor little boy."

"I've seen her laugh."

"Laugh with her baby? That's not odd."

"She's already thrown him into the sea once."

"Because she turned from God and—"

"From herself. Lotte Jansen turned from herself."

"Crazy with grief."

"No, she's amazingly sane."

"Crazy."

"Crazy just that one day."

"I would have put stones in my pockets by now," says the Oldest Person of Nordstrand.

"You should!" says the Second-Oldest Person.

This competition for Oldest Person honor corrupts the beauty of aging, the wisdom of aging. You can be a devoted grandmother, say, only to turn ruthless as you get closer to the title. Winning grows more significant than your families. Instead of being joyful with your grandchildren and great-grandchildren, you brood over your health: cough syrup at the hint of a scratchy throat; long hours of sleep that matter far more than the nightmares of your little ones. As the surviving Oldest Person of the year, you can no longer be trusted.

Your rivalry bonds you. Two may connive against a third, coaching one another: live, live, live; but if the third indeed dies, the feud between the finalists will be epic. Shameless. Not that you'll trip one another on the church steps, or stir arsenic into peach marmalade, though you may contemplate that. Your weapon is compassion. With tales of woe—true and fabricated— you'll remind one another of lost loves and lost children and lost friends, only to push one another deeper into heartache.

Tell me more.

Once crowned, of course, you have to train for the following summer solstice because you may still outlast your rivals. You feel them wheezing behind you, waiting for any misstep, any light-headedness, blood in your piss, god forbid. If you're bedridden for a day, say, or a week, they bring you fatty meals to hasten your end, lean over you to estimate the level of your malady. You, too, have done this. With spite and with intent. Now you know what it's like.

Lotte is afraid of forgetting her children's faces, their smells, the texture of their hair. That's why she has to climb deeper into her grief. Like picking a scab. Below is still the wound, but it doesn't bleed as much. One day before Christmas she bundles Wilhelm into Martin's pajamas and Bärbel's coat, carries him to the edge of the sea, sits down and pulls him onto her knees. "Look at the lights." She points to the cool glow in the sky, blues, and above a band of white that pulls the sky closer. "Lights for your birthday, Wilhelm. One year, you're one year old today."

His narrow back against her chest, thumb between his gums.

She rests her chin on top of his head. "The same sky your sisters and your brother are looking at. This very moment."

Wilhelm rocks his head, tilts her chin up. Down. And up.

"Bärbel and Martin and Hannelore." Lotte tastes their names. "You were eight months old last time you saw them, Wilhelm. Martin's favorite is buttermilk soup. Just like your favorite. He helps me make it, crumbles bread into a bowl of buttermilk, lets it soak . . ." She feels them nearby. It's happening in the telling to Wilhelm. "Our Hannelore, she likes the eggs of seagulls, likes searching for them. Knows to take just a few and leave enough to hatch. And our Bärbel—"

—you cannot cook applesauce without seeing Bärbel's upturned face, lips already open, waiting for that first spoon too hot she says, repeating what you tell her, too hot—

"Our Bärbel is wild for anything sweet. Remember what we call her?" Lotte turns Wilhelm so he faces her. "*Verfressenes Kaninchen.*" Greedy rabbit. She can sniff out sweets even if we hide them. She stuffs them into her cheeks. Like this."

Lotte puffs her cheeks.

Wilhelm pops her cheeks. Giggles. Puffs his cheeks pops his cheeks. *His feet tickle sheep have feet sheep have knees. Sheep have lips and teeth. Lips snatch the fog. Teeth yank it from earth. Make earth tremble. Chomp chomp go the sheep.*

She breathes in his Wilhelm-smell, mud and buttermilk. Another smell then, earth and sweat—Bärbel. She can recognize her children by smell. Cinnamon and milk for Hannelore. *Schwarzbrot*—black bread—for Martin. And she's here for them—

Now—and whenever you'll need me. A different connection than pain and guilt because I've lost you, a connection to you beyond any moment of longing and panic, and I'm here in the world for you with you, a certainty that is stronger than any uncertainty when I will see you again, a peace that won't be mine every hour though I'll recall what it feels like and how it is there for me.

The sky widens into a fan, a swirl, that exalts Lotte, lets her grasp that her children are alive—*BärbelMartinHannelore and a quicksilver murmur in a haze that warps and shimmers—alive on Rungholt that emerges once every spring for a few moments. No one can predict when. But you must be ready for its prelude, the* Schwarze Sonne—*black sun—when the wingbeats of a million starlings block the setting sun while they dance above the marshes in a symphony of light and motion.*

Every time Lotte picks at the new scab—greedily, secretly—her wound gets smaller and her children get closer. She goes back and again to the edge of the sea where it's easier to listen for their voices. To lure them to her, she tells Wilhelm the ancient legend she has grown up with and told all her children. About the *Nebelfrau*—fog woman.

"The *Nebelfrau* simmers the *Nebel* on her stove . . . lets it rise at dawn. But at dusk, she hauls the *Nebel* back down from the sky. It hides the sheep, then settles around their feet until they float on the *Nebel* and—"

"And what then?" asks Martin. Martin who wanted solid food long before the others. Even before he had teeth, he'd suck on a crust of Schwarzbrot, black crumbs around his lips.

"The Nebelfrau lives underneath the sea. Remember, Martin?"

The click-click of Wilhelm sucking his thumb.

Hannelore scowls at Wilhelm. "What did you do with my doll?"

To make her laugh, Lotte gives the Nebelfrau green fog.

"—not green!" protests Hannelore.

Martin chases green fog, stomps on green fog.

Wilhelm slides from Lotte's lap, crawls on green fog.

Bärbel climbs on Mutti's lap.

BärbelMartinHannelore . . . their names taste of sweat, of pollen. Bärbel snuggling against you, listening, Martin half listening, sorting pebbles into rows. Hannelore waiting to correct you in case you change a detail or leave one out. Familiar and unpredictable.

If Tilli picks Wilhelm up, he'll sling his arms around her neck, his legs around her waist; but Sister Franziska, no matter how gently, will pry him off and send Tilli to help with the big children. Still, some mornings Tilli manages to spirit him away to the old Sisters in the retirement wing where the old Sisters tend to their rabbits. And to their lovey-birds: boy finches with reddish cheeks, girl finches with a black streak running from each eye.

The Sisters adore Wilhelm and hoard bites of sweets for him: a spoonful of pudding; a half-eaten cookie. Read him poems they've written with the poet from Niebühl who visits them Tuesday afternoons.

"Boy finches kill weaker boy finches," Tilli tells Wilhelm.

"Nonsense," says Sister Konstanze. "And don't you scare him with that."

"I won't."

"Who told you?"

"My father."

Sister Konstanze scoffs. "Your father is wrong, but we already know that."

Tilli laughs with astonishment and covers her mouth. Disrespectful, she thinks, and it is, disrespectful and delicious. She blurts, "He took my brother away."

Sister Konstanze's lips twitch.

"He said I can never come home."

"My dear courageous child."

Sister Hildegunde praises Tilli. "You have learned so much here that we are promoting you to—"

"Thank you," Tilli says, pleased.

"—to work in the Big Nursery."

Wilhelm, they're taking Wilhelm from me.

The abyss where my own girl lives. And never another breath—

Sister Hildegunde's heart is aching for this Girl with the square chin and apricot hair. "You'll still get to see all the children."

But the impulse to find Wilhelm is stronger than Tilli's hope of changing Sister Hildegunde's decision. Tilli runs. A dusting of snow.

and freckles on Tilli's face on Tilli's breast and the sky tips

"Drink, baby . . . my own . . ."

and the big freckle in Wilhelm's mouth, dry, the freckle is dry and Wilhelm is cold

And Tilli's body makes what her own girl needs and is now for Wilhelm and therefore her girl cannot be so far away.

"Here, drink . . ."

he tugs at the freckle tugs

hum-chuck-hum of bicycle

freckles on Tilli's fingers fly up buttons

"Ssshhhh, my own."

close buttons, hum-chuck-hum

"Ssshhhh, baby."

Sister Franziska eases Wilhelm away from Tilli. "I wish I could help you."

"I won't do it again."

"He is not your baby, Tilli."

"I know." Fear and shame and I'm sorry.

"I'm sorry too." Tears in Sister's voice. "I've asked too much of you."

Tilli cannot envision being in a place where Wilhelm is not. "He opened my buttons. He knows how."

"This is not good for you, either."

"I won't do it again. Please, Sister."

Sister motions Tilli toward the convent bicycle toppled among frozen weeds. "Will you please ride the bicycle back?"

"But—"

"I'll carry Wilhelm. We'll talk when we get back."

25

In the Big Nursery

That night in the Big Nursery, Tilli lies awake in the alcove across from the beds of the sleeping children, four rows of six. As she tries to steady her breath—louder and faster than the breaths of these children—she longs to be an Old Woman. First Sabine will become an Old Woman. Then Lotte. And then Tilli will join that circle. *And never be alone again and no one ever telling me to go away or stay because I'll be the one who gets to say.*

The first time she took Wilhelm to her breast, she made a promise to Lotte to steal Sister Franziska's rosary, a silent promise that matters more than spoken words. She leans over the side of her bed, slides her handkerchief box from the satchel Sister Franziska has let her pack. In the dark she tiptoes past the little beds and down the stairs to the infirmary where she slips the rosary from the key of the medicine cabinet. In the kitchen she melts its amber beads in a jar set within a pot of boiling water. As she waits for the amber to soften, it releases the scent of childhood, of pine and salt. She pummels it into one sticky lump, cuts that into pear-shaped halves the size of her little finger, jiggles the moon clippings of Wilhelm's fingernails from her handkerchief box, and presses them into the amber halves before she connects them again. With her hairpin she pokes an opening for a cord. Come light of morning, she sees the bubbles that have settled around the moons like halos.

The Big Nursery is much bigger than the Little Nursery. Three rooms: The sleeping room. The learning room. And between them the playing room with a big table where the children clamor to stick their fingers into the jam because Tilli did it first, one long finger to fish for the dark speck inside the jam. Not a fly but a bread crumb that looks like a fly but isn't a fly because Tilli gets it out, more jam on her finger than needs to be.

She licks it. Makes her eyes go big.

"Me."

"Jam."

"Since you've finished your barley soup . . ." Barley soup with carrots and bits of apple that she carried up from the kitchen for her children.

"Me. Me."

They lean across the table, try to climb on it.

Tilli holds the jar upside down to make it easy for their little fingers. So what if jam gets the table sticky? She wants to cheer them up. They shriek with delight that comes from the forbidden. Jam on their cheeks. Around their lips. The Sisters are shadows that fade for Tilli when she plays with the children, when their joy restores some of the warmth beneath her heart where her own girl slept till she was born and where Wilhelm lived until she was banished from the Little Nursery. She still sees him, but not enough.

"Fizzy!" the children cry.

"Ticklish!"

They point to her amulet where it lies against the dip of her throat, the shimmer of honey. She keeps it shiny by rubbing it with spit every day.

"The hair on my arm," the children cry.

"Make it stand up, please."

"My arm first."

She slips off her amulet. As the children press against her, she sways the amber against their arms, and they giggle at the sparks. She loves her work with the big children far more than she thought she would when Sister Franziska banished her from the Little Nursery a month ago.

"Slivers of moon inside." She kneels amid the children so they can see the pale slivers inside her amulet.

"How did you get them, Fräulein Tilli?"

"From the sky. They're magical."

Magical. The children sigh with wonder.

As soon as Lotte believes her husband will never come home, she has a dream about waking up to the smell of gravy, rich and brown, and feels a pulling in her groin, a heat—

—*and running downstairs barefoot in her nightgown wondering if you can smell anything while sleeping and in her kitchen Kalle cooks his Sunday gravy, browns a fist-size chunk of meat with onions and bacon, and he doesn't notice her though she stands behind him with her arms around him and her palms on his chest so hot his skin hot the air stirring he's stirring—his miracle not loaves and fishes but gravy he can expand till he has plenty—and just before his gravy is about to burn he adds water, lets it hiss and boil and thicken, and again he stirs and browns until she smells his gravy on her skin and in the mist that surrounds her house and—*

—dawn, then. And her house too cold to hold any smells, other than the smell of cold itself: stone and dampness and snow. Lotte shivers, tugs the bedding around her shoulders. Not Sunday. But a watery Tuesday in February. By late morning she's outside with Wilhelm beneath a patchy-thin cover of clouds, hanging laundry on the line. He takes one cautious step, clutches a fold of her skirt. Yesterday he took his very first step away from her. Now he studies the ground as if considering his next step. Much of the snow has melted, softening earth into mud, but some snow clings to the bottoms of dried grasses, pockmarked where rain has pelted it. Above the darker stones the snow is gone.

Wilhelm takes another step. Tips his face to his mother, astonished by what he can do, beams at her.

"Look at you!" She laughs, sets her laundry basket on a flat stone, and squats, her arms one safe circle where he can walk. Another step—

—and it's then that her husband rides into the yard on a stiff-legged zebra. Its back is damp. So are Kalle's shoulders and hat. And he's already wrong because he sees her smiling and has no idea it's at Wilhelm, not at him, because he smiles at her.

"Please," he says.

His presence intrudes on her longing for him when longing itself has become familiar. She wants to fly at him with her fists raised.

"Lotte," he whispers.

Wilhelm teeters on his baby legs, and she tightens her arms around him, feels the edges of shells he's crammed inside his pockets again, makes herself think of those shells, sees herself emptying the pockets before the wash. *How many times have you turned your children's pockets and socks to get at the stones and shells and sand? Sand is the hardest because it will hide for several washings in seams and in corners. Long after the wave you still find sand in the socks of your children.*

Kalle slides off the zebra, his legs as stiff as the zebra's, as though he's been riding it every day of the six months he's been gone.

"I have—" He clears his throat. "I have an idea."

She won't speak. Won't make this easier for him, though her body is straining for him as if they had no betrayal or death between them.

"An idea for a trade," Kalle says. Away from his family he has felt unmoored, floaty; has sketched his children the way he used to, the easy curve of Lotte around them before and after birth; but they no longer come together for him, are merely charcoal lines on paper that prove how much he has lost. *So much easier to draw animals.*

"The zebra can bring you income." Kalle pats its mangy flank.

"I can raise colonies of moths in that fur and sell them."

"That's the Lotte I know."

"You don't know me."

Wilhelm hides against *Mutti*'s leg, peers at the horse-with-stripes as it smiles, snorts, curls its lips, shows him long teeth. Wilhelm curls his own lips, shows his own teeth to horse-with-stripes.

"I want to help, Lotte, with the farm and—"

"There is no work for you."

"You can rent the barn to the Ludwig Zirkus. I can bring a few sick animals, make them stronger here." Three weeks ago he seized a moment of disagreement over killing this ancient zebra and offered to stable her on the farm his wife brought into the marriage. It gives him cause to stay without telling Lotte he wants to come home. And he doesn't, or at least isn't sure enough to let her know that he doesn't know. "And maybe," he adds, "next winter the entire Zirkus can winter over."

"I've leased the farm to the sexton."

"Old Niessen? Who drinks the piss of sheep?"

"The piss of goats."

"Goats, then."

"And he doesn't drink it. He gets it through a syringe."

"I don't like another man doing my work."

"Your work?" she asks, ablaze with anger.

26

Of Being Alone and Untouched

All Kalle sees is radiance, and for one insane moment he knows she has another man. He's back in that panic of being alone and untouched like the day before Christmas when the others are leaving to visit their families, and he tries to keep that panic at bay by thinking of the jars of Lotte's *Hagebutten Marmalade* on the shelves in the cellar, of the wild beach roses—pink blossoms early summer; scarlet fruits late summer—and he can taste it then, thick jam as sticky as honey with the flavor of summer, countless summers, a history of all summers with Lotte, and still the panic gets in and squats in his soul.

"I haven't been touched," he blurts. "By a woman."

"Why are you telling me this?"

"I want you to know."

"I don't want to listen to this." She covers Wilhelm's ears with her palms and sees Kalle in the embrace of Sabine Florian who can have any man any age. A new jealousy, hers alone, and he has no right to it.

He doesn't have words for this yearning that cannot start with Lotte, because he must ban her from his heart so totally that yearning can only steal in sideways—the length of a woman's step, say, or the curve of a woman's shoulder beneath a dress, or the turn of a woman's neck—sparks of yearning that lead to Lotte. Ignite.

"Here you are, using a mangy zebra as an excuse to come back. Offering me a barnful of mangy animals."

"It's not like that. I want you to have that income."

"I already have income."

"From where?"

"The St. Margaret Home. I'm training to be a midwife."

They trust you to bring children into life? He covers his mouth. Runs his palm across his mouth and chin. Stubble and sweat. She must be disgusted by him.

He asks, "Is the sexton treating you fairly?"

"Is that yours to ask?" It comes out harsh.

But he won't let her push him away with her anger. If anything, he'll fan it, keep it aflame, both of them guardians of her anger. Safer than talking about their children.

"He is treating me fairly."

"Good."

"You cannot be here just because of me. You don't even look at your son." She lifts Wilhelm up so his face floats in front of Kalle's. "Wilhelm, this is your *Vater.*"

Vater. Not *Vati.*

The boy's little arms splash the air as if swimming toward him and the zebra. His sleeves are too long. Bärbel's coat.

Kalle shakes his hand. "*Guten Tag,* Wilhelm."

Lotte turns Wilhelm toward herself, smiles at him. "Your feet are heavy. Sand in your socks again?" All while she's aching to tell Kalle their other children are alive. Saddle him with that knowledge before he decides to bolt again.

Noch nicht. Not yet.

"Sand in your socks . . ." Kalle circles Wilhelm's ankle with a thumb and finger.

.   .   .

Lotte leaves him standing under the gray sky by the barn. Wilhelm on her hip, she runs toward the St. Margaret Home. She's not on duty, but she can't be home with Kalle.

By the front door, Sister Sieglinde walks into her, and Lotte sweeps one arm forward, curtly, motions Sister into the vestibule.

But Sister stops. "What happened?"

"You go first. Please." Lotte doesn't like the chill in her voice.

Sister Sieglinde loves to talk, and if you don't get away, you'll have to listen once again to her rant about papal pomp. It started when Sister Sieglinde was Lotte's teacher and visited the Vatican as a delegate of the Sisters. She was so appalled by the treasures in the Vatican's museum—immense and obscene, squeezed from the most destitute of believers—that she thought of renouncing her vows. Instead she bought a filigreed rosary and two oranges blessed by Pope Pius IX. One orange she gave to the Pregnant Girls, the other to her third-grade students. The rosary she tried to give to other Sisters, but they didn't want it either because its silver tracery snagged their skin. An instrument of penance, they called it.

"What happened to you, Lotte?" Sister Sieglinde asks again.

"I must go."

"You look furious."

Lotte adjusts Wilhelm's weight on her hip and turns away.

She roams the corridors yet can't settle herself. She's in a funk. In a hatchet-wielding funk. If only she had a hatchet. But then what? Too much, even this. Too much of life and plans and birds and choices and now Kalle. Inside the chapel she slams the door so hard that candles flicker on the iron stand by the altar. She nods to herself, opens the door again, slams it harder. There! And again. In the last pew she hides out with Wilhelm. She hums to him. Hums while that crucified Jesus hangs above the altar as if to prove that he, too, was pushed from inside a woman.

27

The Mathematics of Loss.
Of Desire

Before Lotte goes to bed, she sets out food for Kalle on the kitchen table that he takes to the barn and eats alone on the edge of his cot. Pea soup with ham bone. Goat stew. Potato pancakes.

He muddles along, trying to anchor himself in daily tasks. Near Lotte. For now. How he misses the everyday stories he and Lotte used to tell one another—about what they've seen and thought and tasted—looking forward to the telling because they know the other will want to listen. These are not stories you save to write in a letter: they're insignificant to others and therefore all the more significant to you.

If I were to ask Lotte whose hand was in hers, she wouldn't answer, wouldn't tell me whose hand she let slip away when Wilhelm needed all of her. He's been like that, the boy, from the day he was born.

Whose hand? he'll insist, afraid she'll send him away for asking.

I don't remember.

Why did you let go of the others? Pushing at her with questions, feeling cruel. What right do I have after deserting her?

There was no time— For choice.

To console her he'll say, If you had dropped Wilhelm and held on to

the other three—then their weight, their combined weight, would have
pulled you out with them, drowned you all, and I wouldn't have any
family—

But what he sees are his children torn from her hand—Bärbel Mar-
tin Hannelore—while she still holds on to the youngest.

The mathematics of loss. Of desire.

Second Tuesday after his return she waits for him, cheeks
flushed. On the table a yellow wedge of *Rodonkuchen* on a good
plate. To bake his favorite, *Apfelkuchen,* would mean *Willkom-*
men. His Lotte does not pretend.

When she motions for him to sit across from her, he's sure
she'll ask him the question that has lived inside his fear.

Why did you desert us?

Because you would've sent me away—

She says, "I baked *Rodonkuchen* this morning."

"Thank you." He shows his appreciation by taking a bite of
cake, an average bite, not big at all, but it clogs his mouth. He
can't swallow, coughs, face hot, feels the dead children inhabit his
house.

Lotte gets him a cup of water. "Slow now."

Still coughing, he gulps the water, maneuvers the lump of
cake into his fist.

"Promise—" She hesitates.

"I promise."

"You don't even know what it is."

"I can promise to listen."

"Promise to believe me."

"I swear I will."

She hesitates. Then tells it like a riddle. "Small voice? Big
laughter?"

And he gets it right. "Hannelore." It hurts to say her name

aloud, but he continues. "Her voice so quiet, but her laughter always the loudest."

"You think it's because she is the oldest?"

"Could be," he says cautiously and hides his fist with the lump of cake on his knees, then pushes it into a pocket.

"Or will her voice always be like that?"

Always? The skin at the edge of his hairline prickles. "I'm not blaming you, Lotte."

"Because they're alive."

"What?"

She nods, keeps nodding, such joy in her face. "Hannelore and Martin and Bärbel."

He groans. "Oh, Lotte . . ."

She presses two fingers across his lips. "They held on to one another. That's how they made it to Rungholt."

"And how do you know that?"

"From our children." She raises her chin, challenging him.

"Who watches over them?"

"People. There."

"Who plays with them? Tells them bedtime stories? All the things I used to do with them."

"The people who teach them also watch over them. Like at the St. Margaret Home."

"Nuns, you mean?"

"Not nuns. A family. People on Rungholt have found a way to adapt."

"Adapt? Like salamanders? Like in a cave or a grotto or some . . . some Garden of Eden?"

"You— You are a Doubting Thomas. It takes courage to believe, and you want to touch them before you believe."

Oh, to touch you—

"But you can only touch them afterward. The first time you believe, however briefly, it grows. Like healing after an injury . . ."

like when you broke your arm fishing. In the beginning you feel the pain constantly, but there'll come a day when you can't feel it for a minute. Soon, you notice you've been without pain for half an hour. Then half a day."

False starts.

Misunderstandings.

Clashes between reason and hope.

He comes to her along the ocean side of the dike, leaves the cot in the barn where he sleeps, and walks to her bed that also used to be his. Here in the dark room beneath the pitched roof, they lie side by side without touching and whisper about their children away on Rungholt.

This is how it begins. Again. Between them.

"I want to know what you know."

"They live with a shipbuilder and a teacher." Lotte sounds like she used to when they were all still together, joyous and strong. "Their children are grown. They moved out long ago."

"The parents miss them," he says cautiously.

She turns to him. "So much devotion waiting for our three when they arrived."

He shifts closer. Tilts his forehead against hers. "A gift for them to have children in their house again."

For Lotte he'll stop resisting, let her pull him inside her illusion. To keep the children from vanishing altogether, he must give them food, clothes, life. He can do that. Still, what keeps him sane is that he knows the difference. He is not about to leap into the sea to find his children. For Lotte, he will imagine colors on Rungholt. *Doesn't the island emerge from the Nordsee once a year? You believe. That is your offering. And if you do that with all your soul, you'll be with your children again.*

She doesn't stop him when he brings his mouth to her breast, brings himself, and she's ready, is almost ready for him except he's sucking so hard that she instinctively slips her thumb into the seal, something she hasn't done since she loosened Bärbel— the seal of her other babies' mouths was lighter—thumbnail against her nipple, the fleshy top of her thumb toward her daughter, then the gentle plop of letting go.

*—and she's right back to nursing her daughter—not now not now not—*but it's her husband still at her. She bends her elbows, and when he falls from her, she hinges her fingertips in the wide hollows of her clavicle, her forearms a gate of bones. *How foolish to think we can find one another again in the sweet-hidden where our children began.*

He's squeezing his eyes shut—

"Kalle?"

*—*eyes shut till he can see them again, *his children, a string of small shapes fluttering from Lotte's hand, dancing, except he can't tell who is next to her, who in the middle, who at the end of this string of shapes that spools and unspools like the strings of kites he built as a boy, silk paper the colors of church windows stretched across strips of balsa wood, bits of cattail fluff knotted into their tails for steadiness.*

A kite would have risen.

He moans, and she presses the back of one wrist against his left cheek. It used to ease him, bring him back to himself because that's how he must have slept in his mother's womb, curved on his left side, the back of his wrist to his cheek. Moon sculpts the planes of his face. How young he looks, Lotte thinks. *How young we were on our wedding day.* My sixteenth birthday. He just seventeen. She traces the muscles of his neck and down his sternum where she first traced him when she was fifteen, before they dared touch lower, touch sin. It became their code for wanting.

When Kalle awakens in his marriage bed, he can't recall falling asleep, but already he is sleeping again, *dreaming of some animal scrambling across his legs. The smell of piss. Kalle stirs, feels the weight shift, the dream shift, wonders if you can smell piss in your dream. And once again he is losing children. Setting them aside for a moment. Forgetting them. Careless.*

Light then, slanting through the window, and next to him Lotte, eyes still closed. Nestled against her is their lastborn, spindly legs folded to his belly. Kalle can see *the boy pull himself up the railing, scramble across the railing and down to the floor and onto the big bed by himself, burrow between his sleeping parents.* No. Lotte, she must have gotten up, walked barefoot across the cold floor to carry Wilhelm here. *First, she wraps herself into the puckered robe she keeps on the hook by the door to the* Kinderzimmer—*children's room—that Wilhelm used to share with his sisters and his brother, her robe big enough to envelop the boy and herself as she lifts him from his crib and brings him into this bed—*

Is that where the boy has been sleeping all those weeks and months I've been away? Swinging both legs across the edge of the mattress, Kalle stands, his head low so he won't hit it against the ceiling that slopes from the peak above the bed. *The habit of memory. The habit of rising thousands of mornings with Lotte and keeping my head low.*

The boy scuttles to Kalle's side of the bed, pushes something beneath the pillow—Hannelore's doll—and plants his stinky rump on the pillow.

"What are you hiding there?"

Sitting like a tailor with his knees out and his heels together, he rocks himself, eyes deep-set in his scrawny face. To think how chubby he used to be. Now the edges of his body draw inward. Kalle's other children were sturdy at his age.

"If you don't want me to know what you're hiding," he tells Wilhelm, "I don't mind." But he does. He does mind.

Forward and back Wilhelm rocks. Listens to ghost-sheep chomp chomp on dike pull fog from ground chomp chomp fog crawls up unhides legs of ghost-sheep unhides bellies.

Forward and back he rocks, just like Martin, Kalle thinks. Soothing himself. Slow. Quiet. But then faster till he bangs the back of his head, mattes his hair. Martin howled whenever Lotte combed out the tangles, though she was gentle; but he'd sit quietly on the knees of his father who eased the tines of a fork into the knots to loosen the pale, straight hair, inhaling Martin's little-boy smell of sweat and of milk. But Martin stopped rocking himself before he turned one. And now Wilhelm is banging his head, same pale hair. When he sways forward, Kalle slips a pillow behind him to stop him from hurting himself. Startled, Wilhelm halts, wiggles his shoulders to test the softness. Squints at Kalle as if he knew his thoughts. Too thin, too quiet, this one. Kalle's other children always awoke with some sound—giggling or crying or babbling before language became words. He'd plant kisses on their bellies when he tucked them in at night. How they laughed, especially Bärbel. He has not done this since the wave. Cannot imagine doing this with the lastborn.

He turns from him, scoops yesterday's clothes from the birch shelves he built along the low walls. Such fine carpentry, the neighbors say. But fine carpentry is child's work for a toymaker schooled to carve the most delicate details.

Ahead of him black and white stripes. The zebra. Travelers coming upon the zebra in this haze may think they've reached the shore of another continent or wandered into a dream of where they truly want to travel. *And what will they think of me? That I'm a ghost come home? A gentle ghost, I hope.*

He hopes Lotte will let the zebra stay on Nordstrand, grazing with the sheep, roaming, even if he's no longer here. But he doesn't know how to tell her he'll meet up with the Zirkus again come spring. Not yet.

In March she startles him by asking, "Are you leaving again?"

"Do you want me to leave?"

"That's not what I asked." And it's not even the true question, the question she won't ask because she shouldn't have to. *Why don't you stay with me?*

"We can write to each other, Lotte." He wants both, his family and the Zirkus.

Lotte's eyes go hard. "She's too old for you."

"Who?"

"As if you didn't know."

"If you want I'll stay with you—"

"—and with Wilhelm—"

"With you and with Wilhelm . . . that week in August when the Zirkus comes to Nordstrand."

"One week?" she shouts. "One week is not staying."

"One week plus maybe five months in winter. I'll talk to the Ludwigs about wintering here. More space for our animals than in Emmerich. Farmers can board the animals in their barns and sheds, carpenters can repair the wagon wheels, the blacksmith can shoe the horses and ponies. They'll appreciate the income, Lotte. I've thought about this a lot. If they agree, I'll set up arrangements for winter training when I come back next August."

But as March nears April, he doesn't mention winter training again and becomes so evasive that the unsaid between them fills all space. And she is short with him, so distant that he convinces himself she wants him to leave—that's why he must leave before she can send him away; and to her it's obvious that Kalle doesn't want to stay—that's why she must send him away. Their last night together, he tugs her nightgown back down, covers her as if he had not been inside her, as if they had not just loved one another. As they lie side by side without touching, it comes to them that they've never felt this lonely.

PART SIX

Spring 1879

28

A Balance of Bees and Humans

The beekeeper comes to us with bare arms, sturdy arms. His eyes follow the bees that buzz against our walls and windows, not bashing themselves, but establishing their domain. No net over his sun-browned face. Not even a hat. Such is his regard for the bees, that he will not veil himself when he approaches them. And they know. Their buzzing escalates to welcome him.

"They've made your wagon their hive," he tells us.

"We live in a hive," Heike sings. "We live—"

"What can you do?" I ask him.

"Get the entire hive out, or it will lure other bees."

"—in a hive. We live in a hive. We—" Her eyes glisten. "I saw you."

He looks at her with such kindness that I can no longer smell my fear for Heike.

"I have eyes in my head." She points two fingers at her eyes.

He smiles, this tall man, points two fingers at his eyes. "I have to be careful so I don't poke my eyes out."

"Careful!" She drops her hand. Pulls his hand away from his face.

"Thank you," he says.

"I saw you. On the bad day. When Hannelore drowned."

"Yes. That bad day. We were all there."

And then I know—that early. Because I've learned from Herr Ludwig about kindness in men. Not men like The Sensational Sebastian, all flicker and excitement. But men like the beekeeper. With him my daughter will be safe in the world. Because he'll protect her once I'm dead. Because she'll be a child forever, excitable, as close to laughter as she is to tears. Because he is the one I choose for her.

The day he returns for the bees in a horse-drawn buggy with high side panels, I invite him to eat with us in our wagon. When I praise my daughter's *Rouladen*—pounded slices of beef rolled around pickles and bacon—her eyes flicker with tears, and I worry she'll blurt out that Cook has prepared our meal.

Cook likes to tease her about her tears: "*Du hast zu nah am Wasser gebaut.*" You've built too close to water. She'll kiss Heike's forehead. "I'll make you *Pfannekuchen.*"

Cook takes pride in her cooking. Tripling a rabbit stew into soup by adding water and vegetables. Making cabbage rolls or, when we are flush, goulash with much paprika. Most food Cook cannot chew with her little teeth, soft like a child's milk-teeth. Still, she enjoys making them for us: *Reibekuchen* (potato pancakes), *Gebratene Würstchen* (fried sausages).

To distract Heike, I tell the beekeeper, "Your patience with bees is amazing."

"Ideally I remove them and keep them alive."

"Live dowry," I blurt.

Heike claps her hands.

He laughs, startled.

When he detaches the huge hive, he doesn't get stung. The bees come with him, willingly, and he carries them to his buggy. To insulate our wagon, Heike and Silvio cut tall bulrush stems from a pond.

"Moses was in a basket made from bulrush," she informs him, "and he almost drowned."

"I wonder where you got that story."

"From your father, Silvio."

"Are you sure?"

"You know . . ."

Silvio chuckles. "He told me that same story at least a hundred times."

"See? You know." Heike raises a long stem toward his face, tickles him.

They whack the velvet-brown heads against a tree till they burst and collect the white fibers in a sack. Together we seal every crack in the Annunciation wagon.

We eat dinner at The Last Supper, and when we leave, Hans-Jürgen calls after Silvio, "What are you limping for?"

"I'm not limping."

"You're doing a great impersonation of a limping man."

"Just a grown-in toenail."

"Let me take a look."

Silvio shakes his head.

"Big toe?"

"*Ja.*"

"Which one?"

Silvio kicks an imaginary ball with his right foot.

"You need to relieve the pressure before—"

"It'll heal by itself."

"It'll grow into your flesh. Pus and blood and infection and—"

"Blood poisoning," Herr Ludwig teases.

Silvio grimaces.

"Amputation for sure." Herr Ludwig clicks his tongue.

"You're in a good mood," says Silvio.

"Let the man look at it, Silvio."

"He can tell me what to do and I'll do it myself."

"You'll need a sharp knife," Hans-Jürgen says. "Small enough to cut—"

"I'm not letting you near me with a knife."

"I said let the man look at it," Herr Ludwig booms and slides aside on the bench. "Sit here."

Silvio sits.

"Stretch out your leg," says Hans-Jürgen.

Silvio crosses his arms.

His father rolls his eyes. "Leg. Not arm. Stretch out your damn leg."

Silvio stretches out his leg.

Fingers light and fast around his toes. Hans-Jürgen. "Hold still."

A flicker. Touching in public. Silvio does his best to appear bored. "Just do it."

Hans-Jürgen is talking with Silvio's father. Stringy arms, both of them. "If I cut a V shape into the top edge of the toe-nail, it'll grow toward that V and—"

"Good," says Silvio's father.

"—detach from the sides." Hans-Jürgen unfolds a pocket knife.

"Just do it," Silvio growls.

As his father and Hans-Jürgen lean across his toe, shoulder to shoulder, it comes to Silvio that this is what he wants—the not-hiding.

The cut doesn't hurt; change is instant—like a pinch released—when you're still hurting but no longer fighting to get free.

.   .   .

The beekeeper asks us where the Zirkus will be next and bunks with Kalle when he travels to bring us gifts: dried chamomile and fennel; a clay jar with honey.

"Heike admires you," I lie to him.

He says, "I love how your voice rises at the end of each sentence, and how your eyes are set so far apart."

"Heike keeps talking about you."

He describes my face to me as though I'd lived without mirrors. "Such space in the upper half of your face, Sabine. That wide forehead. Slope of your cheeks as if you're forever exhaling after a long breath."

A man I would cherish if I were Heike. But I won't consider him for myself because I've chosen him for my daughter, this decent man who'll honor his promises and his legal duties if he agrees to marry my daughter.

"So lovely and so strong." He brings the side of his hand close to my face. Draws its outline into the air without touch.

Still, I feel the heat of his skin. I can't allow myself to think it's me he wants. That'll pass once he marries Heike.

"Heike has that kind of face too," I tell him.

A lacy bouquet of dried hydrangeas on his next visit.

"The beekeeper brought you *Hortensie* blossoms." I hand them to Heike.

"Dead things." She drops them.

He picks them up. "Preserved. A different phase of their lives. I hang them upside down from rafters to preserve them."

"I don't want dead things." Heike skips away.

While he's left with the blossoms in his arms.

"My daughter is intuitive . . . but not always practical."

Gravely, the beekeeper nods.

"She has so many strengths . . . fearlessness and charm and generosity."

"You have those strengths too."

"Except for fearlessness."

"I see you as courageous."

"I pretend to be more courageous than I am."

First Sunday of May he brings a crate from the toy factory that Kalle's friend Köbi was supposed to deliver.

"I told Köbi I was coming this way anyhow."

Inside the crate: one hundred carved lions; half as many zebras; dancing dogs in tutus; monkeys you can link arm to arm in a chain. The toymakers have also carved animals the Ludwig Zirkus doesn't own—giraffes and seals and elephants—but will sell at the concession stand.

"I cannot see into my own future," the beekeeper tells me, "but I can see into yours."

"And what do you see?"

"That I am there."

"As my son-in-law."

He shakes his head, startled. "It's you I want to marry, Sabine."

"That would make Heike your stepdaughter."

"Yes."

"At the mercy of your new wife."

"Wait— Who is this new wife?"

"If you and I married—"

"That's what I want."

"—and if I died, your new wife could throw Heike out."

"I don't want to marry this new wife. She's mean."

We both laugh, though it isn't funny.

We could still stop, but I ambush him. "As Heike's husband, you'll be responsible for her."

"I'll be responsible for Heike as her stepfather."

"Until the new wife—"

"Enough, Sabine. Enough now."

But his kindness is no match for my perseverance, and I reel him in for my daughter. Bait? I don't know. I'm not proud of that. But I'm not ashamed of keeping my daughter from harm.

When he finally gives in, he looks exhausted. And that's when I feel compelled to be honorable. To give him a chance to walk away from Heike.

"Heike can't have children. An abortion before she turned fifteen. Another the following year. She nearly bled to death."

He winces.

"I didn't go searching for the operation, but when the nurse offered it, I said yes. And whenever I question my decision I come to the same answer—that I had to keep her alive."

"I understand."

"But do you understand that you'll never be a father?"

"You'll be there too. In my house."

"With Heike."

He wraps his arms around his sides; his lips are pressed together, his chin is puckered. He looks smaller, this tall man, thinner, as though I've whittled him down.

And I'm afraid he'll walk away. And I already miss him.

"The three of us together . . . best for Heike." He looks exhausted.

"For her counting to ten is like a song she's memorized . . ." I talk as fast as I can. Lay out her flaws. Rattle them off to hold him. "She doesn't understand what numbers are and how to manage them . . . has no idea she is different. A cello in her arms gives her more pleasure than a child would. At least a cello won't starve if you forget where you left it. She goes from happy to sad—you've seen that." I hesitate. "Ever since the operation—"

"Tell me, Sabine."

"—she's no longer interested in . . . being affectionate with a man."

"Then I'm relieved."

29

The Old Women Set the Stage
by Trusting Gossip

Maria pounded on my door last night with her granddaughter, both of them bleeding—"

"That beast—"

"The granddaughter bit his leg when he beat at Maria again. Then he whipped his belt across her face, laid bare the edge of one eyebrow. So much blood across her eye and side of her face . . ."

"Face wounds can be like that."

"I've offered her my revolver."

"I've offered her my nephews to break his legs."

"Not your sons?"

"Nephews are enough."

"She didn't want our help."

"And now?"

"Now Maria says we must talk."

"Finally!"

The Old Women have been young with Maria and grown old with Maria. They set the stage by trusting gossip to make known that Herr Doktor Ullrich is sinking into melancholy. Twice already—so it travels on the stream of gossip—he has walked into the Nordsee.

"His shoes were lined up in the sand," the Old Women gossip.

"His daughters saved his life."

"Side by side, his shoes."

When the priest arrives to counsel him, Herr Doktor Ullrich chases him off.

"He denies his melancholy," the people of Nordstrand say.

Sister Konstanze arrives with Sister Ida to offer the Herr Doktor a good rest in the infirmary.

"Lies," he yells at them.

But the Sisters don't budge.

"My wife wants to kill me!" He advances, one arm raised.

"Don't you dare," Sister Ida rasps and steps in front of Sister Konstanze.

During their first years at the St. Margaret Home they had cells at opposite ends of a marble corridor; nights they visited one another, terrified to encounter Sister Hildegunde, ready for lies they were willing to confess.

And one dawn it happened. Sister Hildegunde stepped in the way of Sister Ida.

"I was praying," Sister Ida said. "Walking and praying—"

"This is not right." Sister Hildegunde squinted at her, the pale hue of rose petals. "You wake everyone up traipsing back and forth. We must do something about this."

"I'm so sorry."

"After Mass I want you to move into the cell next to Sister Konstanze."

In the cemetery, the people of Nordstrand comfort the Widow Maria Ullrich and her daughters. Nearly everyone is here to see the Herr Doktor buried. Farmers and Sisters and Old Women and Girls and fishermen and toymakers.

"Herr Doktor Ullrich was hallucinating when we visited him," Sister Konstanze tells them.

"Raving mad," Sister Ida adds.

"No surprise he succeeded in killing himself," people say.

"Not by water but by rope."

"He certainly tried before."

"Such a troubled man," says the priest.

"You have done all you can to keep him alive," the people tell the Widow Ullrich.

"You have done all you can," the Old Women tell her.

"You know I have!" the Widow Ullrich says fiercely.

"Ssshhhh . . ." The Old Women pull her inside their circle, arms locked around each others' shoulders *and once again and forever help her drag the Herr Doktor into the barn.* Heavy, he was heavy on the ladder to the hayloft, knocked insensible with a shovel after the feather pillow against his face failed to keep him down. In the loft they knotted a rope around his neck, tied the end around a rafter, and shoved him from that rafter.

One death seen through.

They could have killed him a dozen times.

"Ssshhhh . . ."

The priest blesses the coffin and approaches the Widow Ullrich to offer *Herzliches Beileid*—heartfelt condolences; but the Old Women are a fortress, a black fortress, solid with their black coats and black hats and black shoes. As the coffin is lowered into the open earth, groundwater fizzes around it, bubbles and swells, and the Widow Ullrich emerges from her black fortress. Even if for some implausible reason her dead husband is not totally dead, water will swallow him in his coffin and rise even after his grave gets filled in with dirt, causing a puddle on the grave, a rectangular indentation. *Proof.*

"*Herzliches Beileid,* Frau Ullrich." The priest shakes her hand, eager to return to his bed with a cup of tea and *Lebkuchen. Gluttony—*

No, not gluttony. It's just that he adores eating in bed and drifting into a little nap. The second floor of the carriage house is his apartment now, assigned by Sister Hildegunde, and on the highest shelf in his kitchen he stashes whatever sweet indulgences a parishioner may leave for him in the confessional. To retrieve them, one must get the ladder. A ladder is a fine substitute for willpower.

30

Driftwood Jesus

The following Sunday the priest feels compelled to deliver his gluttony sermon. His gluttony and Rungholt sermon.

"Five hundred years ago, the island Rungholt had gold and treasures from around the world that arrived on ships from tropical countries. On the docks, people could buy whatever they wanted. There was such excess on Rungholt that, soon, the people had no wishes left. Nothing to wait for."

The St. Margaret Girls, who've grown up waiting for nearly everything, are mesmerized.

"Excess led to gluttony . . . led to malicious pranks . . . led to godlessness. I've been researching Rungholt for decades," he says, but leaves out that he's been searching the wetlands for treasures from Rungholt. "You see, in January of 1362, some drunk farmers forced Schnapps down a pig's gullet till it fainted. Then they tied a white bonnet to its head and put the pig into a bed."

A few scoffers and whisperers giggle.

"They covered the pig with a blanket." The priest gathers an imaginary blanket to his neck. Feels the urgency in his voice, likes how the momentum of this urgency makes him feel taller.

He's on Rungholt this very moment, trying to stop those drunks from mocking God. "They sent for the chaplain to give last rites to a dying woman, but when he folded back the ruffles of the bonnet, he screamed and refused to give last rites to a drunken pig. He crossed himself and ran away. But these farmers were so irreverent and demented that they chased him and poured beer into the silver vessel where he carried the consecrated communion wafer. They laughed at him. 'Now your God is drunk too.'

"Again the chaplain got away and hid in a church where he begged God for revenge. And God said, 'Enough! Enough!' And did what He had done before to punish humans. Sent the flood. *Die Sintflut.* Except there was no Ark. Now those of you—" The priest peers at the St. Margaret Girls in the tight rows below the pulpit. "Those of you who are newcomers to Nordstrand would like to know if anyone survived."

The new Girl from Berlin slumps forward. Heavy odors make her queasy. Incense. Liver. Camphor. For her the fainting is not staged; but it is lucky for those Girls who get to support her by her arms and—genuflecting and crossing themselves— usher her from the church into the moist spring air.

The priest waits until the church door slams. His eyes come to rest on the raised faces of the St. Margaret Girls. "Only the priest and two girls survived. The flood took everyone else."

But Sister Ida is not about to let him frighten her Girls with a sermon that assigns all blame to humans and all power to God. After Mass, she takes her Girls for a walk along the Nordsee. They skip ahead of her, chase mosquitoes as if they were butterflies, collect pieces of driftwood. She purses her lips and blows upward, a childhood gesture to cool her face or drive off insects. Once again it startles her that her hair does not lift with her breath. That stiff wimple— *Will I ever get used to that wimple? Or to the shape of my soul?*

"Pure," she was taught as a child, "will happen at your first confession. And the day after you'll wear the white dress of communion to celebrate the shape of your soul. It will be the happiest day of your life." But the happiest day did not come: not when she received first communion; not when she took vows. Not until she met Sister Konstanze with her willful chin and her soft curls, though she didn't see the curls beneath the wimple, of course, not until they peeled off each other's wimples while sitting on the edge of Sister Konstanze's bed.

"Girls." Sister Ida tugs at her starched wimple. "Today we'll build a driftwood Jesus, except—" Her voice gives out, and she taps her throat with two fingers. "Except none of the anguish, none of the agony."

The Girls skip away to find bits of wood shaped like body parts that have been washed ashore: arms; thigh bones; the curve of a belly. One Girl says she can hear the bells of Rungholt, but then she's always the first to hear or see something—even the first Girl to refuse signing the adoption agreement.

"I hear the bells too," another Girl shouts.

"Bells made of gold."

"I can hear them now."

The Girls are exhilarated by the gold and jewels beneath the surface of the Nordsee. *With riches like that, you can take your baby and a story of a dead husband and move to a town where no one knows you, start your life anew.*

"—hire a nursemaid—"

"—and a cook—"

"—a coachman, too—"

"—a seamstress—"

"—a housekeeper, of course . . ."

They yank a frayed fishing net from the mud. Help Sister Ida drag two bleached logs from the sea across the dike. "They're for the cross," Sister says.

They lash the bleached logs together, the short log across the long log near the top. When they set out for more driftwood, they find a cold fire and pull chunks of blackened wood from the sand: three shaped like feet, one like a shoulder blade, several kneecaps, a ribcage, six ears.

For the sake of authenticity, Sister Ida invites Sister Konstanze to lecture on human biology while she and others arrange driftwood pieces into a spine, a neck, two ears, a collarbone . . .

Assembling the Jesus takes six days.

"A genuine act of creation," Sister Konstanze declares.

Sister Ida nods. "Now we rest."

"As it must be."

Sister Hildegunde paints rain and after the rain, her colors more intense in that first light upon wet—sand luminous, roofs shimmering. She'll cover a large canvas with broad strokes that capture vastness rather than precision. Horizontal strokes, deliberate strokes that have a passion and no borders. That cross her eyes, causing her to concentrate on turning her eyes to the side. As she finds new depths in her technique, it's exhilarating to demonstrate to her students what she is learning for herself.

"Not every detail needs to be shown."

"Be the blank canvas."

In the lobby of the St. Margaret Home hangs a new painting of a tiny St. Margaret Home beneath a downpour thick as a waterfall; and yet already light presses through. Sister is mesmerized by horizontal lines—between rough waves and flat waters; between vast sky and vast land—lines that are defined by the uncertainty of shifting where one ends and the other begins, widening, narrowing, and on that line Sister Hildegunde depicts evidence of humans: boats smaller than pebbles; buildings lower than dice; windmills delicate as legs of fleas.

.   .   .

Parishioners like to show Sister Hildegunde their *Hochwasser* treasures.

"We have a painting of *Hochwasser* with tiger teeth and tiger claws."

". . . a bowl with a picture of *Hochwasser* and a sunset."

". . . *Hochwasser* and roses."

"My *Opa* has two carvings of shipwrecks on the backs of whales."

"*Kitsch*," Sister Hildegunde tells her students.

The students laugh.

"*Hochwasser* has inspired people over centuries. Pictures and carvings and painted porcelain. Some of it is art. But most of it is *Kitsch*."

"How can you tell *Kitsch*?" her students want to know.

"You learn to recognize it."

PART SEVEN

Summer 1879

31

August. And the Dresses of the
St. Margaret Girls Billow

August. And the dresses of the St. Margaret Girls billow, graceful and weightless. Wind cradles their bellies so they can run again, laughing with their friends on this sandy path bordered by beach roses. Two things to look forward to: today they'll make jam from the hips of these roses; tomorrow the Zirkus will cross on the ferry from the mainland and the parade is already a presence for the Girls, dazzling in its music and smells and colors.

From the midwife they learn the Latin name for these roses, *Rosa rugosa.* "If you pick them too soon," she says, "they're hard and sour."

"But if you wait too long, they're pulpy," says Tilli, who has lived at the St. Margaret Home for an entire year, longer than any other Girl.

Pails swing from their hands as they fill them with the ripest fruits of wild roses. They want to keep their new friendships forever because they feel closer to St. Margaret Girls than to any friends before—*except for your first best friend who was you and you her with no fences between*—but some of the Girls will get away as soon as they can, flee from the shame of getting big, rip these new friendships from their souls so that nothing can tilt them into memories of the St. Margaret Home.

Hagebutten Marmalade—rosehip marmalade from the recipe of Old Women. In the kitchen of the St. Margaret Home, Tilli warns the Girls that the tiny, sharp hairs on the hips can lodge in your fingers.

"Like splinters."

"To get them out," the midwife says, "you must scrape your front teeth across the tips of your thumb and forefinger. Like this." She sticks the tip of her thumb into her mouth, presses it against her upper front teeth as she pulls it out.

"Just don't swallow the splinters," warns Tilli.

For the rest of the day, she works with the Girls: they trim tops and bottoms from the rosehips, cut them into halves, and scoop out the white seeds. Next, they chop the halves and boil them in water. Once the rosehips bubble in the big pots and turn the water brickred, the midwife demonstrates how to strain the mixture through sieves to get rid of the last splintery hairs. Tilli gets to add honey before they ladle the *Marmalade* into jars and seal them in a simmering water bath. For days the Girls' fingertips are scarlet.

"When you leave us, I'll send a jar with you," the midwife promises.

While roustabouts unfold the unwieldy canvas for the tent, three St. Margaret Girls drag a ladder from the carriage house to the huge driftwood Jesus who raises his left arm as if giving orders to them; they stick wildflowers—*Butterblümchen und Kornblümchen und Kleeblümchen*—into his thorny crown to welcome the Ludwig Zirkus. The Sisters are delighted by their *Übermut*—exuberance.

As the roustabouts pound stakes into the ground, one stake dislodges a dirty clump of gauze.

"Look at this!" The blacksmith holds it up, flings it away in an arc.

"Must be from the war with the Danes," says a farmer.

"Would a bandage keep a dozen years?" asks the baker.

"You think there're still bodies down there?"

A toymaker kicks at the ground. "Wouldn't surprise me."

"My uncle had to fight on the Danish side," a fisherman says.

"My father had a leg amputated," says the blacksmith. "Green after a bullet."

The first time Lotte sees Kalle again is when he comes to the house to get the zebra for the parade. But it's agitated, staggers in a circle, whinnying, ears standing up.

"What's wrong with you?" He pats the zebra's throat and jaw.

"I haven't seen her like this." Lotte strokes the silken length between the animal's nose and eyes.

"Something is upsetting her," Kalle says.

"Maybe the smell of the Zirkus animals. She must know they're back."

"She'll see them in the parade."

The zebra butts her head against him, nearly knocks him over.

He laughs. "Getting stronger, are you?"

He swoops Wilhelm onto the zebra. Holds him steady with one arm around him. Children and dogs run to follow the parade.

"Some earthbound Ark we have here," *Vati* tells Wilhelm.

Verrückter Hund raises his leg. Wobbles topples.

Vati says it's because the Sisters don't teach him how to pee like a boy dog. "But you can show him, Wilhelm. Butt your shoulder against his side. Keep him from toppling."

Pee like boy dog . . . Dove flies at church door. Nest above door.

"See the shadow of the steeple," *Vati* says, "how it points at the St. Margaret Home?"

Wilhelm sees. Rides over shadow of steeple.

Flies teem around the eyes and nostrils of the Zirkus animals, not moving if the animals swing their heads or tails. Mud sucks at the shoes of the spectators, darkens the tips of their umbrellas. They swat at flies, lift small children who've slipped in the mud, but all that is part of the festivities that will include their purchase of tickets—Saturday and Sunday performances sell out quickly—and the blessing of animals once the priest and two altar boys appear in a puff of myrrh that scares off the flies.

When Kalle brings Wilhelm home on the zebra, they stop in the barn to get more ropes. He lifts Wilhelm off the horse, lifts him high, higher yet, and that's when he hears it—laughing in his kitchen. A man's voice. Then Lotte's. *She doesn't laugh like that when she's with me.* An icy-hot stab behind his eyes. He sets Wilhelm down. Riffles through the shelves above his workbench, looking for chores that'll postpone entering the house.

"Can I ask you a question about a Sister?" Köbi asks Lotte.

"Which Sister?"

"The one with the long legs."

"You cannot see a Sister's legs."

"I know what hers look like. She's younger than the others and walks fast. If you watch closely, you can picture her legs. You'll notice it in her walk . . . the way only long-legged women walk."

"You must explain something to me."

He flinches. "Explain what?"

"How does a long-legged woman walk?"

He blushes as he used to in first grade.

"You're blushing."

"And you—you have no mercy."

"Must be the new Sister. Sister Bertha."

"Sister Bertha . . ." He sighs. "Those sweet legs. Almost too long. And that swivel . . ."

"What swivel?"

"Of her . . . her personality. Her hips."

"Women adore you," she teases Köbi. "Women melt just looking at you."

"I know."

She laughs aloud. When's the last time she heard herself laugh? "Women cannot wait to get engaged to you."

"A sad thing."

"It is a sad thing."

He grins. "Abundantly sad."

"Why a Sister?"

"Love chooses for us. Love chose for my ancestors. My great-uncle took a year to walk through Germany and met this young woman on Nordstrand."

"Don't tell me another Sister."

"A weaver. His entire family traveled to Nordstrand for his wedding and never returned to the Schwarzwald. Now—this Sister Bertha? Do you know her well?"

"Well enough."

"What is she like?"

"Why?"

"I must know."

"And then what must you do? Get engaged again?"

He winces. Four broken engagements so far.

"You love getting engaged but not being engaged because that leads to marriage. So—let's imagine Sister Bertha leaves the convent for you."

He looks startled.

"She moves in with you and—"

"Oh no."

"—and her beautiful love for you replaces her beautiful love for her eternal bridegroom—"

"No."

"—and she ends her engagement to her eternal bridegroom. Devotes herself to you."

He groans.

"Hungry, *Vati*."

"First we must clear this out."

All around them sharp tools . . . a scythe a shovel an ax a pitchfork . . .

Wilhelm tugs at a bucket of nails.

"That's heavier than you. You'll get hurt if you drop it on your feet."

"*Nein,*" Wilhelm cries.

"Stop it!" Kalle yells, instantly ashamed. He hands him a wooden ruler. "You can carry this."

"I help." Wilhelm tunnels his little hand into Kalle's fist and—

No— Martin tunnels his hand into Kalle's fist. That's the hand Kalle wants in his, not the hand of his lastborn whose eyes are too mild to match Martin's.

In back of the lowest shelf he finds a nest of shredded rags, evidence of mice. Kalle grabs the shovel, ready to kill, but when he flips the nest, a female falls from it, three tiny mice latched to her teats, sucking and still latched to her while dropping to the floor where she lies on her side. Kalle can't raise the shovel. He's killed mice before. And now is saving them. Because of the nursing. Because of the not letting go. Because he is still a father with one child hanging onto him.

He drapes a burlap sack around the milking stool and sets it above the mice. To shelter them? To give them privacy? He shakes his head. *Privacy for mice.*

"You stay away from mice," he warns Wilhelm. "They're filthy. They get people sick." Then he positions Wilhelm on his shoulders—his armor, his conscience—and walks toward the house, pushes the door open.

"I'm already over her," Köbi says to Lotte.

"I don't believe you."

Kalle bristles. "What are you doing here?"

"You said you'd meet me here." Something cocky in Köbi's voice. "To talk about wood shavings."

"Well . . . last time they were too small."

"I'll tell them at the toy factory. Again."

"Our animals sneeze when they breathe them in. You should know that."

"I know that." Köbi organizes the collection of wood scraps and leases barn space from farmers to store mounds of shavings and sawdust that settle and dry from brown to silver. If the sawdust doesn't get replaced often enough, it gets nasty from dung and piss.

Wilhelm's heels thump against Kalle's chest and he catches them in one hand. Holds them still. "You must explain to the toymakers the difference between sawdust for the arena and wood shavings for bedding that must be large enough so they cannot get into the animal's lungs."

Lotte raises her arms to Wilhelm. "Come here, *Kindchen*." She won't look at Kalle. Won't step in front of him. Just reaches for her son from the side and lets him glide into her arms without touching her husband.

32

Lure of the Island

That night she barely talks to him.

Long hours of work with the Zirkus the following day, and he gets back to Lotte late.

Morning, then. In the kitchen. And she lets out a shuddering breath. "I cannot do this by myself . . ."

"I understand," he says, though he doesn't.

"Some days when I'm alone . . . I cannot see them anymore."

"Here. Here now." He pulls a chair away from the kitchen table, settles Lotte on his knees. "We see them better when we're together."

"When we talk about them."

"They're playing in the sun." He spins the story for her, embellishes, to lift her from her despair. And be with her.

"Hannelore . . . she's in second grade. Her teacher says she's eager to learn."

"She's always been curious. And Martin has been wanting to go to school ever since Hannelore started."

"Sometimes he gets envious of her."

"I hope the other family knows how to reassure him. Not punish—"

"They're kind people," Lotte says.

"Bärbel loves to play with the family's animals."

He restores Lotte to being with their children. He can give her that. Can give her Bärbel as she tags behind the teacher and the shipbuilder and tries to help with chores, not one bit afraid of the horses and cows. Can give her Martin trailing Hannelore, imitating how she arranges her bedding around herself, the two of them plumping and shifting and hiding like starlings in their pockets of leaves. Can give her Hannelore on her third birthday, songs and *Kuchen* and the wooden doll with the yellow dress that Wilhelm likes to drag around.

Lotte sighs. "But now the other family gets to celebrate her birthday with her."

He runs one palm up and down her spine.

"I wish . . ." She lays her head on his shoulder.

"Have I told you about the playground at their school? Just like here. Sundays they take our children there and show Bärbel how to pump her legs on the swing—"

"—but not too high."

"They always look out for Bärbel."

Wilhelm tugs at his sleeve. "*Vati? Vati?*"

"Not now," Kalle snaps, wishing he'd said it softly because Lotte raises her head from his shoulder.

Wilhelm keeps tugging, and what feels clear to Kalle is this: the boy does not fit into the world he and Lotte inhabit with their older children. He, who has never slapped a child, wants to demolish the boy and—in the waning of his flesh and spirit— get back his other three.

Where did that come from? Demolish? Certainly against my will.

"I'm not capable of that," he blurts, mortified.

"Capable of what?" Lotte asks.

He shakes his head.

"So good with animals, aren't you? But you don't want to love your son."

"That's not so." But the sweet trusting gaze of the boy makes Kalle uneasy, a glance that will suck all life from you if you let him. He must shield the boy from knowing. Wilhelm was already thrown away once—nothing can undo that.

"I'm sorry," he says. "Also about how I was with Köbi."

"You only want what you can't have."

Lotte stands up, but he pulls her back, pulls the boy up onto her lap, enfolds her between the boy and himself. She brings her arms around the boy's back, settles in. When Kalle's legs go numb, he doesn't lift the boy back down; she'll take it as a sign that he's trying not to love Wilhelm.

Words that make pictures of their children. To be with her, he must remember the words she has told him, remember the sequence to establish their children for her. He must not miss one detail because he'll need it to build the next detail. And the one after that. If he holds on to the power of reason he can let her slide into her make-believe but remain separate, ready to comfort her when she emerges, to caress her till she opens herself to him.

"Tell me what they are doing. This moment?"

He feels burned by her intensity. Is she testing him? The strength of his belief?

"Tell me they are on Rungholt now."

"They are on Rungholt now. Probably still asleep."

"Not probably."

"They are still asleep."

"It's our secret."

"Has the secret taken the place of our love, Lotte?"

"You're not the only one who gets jealous."

"Who?"

"As if you didn't know."

"I don't."

"It's still early on the island," she says and waits.

"Hannelore will wake the little ones . . . tickle them awake. You know how she is." *Hannelore, their firstborn, raising her chin when she asks yet another question. Hannelore who wears down the surfaces of her doll with her love, drags it around by the braids, sleeps with it facedown across her belly. No one else knows the children the way he and Lotte do.* "Soon they'll have breakfast."

"Slices of boiled ham?" Her voice is raspy.

"*Ja.* And Dutch cheese."

"Exotic fruits . . ."

"They'll eat pastries," he prompts her.

"Pastries so delicate they'll pass their lips like—like breath," Lotte murmurs, yielding to the lure of the island where it's always balmy, where she can dress her children like royalty, feed them with delicacies they've never tasted but only heard of.

"What kind of exotic food?" he asks.

"Oranges . . ." Her throat swells with sudden wild joy for her children who can eat oranges every day. "Once I tasted an orange."

No—almost tasted an orange. One slice of one orange. In third grade, when her teacher, Sister Sieglinde, brought an orange to class, blessed by the Pope in Rome. If Lotte had been at school and not home with the measles, she would have seen Sister Sieglinde pull the orange apart, golden half moons that she slid on the tongues of her students like communion wafers. Juicy and sweet, her classmates told Lotte, till she came to remember that taste on her own tongue.

"All the riches of all the world," Lotte says.

33

You Must Be Kind to
Your Husband

Y ou must be kind to your husband," I remind Heike the morning of her wedding.

"My husband is boring."

"Your husband is kind and generous."

"He is old."

"Younger than me."

"He talks old."

"He's only thirty-two. Halfway between you and me in
age."

"Then you marry him."

"Heike!"

"He likes you. I have eyes in my head."

My neck burns red.

"But he'll die soon." She picks up the dotted feather of a
seagull, sticks it into her wedding bouquet.

"Why do you say that?"

"Jesus died when he was thirty-three."

"Not everyone dies at thirty-three."

.   .   .

If you turn your attention on Heike, the light comes back three-fold. It's been like that ever since she was a girl; now, as a bride she is radiant, lovely; and you can almost forget that she's not always like that. She adores the ceremony, the gifts, especially the inlaid cello the beekeeper has commissioned for her. She wants to play it right away but the priest makes her wait till after the vows. But then the people of Nordstrand urge her on, and they dance.

Not all of them, though. Some fret how painful it must be for Lotte and Kalle to celebrate on the anniversary of their children's drowning, and this awareness makes them so anxious that they feel compelled to console the Jansens.

But their reaction is bizarre. Crazy, even. Lotte and Kalle smile before they speak. Smile at each other and then at the people and say, "We have reason to celebrate." And: "Soon there will be good news." And then Kalle, going on about winter training, how he'll arrive early winter and set up everything. Already he has brought three more Zirkus animals the Ludwigs have entrusted to him, ailing or too weak to be on the road. They'll stay on Nordstrand until they recover or die, sharing his barn with a cow, a horse, two pigs, and sixteen sheep.

He encourages the people to stable animals. "Get your choices known. The Sisters have signed up for the monkeys," he says. "I'm keeping a list."

The beekeeper has given Heike his bedroom on the second floor, next to my bedroom. For himself he sets up a bed in his workroom downstairs where the walls are covered with shelves for books and honey jars, and scales and countless tiny drawers with herbs.

On his walls hang two of Sister Hildegunde's paintings. Heike's favorite is called *Blue Train*: Girls carry their babies from the bishop's mansion and board a blue train on the dike. One third of the canvas depicts, in miniature, the Rhein where families wait by picnic tables laden with cakes and flowers.

"Was it expensive?" she asks the beekeeper.

"I traded honey."

"I— I gave you my bees."

"A quarter of a million bees."

"My bees. My honey. My picture!"

He laughs. "I agree. Would you like me to hang *Blue Train* in your bedroom?"

She claps her hands. "*Ja.*"

In the other painting umbrella-shaped clouds carry peafowl and babies while big-bellied Girls tug at the handles of the umbrella clouds to bring them closer.

Babies . . . all those babies in the paintings. How will he be with not having babies of his own?

34

A Frantic Summoning

Together, Lotte and Kalle chart their children's day, a sort of heaven far beyond—except the island is closer than heaven, its world shimmering at the edges, expanding. Until now, Lotte was the one who started, but today the toymaker takes her to the island: *she is there, with him, where their children play and breathe and run ahead of them when they go for walks and Lotte laughs her deep and loud laugh, mouth open, head thrown back.*

"I've missed your laugh," he says.

"Have you missed their voices?"

"Of course."

"The voices of our children. Do you want to hear them?"

"Yes," he says. "Yes."

She gets Wilhelm from his crib, props him on her hip, and Kalle follows her outside and up the dike and across to the *Watt.*

"Listen," she murmurs.

"I don't hear—"

"Not yet. Listen."

But he's restless.

"They don't come every day I wait for them, but if they're near, it begins with a murmur so delicate—"

He sighs. "I still don't hear anything."

"Ssshhhh . . . soon . . ."

He raises his face. Hears nothing until all around them *now rises the quicksilver murmur of children and the border wavers and glistens and what's on the other side is tempting, the chance to find your children alive on Rungholt. A promise if you can believe. Which you long for, this moment. Quicksilver murmur . . . and the voices of Wilhelm's children far away in the future? And yet already here. Three grandchildren who will come to you from Wilhelm. Solace in that. Rejoicing. Three for the three taken away. The tallest a girl with black hair. Daughter of Wilhelm but not of Wilhelm. Two little boys, fair like Wilhelm with his delicate features.*

Kalle scans the dark band of horizon and beyond where their children live. *Let them be on Rungholt, then.* At least he and Lotte are in this world together where planning to be with their children lifts the pain. But you must move swiftly before reason can stop you.

"Just a few hours by rowboat," he says.

That night she pulls Kalle beyond his edge of reason. Turns on her side, knees and forehead against his while winds bear down on the house her grandparents built against the dike. He presses his forehead against hers, shifts his knees toward hers. The center between them is empty, shaped like a heart. *Oh—to have you again.* She strokes his sternum, opens herself to him, body and soul, an instinct more urgent than making a child: this here is a frantic summoning of the three already born, a frenzy of tearing and tasting and biting they would have been shocked to imagine before, all for the sake of reaching their children in this world where wanting to believe becomes believing. Falling then—

into faith, into absolution—and he plummets with her toward Rungholt, feels the heft of his children as he clutches them into his arms. *Alive and we're not to blame.* No stranger than miracles we've grown up with: *Jesus strolls on water; the crippled rise; a dragon spits up a saint; priests drink Jesus's blood; the dead come to life* . . .

He will bring them home: Bärbel, quirky and giggly, no eyes for anyone else when her *Vati* is there; Hannelore with her remarkable questions, certain her *Vati* will answer them; Martin, smart and moody, who may become a quarrelsome man if not guided by his *Vati*. And guide him Kalle will. Guide them all with patience and kindness.

At the school museum Lotte and Kalle examine journals and letters, unroll a brittle vellum map from the seventeenth century and weigh down the yellowed edges with books. Over centuries, the museum has grown, curated by the Sister who has her office in the museum where she's allowed to sit in the embroidered armchair or rest on the sofa, prepare for classes at the fourteenth-century marble table, surrounded by seascapes and framed documents.

They find letters tucked into pages of church records.

A warning from a survivor:

> Stay far from Rungholt during slack tide just before the current reverses.
>
> Be vigilant. I nearly drowned.

A priest advocates in the 1683 church records:

> If you see Rungholt, you must turn back, or the vortex will drag you down.

The beekeeper's great-aunts write about fishing one spring when the island rose up in front of them:

> We were lucky the water pushed our dory away.
> When Rungholt sank again, we were already beyond
> the outer ripples.

Lotte and Kalle discover circled entries that span two centuries:

> I am preparing to leave for Rungholt.

> We'll wait for the first high tide after the black
> sun of spring.

> My ancestors own a brick kiln on Rungholt.

> A shipyard.

> A farm.

The same annotation with each circle:

> Nicht zurückgekommen. *Did not return.*

What Kalle and Lotte take from those entries is this: you must row out and wait directly above Rungholt; you must be prepared for that brief lull of slack tide when the island will rise—earth and structures—and lift your boat, allow you to enter and seize your children.

"It has to be next spring," she says.

"That's the soonest. Yes."

They resolve to listen more closely to stories that have always been there of people who rowed out and witnessed Rungholt rise from the sea.

"I'll prepare in the meantime."

"But after that—how do we bring them back home?" Kalle asks.

"We don't have to figure out the how. Not yet."

I Know I'm Bossy

Heike screams when we tell her she cannot leave with the Zirkus, whips her hair from one side to the other as if shaking out water, brief flashes of face as she hides from us, from herself. *Oh, Heike.*

The beekeeper steps back.

But I walk into her, brace her with the momentum of my body, her head against my shoulder, until she quiets in my arms. "Oh, Heike."

In the morning she's gone. We search all over Nordstrand.

"I held her back," I tell the beekeeper.

"You held her safe."

"She wanted to fly at the trapeze since she was a small girl, but I insisted she become a musician."

"You encouraged her to be a musician."

"So much of raising her has been like that. Encouraging and insisting without telling her she's not like other girls."

"A secret between you."

"That part of it. Yes. But there's so much more, her joy, her—"

"When she is joyful. But today—" He pulls up his shoulders. "That was horrible, seeing her like that."

"I'm sorry."

He waits.

"I'm sorry I didn't tell you about her rages before."

"What else should I know?"

"It doesn't happen very often."

"That's not what I asked you, Sabine."

I'm not surprised when Silvio rides back with her on his horse.

"You and I can go," she whispers to me.

"We live on Nordstrand now. Remember?"

"I want to live with you and the Zirkus."

"You have a husband now."

Heike groans. "I don't want a husband."

When she runs away again, the beekeeper and I know where to search and follow the Zirkus route in the carriage. But Heike refuses to return with us. First I try with words—I always do with her. When I pull her toward the carriage, she throws herself on the ground and shrieks.

"I cannot force her," the beekeeper says.

"You don't have to," I tell him.

"I won't force her to come home."

Silvio lays a hand on the beekeeper's shoulder. "Give her a few days with us."

Heike doesn't return the following day. Or the day after. Instead Tilli comes to our door and offers to keep Heike from running away. Before we can say a word, she thrusts an embossed certificate at us that qualifies her to work as a *Kindermädchen*—nursemaid.

"Sister Hildegunde says she'll give you her personal recommendation."

"Heike is not a child," the beekeeper says.

"I know, but—"

"Thank you, Tilli," I interrupt, "but Heike can wash herself and feed herself and—"

"But I can keep her safe. Make her want to stay at home."

"How would you do that?" The beekeeper watches her closely.

"I'll find ways to make her want to stay. Maybe I'll start by playing Zirkus with her. Take her on long hikes until she's too tired to run away. Let her help with the zebra and the other Zirkus animals."

We talk. And keep talking long after Tilli has left to get her belongings from the St. Margaret Home.

"That girl needs a family," the beekeeper says.

"That girl wants Lotte's family. Lotte lets her visit a lot but not move in."

"And now she'll live next door to her."

But when I tell Lotte, she says it's a brilliant idea. "A very brilliant idea, Sabine."

"This close to your house?"

"She and Heike will be good for each other."

"Tilli adores you."

"I'm in her way. It's all about Wilhelm."

"It may have been at first, but I see how Tilli looks at you."

Four days later when Silvio brings Heike home, she won't look at us. I try to embrace her, but she steps aside.

"Heike?" The beekeeper smiles at her. "We have a surprise for you."

"What?" she snaps.

"The surprise is in your room."

She shrugs.

"A surprise?" Silvio raises his eyebrows. "Can I go and look?"

"I don't know," says the beekeeper. "You'll have to ask Heike."

She grips Silvio's wrist. "We'll look together."

We follow them up the stairs. When Heike opens her door, Tilli pulls her inside.

"Where's my surprise?"

Tilli points at herself and curtsies.

Heike points at herself and curtsies. "What are you doing in my room, Tilli?"

"That's where I sleep when I live in your house."

"No, you don't live in my house."

"Yes, I do."

"You're bossy."

"I know I'm bossy."

"Were you bossy when you were a little girl?"

"*Ja.*"

"Did you have sisters or brothers to boss around?"

One breath we are, Alfred, not knowing where it leads . . . but a given, natural . . . we no longer have that—

"Tilli!"

—don't think about him don't—

"I asked if you have sisters or brothers."

"Only chickens and cows to boss around."

"Do they listen to you?"

"Oh *ja.*"

"Where is your family?"

". . . a fire . . ."

"My *Vati* is dead too. He could fly."

"Fly where?"

"Everywhere. He flew away away from the trapeze the day I was born. But then he crashed."

Tilli asks, "What side of the bed do you want?"

"My side," says Heike.

·   ·   ·

"There's a painting I must show you."

I take Silvio to the St. Margaret Home where several of Sister Hildegunde's paintings are exhibited in the lobby along with tapestries and paintings by students and Sisters. I don't have to point Silvio toward the one called *After the Zirkus* because he's already approaching the canvas of a stark Nordstrand landscape that holds the glitter and hum of the Zirkus, superimposed in fine layers, long after the Zirkus has left. Such a painting, Silvio understands, *will pull you inside, make you sweat because you cannot imagine the painting in someone else's house; make you decide to buy it before anyone else can.*

I motion to him but he rushes toward a Sister who's cleaning the birdcage and tells her he wants to buy *After the Zirkus.*

"It's already sold," she says and points at me.

He wheels toward me, scowling.

"We bought it—"

He slices his hand through the air, dismissing my words.

"—for you after Heike ran away again. We knew you'd bring her back."

Silvio hangs *After the Zirkus* above the foot-end of the bed he shares with Hans-Jürgen. After weeks of gazing at the painting before sleep and upon waking, he fathoms that Sister Hildegunde must have taken a fragment of what he's seen and dreamed and yearned for—all his life or for one moment—and reflected that in her painting, validating what Silvio has sensed, yet making it more significant so that, in memories-to-come, it will always be significant like that.

How did you know so much about me, Sister Hildegunde?

36

Our Own Hidden Wildness

Heike is exuberant now that Tilli lives with her. They roam the wetlands. Long steps, against the wind. Both strong. Heike lithe, Tilli solid. They take Wilhelm to the playground on the school hill. Push him and then each other high on the swings. Flying, legs pumping.

"Hold on now, Wilhelm." Tilli has angel hair.

Heike pushes him higher, her hands on his back. "You like having wings?"

Wilhelm laughs.

They row out in Kalle's dory, but Wilhelm is only allowed in the boat when his mother is with them. Patient and inventive, Tilli plays Zirkus with Heike and Wilhelm. Rewards them with food. They make the rounds of the neighborhood. At the St. Margaret Home Heike reads to the babies, pretend-reads, turns pages while Wilhelm makes singsong words of what he sees in the pictures.

Heike wants to please Tilli whose presence outshines the lure of the Ludwig Zirkus. The beekeeper is fascinated by their interactions. Heike looks to Tilli for information, which Tilli whispers to her so that Heike can present it as her own, believe it is her own. Emboldened, she'll tell the beekeeper she loves mathematics, asks him to test her. Cheerfully she'll call out some number, any number—eleven or twenty or five—and laugh when that's incorrect. When Tilli corrects her, Heike asks him to test her again.

The beekeeper laughs. "You're throwing into the dark."

Moments like this he can love Heike, not as a wife who makes him wonder if this marriage should have been—a question he only allows himself in his loneliest hours—but love her as a stepdaughter who is crafty and funny and slow.

Most evenings she practices her cello for hours, and he listens, mesmerized.

"Your mother told me you are talented," he says, "but I had no idea how talented.

"Would you like to give a concert?" he asks her.

"Can Tilli come to my concert?"

"Anyone you want to invite."

"I'll be there," Tilli says.

I like doing the design and major sewing projects for the Zirkus that the Twenty-Four-Hour Man delivers once a month. The Ludwigs have hired a woman to help with cooking and small mending jobs.

Now that Lotte and I are neighbors, I bring to her all I've learned about friendship while on the road, try to charm her with candor, with praise, with the offer to design a dress for her. We walk along the shore and talk; sit by the *Kachelofen*—tile stove—and talk: about us, about Heike, about Wilhelm—but not about Lotte's other children.

Not until I'm on my knees, pincushion on my wrist, adjusting the hem of the new dress while she stands on my sewing stool.

"That afternoon on the flats . . ." she starts.

That afternoon on the flats . . . I wish I could tell her how futile my fear for Heike felt when Lotte lost three children, healthy children—not like Heike. Too soon to tell her, I think. Not at all, I think.

"That afternoon you said you'll do anything for me."

"It's what I felt."

"Still?"

"Still." I wait for more. Stick another pin through the fabric.

"So if I ask you something indiscreet—will you tell me?"

"Ask, then."

"Kalle—" She looks embarrassed, angry. "Were you with Kalle?"

I sit back on my heels, pins between my front teeth. "No!"

"Ever?"

"How long have you—"

"Since the first time he left. About you or some woman."

"Have you asked him?" I motion for her to turn to the right. "Not that far."

"Like this?" One small step. "He says he hasn't been touched."

"I believe that."

"Why should I?"

I stick in another pin. "I stuck Kalle with a needle once, no, twice. The first by accident, the second on purpose—that's how furious I was. I didn't want him to get away like that, leaving you with the loss of—"

"You still haven't said why I should believe him."

"Kalle isn't . . ."

"Isn't what, Sabine?"

". . . awake. In that way."

One corner of her mouth rides up. "With me he is."

"Then I'm glad for you. For both of you."

Whenever we go near our hives, Heike, Tilli, and I wear white hats with netting like the lady missionaries on the collection box in church, and we put on accents, the way German missionaries might talk in Africa. The St. Margaret Home is our best customer. The Girls love honey. So do the Sisters.

To hold him for my daughter, I pamper the beekeeper. Show Heike how to iron his shirts, twice, so that the collar feels like silk against his neck. Ask him about his favorite meals—"*Entenbraten*," he says; "*Weinsuppe; Zitronenkuchen*"—and teach Heike how to roast a duck and simmer wine soup and bake lemon cake.

People claim I moved with my daughter into her marriage because that marriage would provide for me, too. But the beekeeper wants me here, grateful I look after Heike.

While dusting his workroom we find loose pages with puckered edges. Behind the bookshelves in Heike's bedroom Tilli discovers stacks of overdue library books. Before I wash his clothes, I empty his pockets: coins, handkerchief, pieces of thin twine. If Tilli stays by her side, Heike finishes what she starts; left alone, she'll try to get away, roam the meadows and dike with long strides. But now we have Tilli who always catches her and roams with her, brings her home with her hair tangled, face flushed, words tumbling with shifting clouds and sun, with thunderstorms and rainbows, with people and willows arching away from wind.

During Heike's performance I sit with the beekeeper in the first row. We arrived early, amazed as the auditorium of the St. Margaret Home filled. Tilli is in the audience as promised, two rows behind us with Lotte and Wilhelm.

As Heike plays the cello, she pulls it against her body, into her body as if it were part of her, long arms reaching forward and around it. In her face every expression I've witnessed since her birth: first, of course, the coming into the void from the shelter of my womb, and spreading her arms wide; the enthusiasm of the small girl in motion, face tipped toward me, always, and the look-at-me, look-at-me; the sullen fifteen-year-old eating starling soup at the long table in The Last Supper, shoulders curved inward, face turned away from me.

And I see what I have not yet witnessed: Heike five years from now; Heike at my age, still child-like. I feel warm and take off Pia's woven shawl, fold it across my knees, spellbound as a confidence comes into Heike, and she draws the bow across the strings. I know what her hair would feel like under my fingertips were I to brush it from her temples. Know how her wildness funnels into her music, only to claim her again—*as it claims me; claims me again and again, though I can outdistance it*—and I wonder how many in the audience recognize our own hidden wildness.

The beekeeper, too, is taken by the wildness in Heike's music, rushing ahead of her into brilliance. As she wraps herself around the cello, face dipping into the hollow between its neck and belly, I wonder if he understands he'll never be as important to her as a cello. His eyes fill with tears—of relief? of exhilaration?—and he reaches for my wrist where it lies on my scarf. I keep my eyes on Heike, though my pulse thuds in my wrist, my throat. He gathers one edge of my shawl across our hands, links his fingers through mine. I'm astonished his skin is softer than mine.

PART EIGHT

Winter 1879–1880

37

Old Rifts Mend

In November Kalle arrives early to meet with farmers about boarding Zirkus animals in their barns and sheds; with toy-makers about repairing wagon wheels; with the blacksmith about shoeing horses and ponies. Old rifts mend once the Ludwig Zirkus winters over and people help care for animals they've only seen in parades and in the arena. They visit one another with tales of the ponies' fancy footwork, say, or with worries about the lion whose scent agitates the cattle. Already he's been relocated from the Knudsens' barn to the Bauers' goat shed where he has to crouch. Now the goats live in a barn with the Bauers' cows; disoriented by the high rafters, they knock into each other, and bleat in that indignant voice only goats have.

The Sisters invite the eight monkeys into their aviary, and even church families bring their children to see those mon-keys swinging and eating and scratching where children are forbidden to scratch their own bodies. The children's shriek-ing matches the monkeys' shrieking, behavior not tolerated at home or at school; yet, at the aviary, their parents become le-nient, wander into the lobby to show their children the exhibit

of paintings and weavings by students and faculty. Some ask the
Sisters if they'll have another recital.

Such excess of good will causes church people to nod greet-
ings toward St. Margaret Girls; causes the blacksmith's wife
to rip the double seams of her husband's uniform from the
German-Danish War, turn the blue fabric inside out, and sew a
skirt and fitted jackets for Hedda who lives with her baby above
the smithy.

Through much of the winter the ground will stay muddy
because all those hooves won't let it freeze; no matter how carefully people will wipe their shoes, they'll drag dirt into houses
and churches, especially into school where the children will
study the biology of animals.

*You map out your lives with your children. Immerse yourselves in prepa-
rations that become as immediate as your lives in your farmhouse on the
land side of the dike. And though you cannot reach your three oldest—
not yet, not yet—you can keep your love for them tucked away, your
worries, too. Until you see them again. And you feel calm. Ready for
the first high tide after the Schwarze Sonne when you'll row out and
bring them home. Rungholt has entered your souls: more vibrant now its
colors; more defined its structures; while the familiar landscape of Nordstrand is blurring.*

Kalle trusts his dory. He and the beekeeper built theirs together.

"I'll chart the location, the exact location above and around
Rungholt."

*Once the boat is centered above the island, you'll wait for it to rise.
Reveal its point of entry.*

"We'll only see it if we're right there," Lotte says.

"If we're too close to the rim, we'll get sucked into the waters
that pour from the edges of Rungholt."

"Like waterfalls."

You will enter the island together and bring your children back home.
This is how it will be.

Every day Kalle stops by his boat, checks oars and oar locks, checks its flat bottom, its high bow that points in the direction of Rungholt, and proclaims it safe for his entire family. It's a fine boat. To test their plan they row out while Wilhelm plays with his wooden zebra and his wooden monkey on the bottom boards, listens closely.

Vati says, "We know where to wait. Above the center when the island emerges."

Mutti says, "Careful with what you say. Wilhelm understands too much."

Vati lowers his voice, but Wilhelm still hears him say, "In that lull just before the tides reverse."

Mutti says, "I wish it could be today."

Wilhelm's zebra walks up *Vati*'s leg.

Vati says, "The time is not right. The *Schwarze Sonne* hasn't come back."

"We cannot tell others," *Mutti* whispers.

"This is just for you and for me."

Wilhelm's zebra bites *Vati*'s leg.

"And for the children. Who do you think will greet us?"

"Hannelore."

"*Ja.* Or Martin."

Wilhelm's monkey jumps. Up and down. "Sketch, *Vati*?"

"Bärbel will try to run ahead of them, forgetting she is still little," *Vati* says. "Always so surprised when Hannelore and Martin pass her."

"Maybe Hannelore won't like being lifted up. Too old for that."

"Then I'll kneel in front of her and hold her." Kalle closes his eyes, suffused with love for his Hannelore as he holds her in his arms; but when he opens his eyes, Wilhelm's face bobs in front of his, lips puckered around his thumb.

Voice muffled. "Sketch, *Vati*?"

"Not today. Too many chores."

That quick glaze of hurt.

"But soon," Kalle says.

He decides he won't make Wilhelm wait as he did with Hannelore, even after she turned six and begged him to teach her. He wishes he'd shown her to lean the weight of her hand into a pencil stroke; how to play with the fluidity of a stroke: where it lies heavily on the paper, widening; where it is light and narrow. And then of course the spaces left bare to suggest the body, motion. But there will be time for that now. And he'll start with Wilhelm.

As they head back to their house, he says, "Do you know that animals are never without motion? Even while they sleep. A tiger about to wake up. A bird about to catch a fish. A monkey about to . . ."

"Leap!"

"Good." Kalle eases the thumb from his son's mouth. "What other animals can you think of?"

Shadow of stork on steeple . . . Wilhelm claps his hands. "Stork about."

"About to eat?"

"Fly!"

"Something is always about to change." Kalle squats next to him, faces at the same level. How wasteful he's been with his son's devotion. How afraid of failing him. He did not keep his other children safe. What chance does his youngest have? "Would you like me to carve a stork for you?"

Wilhelm nods.

"Shall I carve it flying?"

Wilhelm nods.

"Or standing on one leg?"

Wilhelm raises one knee—*stork I am stork*—teeters on the other leg.

Kalle catches him before he can fall, steadies him by his skinny shoulders, feels the quiver in his son's bones. And tears up. "We'll draw it together."

"No."

"Why not?"

"Chores."

"Is that how I answer you? Thank you for reminding me. I want to stop with chores and sketch with you. Now. Let's find some storks."

Storks on steeples. Storks in wet meadows. Ruts of water. Wilhelm is cold, scarf dragging. Clack-clack of storks. Long red beaks. Long red legs.

Vati ties scarf around Wilhelm's neck. Says, "The knot is in back so you can't undo it."

Clack-clack. *Vati* crouches. Draws lines in mud. Muddy fingers. Draws storks on steeple. "Soon, you'll be able to draw birds in motion, Wilhelm. Other animals too. If you imagine the animal the moment before it moves, you know the bones beneath the feathers or the fur . . . even the muscles and the blood vessels. You can teach yourself to see."

Wilhelm frowns.

"By looking . . . By imagining. I'll show you how." Kalle tugs Wilhelm's scarf over his mouth. "Hold on to my sleeve so you won't fly off."

"I can fly."

"I know you can fly. Just don't leave me behind."

Wilhelm breathes warm through his scarf. Cold where his nose drips. *Snot icicles hurrah.*

In the houses of others they come across Sister Hildegunde's paintings, expanses of green and yellow and blue that can hurt your eyes if you forget to blink. Wind hunts the clouds—gray clouds, purple clouds, pink clouds—across endless skies. And windmills. Windmills. So much land and so few houses in that flat, flat landscape, heartbreakingly beautiful.

Sister Hildegunde gives breath to the landscape Kalle longs for while on the road: winds ripple fields of grasses and fields of rapeseed and fields of wildflowers as if they're waves. The slopes of dikes flecked with sheep: most white; a few black. Yet, when he's on Nordstrand, Kalle longs for the Ludwig Zirkus; and gradually, the Zirkus makes it into Sister Hildegunde's paintings as if summoned by Kalle's longing. Like a girl in her joy, Sister paints from the angle of her childhood—radiant animals and performers—summoning the magic and colors that arise from what you conjure and give credence to.

38

Sabine and Lotte

I confide in Lotte. Wish I hadn't confided. Wish I could ask her if I stop by her door too often. Not often enough. If I ask her invasive questions. If I don't ask her enough about herself.

Luzia would know. She'd tell me, *"You're so used to starting anew each week in another place that you try too hard with Lotte. You're both on Nordstrand to stay, neighbors, and you don't have to rush. Lotte is not going away."*

How I miss Luzia.

Once again I'm at Lotte's door.

"How do you go on after—"

Lotte blinks.

"I shouldn't ask."

"I saw you at dusk. On the dike. You stood close to the beekeeper . . ."

Claws. Lotte has claws, I think. That's how she goes on. She won't say anything she doesn't want to say. And I'm glad for her.

". . . the kind of close that reveals—"

But I know what she stopped herself from saying: *that reveals your bodies want to couple.* I know because it's true and because I can tell with others—by the distance between their bodies, the charge between them—if they've slept together or if they want to sleep together or if they haven't caressed one another for years.

"People talk," Lotte warns.

I shrug.

"You must be discreet. For your daughter's sake."

Between Luzia and Oliver that charge is almost constant, stronger than at their wedding two decades ago.

I rush to their wagon first, Heike and Tilli and Wilhelm trailing along. With Pia they play family—*Mutti und Vati* and their son and their tiny daughter, their favorite game because Pia is little forever.

Except they must not tell her that, Pia's father says. "It will make her sad. She doesn't know yet."

Luzia paints butterflies on their cheeks and foreheads.

When we leave their wagon, Pia comes along. Heike wants to carry her on her hip but Tilli won't allow that. Whispers that Pia's legs are too short for that. So Pia walks between Heike and Wilhelm, her hands in theirs, and hiccups with delight.

At Herr Ludwig's wagon Heike has to knock twice, and when he calls for her to come in, his voice flutters. She pats his skinny arm that make his hands seem huge. Crusty specks on his wrists.

"Heike," he says to Pia. "My dear Heike. Will you play the cello for me?"

"Not Heike." Pia shakes her head.

Heike doesn't know what to tell him. If she offers to play, he'll get embarrassed that he called Pia by the wrong name.

"Pia is too little for the cello—" Tilli starts.

But Heike interrupts. "She means too young. I can play the cello for you."

"Every rehearsal," Herr Ludwig reminds Pia.

On the way out Heike whispers to Pia that she'll share the name Heike with her. "But just for Herr Ludwig."

At the rehearsal they perch on hay bales, clap and holler just as real audiences will clap and holler. The Whirling Nowack Cousins are still amazingly agile, slower but more precise, a choreography that lingers on the play of muscles in their arms and legs, demonstrates the confidence of their bodies.

"Pia Pia! Look—" Wilhelm yells as Oliver rises and spreads his arms and legs. "Your *Vati* flies!"

Pia paddles the air with her hands to reach her *Vati*.

"But your *Vati* will come back to you," Heike assures her.

Just before Pia's *Vati* lowers himself to the ground, he stretches up, bends at the waist, then grasps the ankles of Hans-Jürgen. Together The Whirling Nowack Cousins flip into a kneeling stance, heads thrown back, throats arched.

Pia clambers across Heike to sit on Kalle's knees.

And he whispers to her his silent chant, silent no more, "You are part of my story . . . And I'm part of your story."

Her gaze is on him.

So is Wilhelm's.

Kalle reaches for his son, pulls him up next to her. Pia, so fierce while Wilhelm is cautious. Black hair and olive skin while his son's hair and skin are pale. "Your story, too, Wilhelm," he says. "I'm part of that and you're part of my story."

In the Whirling Nowacks' wagon, Silvio stretches out on the bed and Hans-Jürgen strokes his lean face as he listens to how Silvio used to adore his parents when he was just with one of them.

"But not when they were together with me the only spectator to their melodrama. The promises and the love and the fights and the hurling and the passion."

"Performing?"

"Like being in the arena with a huge audience."

"You think he knew about you all along?"

"I don't know. He's never said anything like that before."

"Maybe he knew before you knew."

"Then why all that matchmaking with Sabine and me?"

"He wants her to be his family, her and the little girl. But he can have that without turning you into her father."

"And now he's losing more of himself every day."

Hans-Jürgen traces Silvio's hairline, the peak just off-center, and lets his hand be caught.

"Why are you so . . . sweet to me?" Silvio asks.

"We could fight?"

"Too easy."

"Lots of experience, though." Hans-Jürgen smiles with that lovely laziness that comes before embracing. "Now?"

Now—

"They fuss over him like he's their child," says the Cook, but she fusses just as much, makes *Vanillepudding* for the old man who has trouble eating and forgets her name.

Most of his hair has fallen out, and his flat ears have grown huge. If you were to see his face for the first time, you wouldn't know if he's a man or woman. Along the route, people hear crying from the biggest wagon where he lies in bed, curved into himself as he waits to sleep in the arms of Silvio or Hans-Jürgen. When he confesses that he didn't like him at first, Hans-Jürgen says it's like that for most people and massages the old man's shoulders.

For the parades, Silvio organizes the animals in the same order his father used to: Egypt's cage is in the last wagon, the first to be loaded, the last to unload, so that the smaller animals don't have to be led through Egypt's wagon. Still, some get spooked by his big-cat smell that lingers when they return to their cages.

When Silvio offers Hans-Jürgen the job of ringmaster, Hans-Jürgen says he'd rather be the ringmaster's assistant. He suggests carrying Herr Ludwig into the arena on a gold-painted throne, still the official ringmaster in top hat and tuxedo, the whip across his knees.

"To represent the magic," he says.

"Even if he falls asleep on his throne?"

"He is the magic. Especially if he falls asleep on his throne."

39

To Feel Your Skin Despite the Layers of Our Habits

The marble stairs are still there, but the bishop's peacocks are long dead—frozen in snow or boiled in stew—and the cries, laughter, too, that you hear come from new babies, and from older children who still live at the St. Margaret Home. Wilhelm loves to visit the old Sisters. Loves to scramble up those stairs, no matter if with Tilli or his mother, then slide down on his rump to the babies—down and up again and down and up again—recognizing the faces of the old in the babies, and the faces of the babies in the old. *Faces alike. Shapes, too.*

Some days he gets to help push a wheelchair with an old Sister along the corridor of the retirement wing with the vinegar smell of sweaty illness. When he feeds the rabbits and loveybirds, even the forgetful Sisters turn their heads to follow the movements of their animals, and their faces are no longer so tired.

Sister Ida sleeps a lot, clutching her rosary; but as soon as she wakens, the rosary hops through her fingers, hour after hour, bead after bead of prayer, each decade a sorrowful mystery: the agony in the garden, the scourging at the pillar, the crowning with thorns, the carrying of the cross, and the death of Christ on that cross. Then the rosary hops all over again.

Sister Ida can no longer speak, something with her throat no *Doktor* can diagnose, though Sister Konstanze traces its beginning to the night Sister Ida first lost her voice to Sister Hildegunde. But Sister Ida thinks constantly, especially about the axis, the St. Margaret Home as the axis, with Sisters and Girls and babies revolving around this axis. On Sister Ida's birthday the midwife gives her a little chalkboard to write words and sentences.

But Sister Konstanze understands her without words. Sits on the edge of the bed and strokes Sister Ida's arm. To feel your skin despite the layers of our habits . . . stirs memories of so much more. Some nights Sister Konstanze slips from her cell, slips into the retirement wing, slips into Sister Ida's bed. *You're accustomed to making one space fit two.*

Sister Ida lets Wilhelm draw on her chalkboard. When it squeaks, she grimaces and taps her ear. Takes the chalk from him and shows him how to guide it gently across the chalkboard.

Wilhelm nods. Gets the chalk from her. Draws *Verrückter Hund.*

Sister grimaces and taps her ear.

Wilhelm grimaces and taps his ear. Pulls up his shoulders to make his hand lighter, draws a tree—no squeaking—next to the dog's hind leg.

Sister smiles, holds out her hand for the chalk, writes words Wilhelm can't read. "How I miss the certainty of waking next to you."

But what Sister Konstanze reads aloud is this: "What I look forward to all year is that first delicious green of spring."

"How I remember that . . ." Sister Ida writes. "With you."

40

Their Own Patron Saint

Sister Franziska is the first to notice. With Lotte Jansen as midwife there have been no deaths—no infants, no mothers—going back to Hedda and her infant a year ago.

When Sister Franziska tells the other Sisters, they're stunned.

"Of course," they say, "but only in looking back."

"I didn't notice it till now."

"No fresh graves since Lotte Jansen began to midwife."

"Compensation for her terrible losses."

"That's why God is sparing her."

"But for how long?"

"Until He has taken enough from her."

"Who are we to question—"

"If we don't, who will?"

As stories about the young midwife spread through the St. Margaret Home, the Girls come to think of her as their patron saint. They're ready for a saint who soothes them, lightens their burden. What matters most is that the midwife will not judge them. The Girls believe it's because she has done something far worse than they ever will. To give away one child to be adopted, two if you're ill-fated to bear twins, is nothing compared to the midwife losing three children to the sea and throwing away the fourth. One St. Margaret Girl will tell a new Girl, and nearly all come to take for true that the midwife Lotte Jansen has sacrificed her children for them. *Sinner and savior in one. You can identify with her. Though you're not as craven a sinner. Or as selfless a savior. You have been longing for this saint, your own patron saint. You steal items she has touched—a comb a pencil a spoon. Stow them away. Relics.*

Still, a few Girls fear the midwife's power more than God's. To Him they can pray for a stillborn; jump rope till they fall; probe with knitting needles to dislodge the parasite that has grafted itself to their insides; leap from the roof of the aviary and break both legs.

Sister Hildegunde paints countless versions of the mansion, some set on Nordstrand, some in Burgdorf where she grew up. Gradually those two landscapes morph into one: a sea that flows like a river; a river that fills the horizon. Dikes shelter both landscapes from floods. She gives the mansion wings so enormous she hears them flapping and feels blasts of wind. Barges and whirlpools she paints; flocks of nuns and flocks of babies; bridges and willows teeming with finches and monkeys and peacocks. What remains the same is how the mansion levitates on layers of mist.

"It doesn't have to be like it was," she teaches her students.

Inspired by the eternal feud between humans and sea, Sister Hildegunde finally captures the wild beauty of flooding in *Hochwasser*. If humans were to halt, the sea would surge forward, drowning their fields, their sheep, their families.

Hochwasser. And with it the abandoning of all you've worked for.

Hochwasser. It will herd you to the mainland, perhaps come after you as it often does in a nightmare.

. . .

Sister Hildegunde discovers Wilhelm in front of the dragon painting, looking up, though his hands cover his eyes.

"Such a funny dragon," she says. "Let's show our teeth to the funny dragon."

Wilhelm watches her through spread fingers.

"Like this." Sister pulls back her lips and hisses.

Wilhelm pulls back his lips and hisses. Drops his hands and hisses louder.

"Most excellent," says Sister Hildegunde. "Now let's roar at the funny dragon."

"Moooooooo," Wilhelm roars, eyes wide-wide open, roars like the dragon. "Moooooooo."

And that's how Sister Hildegunde will paint him, this boy facing a dragon, both roaring.

41

Nineteen Days

The beekeeper gets up during the night, fetches hot water from the boiler in the *Kachelofen* that's set into the wall between the kitchen and parlor. He pours the water over dried chamomile blossoms, stirs in rapeseed honey, sits alone at the kitchen table with the cup between his palms, and raises it to his lips.

I know this.

Because one night I hear him. I get up to sit with him. Across from him and the steam from his cup and the wide span of his hands around the cup. Where does the warmth of his hands leave off and the warmth of the tea begin?

We talk about Heike, worry about her as if we were her parents. Between him and me there is a constancy I haven't known with men. And yet, it feels familiar because it's been there for me with women. With Luzia. With Lotte. *A constancy and a comfort.*

I make sure he sees me enter the path between the tall grasses, and I linger until he steps from the house. Then I let him find me. Wait for him to pretend he doesn't know I'm here. That's before I know that he does not pretend. He tells me he saw the bobbing of my shoulders and head above the grasses, always a few turns ahead of him.

We spread out my shawl, a flicker of threads, and when we lie down, the weave adapts to our bodies and the space between them, rearranges itself in hues of purples and blue.

"Now I know why the bees came to us," I tell him.

"Why?"

"So that I had to summon you."

In mist like this, you are gorgeous. It smoothes your skin. Makes your hair glisten. Mist is content to hold you, shrink your surroundings, lets you see the hidden till you emerge stunned, changed. For that's the quality of mist. Waves and wind may rage, but mist does not need to show off.

We don't talk about what we're doing. Because then we'd have to stop.

From then on, I listen for him at night, sit up against my pillow so I won't be caught by sleep. Soon, he is steeping two cups of his tea. Mine waits for me when I join him.

He slants the honey jar toward me. Rapeseed honey flows toward the edge of the rim.

"People will say . . ."

"Say what, Sabine?"

"That this is how I keep you for my daughter."

"You're making a sacrifice then." He teases me.

"Being with you is no sacrifice."

"What else will people say?"

"That I was searching for a man to keep Heike from harm if I were to die."

"I'll keep both of you from harm."

"I would never take you away from Heike."

"I don't matter to her."

"But if she wanted you—"

"It was never about her, Sabine."

"For me it's always about her."

"I know that. But for me she is a child."

After a few weeks of this—

No—

Nineteen days.

I remember exactly.

After nineteen days of this we stand up from the table and go to my room and lock the door.

Who has the right to say what should and should not touch?

How many of you have longed for desire to overtake you once again?

For the rush of your beauty to amaze you?

Who is to say what is sin?

We're discreet. Of course we are discreet. In public we hold one another with our presence, not with touch. And it's even more exquisite like that because only we know. That's how I have him for myself. He tells me he did not expect the passion that claims him, crazes him. For me such passion is instinctive. I show him. *You tuck your toes beneath my feet, press them upward against my soles while your palms press downward against the crest of my head, and as you sink into me, bordering me inside and out, I strain against that sweet hold, break through with a cry.*

Steadiness of a Thief

The Old Women are the guardians of legends. The Jansen children have entered legend. Definitely. The suicide of Herr Doktor Ullrich is gossip. The *Nebelfrau*—fog woman—has belonged to legend since before all time. *Since before Rungholt. She can hide anything with* Nebel. *Confuse you. But if you look deeply into her* Nebel, *she will reveal the unseen to you. For some that's courage.*

"Eighty-five Hail Marys," Maria Ullrich volunteers when the Old Women meet at her big house. Lace tablecloth and napkins. Her best silver. Candles though it's the middle of the day.

"That's nothing," says Frau Bauer. "He gave me a headache."

"In addition to the headache."

"Twelve Our Fathers."

"Three of each."

"*Eine ziemlich unschuldige Woche?*" A fairly innocent week?

"I got done sinning when I was a girl."

"True enough."

Maria pours coffee into her porcelain cups. Hand-painted by

her dead husband's grandmother. Used only on Christmas Eve. But now every day. Despite her creased cheeks and neck, she feels more inside her beauty than when she was a young woman.

"I bet the beekeeper and Sabine got fifty Hail Marys," says Frau Bauer.

"And fifty Our Fathers."

"So let them. I get bored searching for what is sin and what is not."

"The church's way of keeping us timid."

"Timid? Good luck with that."

"If they tell you it's a sin you won't do it."

"Hah!"

"Or not as often."

"But eighty-five Hail Marys? Whatever did you do, Maria?"

Maria whispers, "Would you like to know?"

"Yes."

"If I wanted you to know . . ."

They lean toward her. "Yes?"

". . . then I would tell you—not some priest."

"Oh—"

"You can be so . . ."

". . . exasperating."

"Stubborn," Maria corrects them. "Stubborn."

"Did you know the saintliest men sin the best?" I ask the beekeeper.

"And do I?"

"What?"

"Sin the best?"

"Oh yes," I murmur against his throat. "It was mystical, the way you came into our wagon . . ."

"For the bees?" he teases.

"For me."

"What if I was the one who sent the bees to invade you? Courting you with the sweetness of my honey."

"Courting both of us?"

"You. It was always you, Sabine."

I raise myself on one elbow, bring my face above his, and am stunned because my skin feels looser than when I lie beneath him. With The Sensational Sebastian I never thought of that; but now, with a lover a dozen years younger, I feel my features sag toward his. Is that what he sees? Quickly, I roll on my back. Feel my features adjust to gravity. Pat my cheeks and neck. Firm now.

He kisses my breast. "What if you outlive me?"

"One of us, then, the one who's left over, will watch over her."

The beekeeper talks to me while I'm sewing, lets me know if he'll be away all day, or if he is hurt or puzzled. He talks to me before saying anything to Heike. And I listen. Assure him. Don't let on I'm worried he'll leave Heike. Fear has found a new target.

When he can't find his amethyst letter opener, I offer to help him search for it.

"No, it was in my life a long time. I was fortunate. I expect losses. My first impulse is to get over a loss in a way that won't take away dignity."

"Dignity?"

"From others and from myself. It would be naïve to expect loss to bypass me."

"I tend to hold on."

He nods.

"Were you always like this?"

"*Ja.*"

"You must have been wise from the time you were a child."

"It gets easier to lose things . . . even people. That's why I dared marry your daughter."

"You have the steadiness of a saint—"

"—of a thief."

"A thief of what?"

"Books. I steal them from the library. It started when I was ten and the spine of my favorite Greek legends was torn. After I glued it to make it last, I returned it to the library. But that night I couldn't sleep because I was afraid others would tear it up again."

"You were a child."

"I took it without borrowing."

"You were a child!"

"I wanted to keep it safe for a few days or a few weeks and then take it back to the library and put it on a shelf when no one was looking. But I couldn't . . . other books too. Later."

"Always books that were torn?"

He nods. "I confessed to the priest. Still, I couldn't stop."

"Some of the greatest readers of the world stole books."

"How do you know that?"

"Everyone knows."

"No proof."

"It must have been like that."

He laughs. "Oh, Sabine."

"You still do it?"

"No."

I purse my lips. Wait.

"Not entire books. I take a piece of twine with me. If I want a certain page, say, I put the twine inside my mouth till it's wet and then insert it on that page next to the binding. After it soaks through, the page comes out."

Spit and missing pages. Disgusting. I see the pages with puckered edges Heike and I have found, the bits of twine we emptied from his pockets. "How about readers who check out those books after you're through?"

"I take only a few pages. In a respectful manner that preserves the books."

Respectful?

He watches me intensely.

Waiting for me to praise him for his thoughtfulness?

"We all lie to ourselves. This is just how you do it."

He looks surprised. "I don't lie to myself."

"Of course you don't," I say quickly. After all, this is his house. And I must not let myself forget that. "I'm talking about the lies people come to believe about themselves. Lies they make up to spite or boast or get what they want."

"Do you lie to yourself, Sabine?"

"What did you answer him?" Lotte says when I tell her.

"I put on my most mysterious smile for him."

We're in her kitchen, making Venetian candy with honey from our hives while Heike and Wilhelm and Tilli build bridges and houses with building blocks and feathers.

"I want to see that mysterious smile."

I demonstrate. Smile with my lips closed. Hold it.

She turns her eyes to the ceiling as if struck by some divine insight.

"What?"

"That . . . is not mysterious."

"Yes, it is."

"Looks like sour stomach to me."

"The Sensational Sebastian said my smile is mysterious."

"Of course. Everything that man said was true."

I pretend to frown, but I have to laugh.

"Did you ever hear from him again?"

"Not from him. But about him. Still a trapeze artist but always for a different Zirkus. Bremen. Köln. Danzig. Running from one woman while chasing after the next, telling her she's not like other women."

"That's supposed to be a compliment?"

"It's his line. I tried to prove him wrong."

"Do you ever wonder how many other children he has fathered?"

"Abandoned."

"True. He never was a father to your Heike."

"Probably starts a new child with each new woman. Until he gets too old for the trapeze and stays with one woman for so long that, indeed, he turns to stone."

"More, tell me more." Lotte is fascinated and revolted by him.

"You're far too interested in him."

"I confess. Now tell me more."

"We need more feathers," Tilli announces from the door.

"Feathers for my hat," Heike says. "A hat like Tilli's."

"Me too," Wilhelm says as Tilli bundles him up.

"Stay together," I say, though Tilli does that instinctively.

"A hat with a million feathers," Heike says.

"Beautiful," Lotte says.

"So . . . one day the Ludwig Zirkus sets up in a village where his statue stands in a square, bird shit on his shoulders . . ."

". . . and you go up to The Sensational Sebastian and—"

"I don't want to."

"Just imagine . . ."

I don't want to think about The Sensational Sebastian, but for Lotte I will. I'll stand on my head to make her my best friend. Sometimes I believe she already is, but that doesn't last.

"So . . ." Lotte prompts.

"So . . ." I sigh theatrically. Clasp my hands to my breasts. "Let's say I'm with the Ludwigs that day they find his statue."

"Don't forget the bird shit all over him," Lotte says.

"Right. Bird shit."

"And you walk up to him and you tell him he's finally found his place, but he cannot answer you because he's all stone now and you can say whatever you had to hold back."

"I don't hold back much, Lotte."

43

You Don't Have a Brother

Usually Lotte and I can talk about everything. It sustains me. Is part of our days, our thoughts, our laughter. That's why it's so troublesome when she and Kalle isolate themselves. Of course we see them—they're our neighbors—but every sentence they speak to us already aims toward its ending while they press on past us; every word has that rush forward, even when they walk slowly along the crest of the dike.

They whisper, those two, as if afraid wind will scatter their words through our neighborhood. Is it because I've told her too much about the beekeeper and me?

As Tilli weaves back and forth between our families, the balance changes. Heike starts running away again. To Lotte's house. And Tilli brings her back. Part of the time Tilli lives at our house, but more often next door.

When Heike wants to go with her, Tilli says no one else is invited.

As if Lotte and I ever needed an invitation.

Heike asks, "Who says so?"

Tilli hesitates. "Lotte."

Heike bawls. Like a child, only louder.

I put my arms around her.

"I'm sorry," Tilli says. "I'll help here, too . . . with anything you need."

"You know we need you to be around Heike. What is happening with Lotte?"

She blushes—that is, the white around her freckles turns pink so that her freckles are lighter now. "I don't know what is happening."

But I don't believe her.

With each absence Wilhelm has claimed more space in Kalle's soul. His wordless attachment competes with the space his siblings occupy, a struggle when Kalle still tried to keep Wilhelm separate from the other three, when he didn't understand his quiet and unyielding persistence that he has come to admire.

In November Kalle returns with an early Christmas gift for Wilhelm, two brushes and a metal box with watercolors. He also brings a pony, rendered worthless by the impatience of its previous owner, and promises Wilhelm to teach him how to nurture the pony to strength, earn its trust.

Heike takes Wilhelm and Pia to the barn to visit the pony. Smell of dry hay. Wilhelm has to sneeze.

Heike lifts him up. "You can pet the pony's head."

Above the pony is a spider's web where a wasp whirs and spins like a carousel. The spider scrambles down the thin-thin that comes from its body but stops when it's close to the wasp that thrashes like the whale in the picture at church harpooned by a little boat.

Tilli comes up next to them. "I was looking for you, Heike."

"I got away."

"You're good at that."

Heike laughs. "I know."

"And you know that you're not supposed to get away with the little ones by yourself."

"Not little," Pia complains.

The web bulges, but no wind. Up and down the spider works, wraps the wasp. A bee Tilli would free with a twig, poke it from the net. But not a wasp.

"Bees have round rear ends," Tilli says. "Wasps have pointed rear ends. That's what my brother says."

Heike says, "You don't have a brother."

"My cousin. I have . . . two cousins and they are brothers."

"But not your brothers."

"Not brothers to me."

"Down. Now." Wilhelm squirms in Heike's arms.

"But then you can't see the wasp."

"Wasps mean."

"Bees make honey," Heike says. "The beekeeper is my husband because I gave him my bees."

"How many bees?" Pia asks.

"Two million."

Tilli asks, "Remember when the wasp stung you in the foot, Heike? You were running in the tall grasses."

"Grass waves like water."

"You cannot drown in grass," says Tilli.

"I was running and then I cried because of the wasp."

Wilhelm sneezes.

Pia tilts her head back to watch the spider climb all over the wasp, all around the wasp. "Up," she demands. "Now."

Tilli props her against one hip, careful to keep the short legs together. She can't carry Pia like Wilhelm who'll clamp his legs around her waist.

The spider up and down fast. Stock-still, the wasp.

"You picked me up from the grasses," Heike says. "You put your spit on my bite."

"To stop the itching. Spit does that."

"You got a big knife—"

"—a little paring knife—"

"—and stuck it into my foot."

"No. I scraped it across the stinger."

"Until it came out."

"Out," Pia repeats.

The spider spins with the wasp. Both spin till the wasp is stock-still again. Then the spider crawls all around it. Swaddles the wasp.

"It's nature," Tilli says to the little ones. "Spiders numb their victims."

Pia grimaces.

Wilhelm grimaces.

Come morning wasp is gone. Net is gone. Above hangs a tiny dark bundle.

"Our wasp," says Pia.

"Our spider hoisted it up," says Heike.

I wait until Kalle is away for a few days. Then I rush to Lotte's house.

"I've missed you," she cries when she opens the door.

My face is wet. "I've missed you, too."

"If—" Her fingers sweep the wet from my face. "If anything happens to me—to me and to Kalle—will you raise Wilhelm as your own?"

I take her by the elbows. "Are you ill?"

"No. No, I just need to know what if—"

"For me to raise Wilhelm. As my own. I will."

"Just if.

"I will."

"So we both understand."

"You would tell me if you were ill?"

"I would tell you."

"Then what is it you're not telling me?"

PART NINE

Spring 1880

44

Maria Ullrich Is Hungry
for Colors

Maria Ullrich is hungry for colors.

She wants a red dress, hussy-red.

But it's too soon for red, especially a red wedding dress. I promise Maria to sew a red blouse for her. For now I store her secrets and the clothes I've sewn for her.

One more month of mourning.

One more month of black clothes, Maria tells me. Then she'll let herself be seen with her fisherman. First in church—nest of most gossip. Her church clothes I have ready. Pale blue. For walks along the dike with the fisherman she'll wear pale green. Sundays after Mass she'll invite him to her house for *Mittagessen*. He'll bring the fish, she tells me, prepare it as he has countless times for her and himself—delicate with butter and with herbs. Her daughters will like him—he's modest and kind, curious about them. Afterward they'll be surprised he's spoken so little but listened to everything, his expressions playing back to them what has pleased him, say, or moved him. Too soon to tell her daughters what she and the fisherman have decided decades ago—that he'll claim them all as his daughters—and it is true, could become true, moving them toward an outcome both simple and merciful, unassailable by even the most rigid conscience. A wedding planned for summer.

In the weeks before the black sun, Lotte and Kalle cocoon. Let everything fall away from what matters as they prepare for their children's return. They air out the little featherbeds. Arrange with the sexton's hired man to tend to their livestock for one night and one day. As the Old Women observe that the Jansens are painting their shutters and repairing the back steps, they ease their concerns. After all, Lotte and Kalle look happier than they have in many months.

Together Tilli and Lotte wash bedding and make up the beds in the *Kinderzimmer*.

"Who'll sleep here?" Tilli asks.

Lotte smiles.

"Are you expecting guests?"

"Better than guests."

"Can you tell me?"

"Soon. But not a word to Sabine."

They pull fresh covers over the featherbeds. Shake them till they plump up.

"Not a word."

"Just that . . . it's still a surprise."

"What kind of a surprise?"

"The best of all surprises." Lotte is feverish in her excitement. "Oh, Tilli, you'll be so happy—"

"About what?"

"You'll know in a few days."

"Can you give me a clue?"

Lotte purses her lips.

Tilli waits.

"Our family will be bigger."

Tilli's heart skips. Soars. *It's going to happen. It's finally going to happen. I'll move in with Wilhelm and Lotte.*

Lotte widens her arms, and Tilli is about to step into her embrace when Lotte hugs her arms around herself. "We're bringing them home, our children . . ."

Tilli stares at her. "But they drowned."

"They're alive." And what Lotte first revealed to Kalle with such hope and trepidation now pours from her, faster and louder, words tumbling and spiraling.

Tilli stands frozen, arms hanging. *Has Lotte gone mad?* Those children are dead.

"You'll like our children."

"I saw them," Tilli says.

Lotte waits. Rocks back and forth on her feet and waits.

"At the Zirkus. With you. That day . . ."

As Lotte tells her how she and Kalle will row to Rungholt and return with their children, she feels closer to Tilli who believes her, mirrors her own magic. Still, Lotte has to ask her, "Do you believe me?"

Tilli nods and already she's veering into what she's best at: being useful to claim a place for herself. "You'll need help with your children. They've been away for so long."

Tilli will calm Sabine if she gets suspicious. Will keep Wilhelm safe until they're all back.

Lotte lets Wilhelm help her while she bakes and cooks. "For your sisters and your brother."

"When?"

"Soon."

Wilhelm is afraid that Hannelore will take the yellow doll and that Martin will break his toys. Wilhelm must hide the doll in Heike's room, make her promise not to tell.

.   .   .

Done with the heavy lifting of life, the Old Women help with the cooking. Help with their grandchildren. Teach them good manners and how to scrape the soles of their shoes and brush off sand so they won't drag it through the house. Still, sand makes it indoors, and the Old Women sweep it away. Sweeping. Always sweeping. Sometimes four generations live in a row house or next door to you. The youngest and the oldest are most revered: the youngest adored; the oldest valued for the wisdom you can read in their faces. As you age, you grow into your true nature: more loving if you are born loving; more envious if you are born envious; more patient if you are born patient; more greedy if you are born greedy. The imprint of your life maps your features.

45

Schwarze Sonne

Oh, there—"

"Listen."

"The noise of all those wings."

Dusk, and they've spread their blankets in the field: Heike leans against Tilli, makes finger wings; Wilhelm sits on Tilli's knees; Kalle and Lotte whisper, their heads close; while Sabine and the beekeeper make sure to sit at a proper distance from each other.

Tilli is the one to draw us all together, Kalle thinks.

"The starlings."

"Like a storm."

Heike pinches her nostrils. "They stink."

Tilli pinches her nostrils. "They stink worse than sheep."

"Because there are so many," the beekeeper says. "They gather in one huge cloud before they go down to their sleeping grounds. Because of the predators."

With her free hand Heike pinches Wilhelm's nostrils shut, but he swivels his head, shakes her off.

"Don't do that." Heike catches his face between her palms.

"Let me help." Sabine lifts Wilhelm from her.

"Wilhelm," Heike cries, "hold your nose shut."

Starlings tumble from the sky in fabulous and iridescent formations that scatter as birds of prey—falcons on tapered wings, hawks on broad wings—give chase to this feast of starlings that veers and dips and soars as it enfolds its loss; and if you have not encountered such loss, you may assume the flock has always been like this, whole, the sum of all transformations, as it flings its devastating grace and splendor at the heavens. *But what if you don't understand what you're about to lose?* With her own girl Tilli should have known. *Worst thing is you cannot know until after.* Like the morning before the drowning when the Jansen family reveled in their happiness and Venetian candy.

Wilhelm lifts his face to the black swirls. Tastes his amazement like sugar on lettuce.

Kalle drinks in his son's wonderment. "The starlings," he tells him, "are so tired that the urge to sleep is greater than caution. They know they must get down to the marshes swiftly, together, to be safe." He describes how *Raubvögel* wait for the starlings to descend. "Falcons attack from the sky, hawks from below. Most—"

"Hawks need to eat too," Tilli says.

"Falcons, too," Heike says.

"True. Most starlings pass through the attack of the hawks and reach ground."

"Yes," Lotte says. "They clutch reeds, one claw here, the other claw there, and press down the tops to stabilize them, make a pouch of leaves where they hide and rest through the night."

Heike swats at mosquitoes.

"They must sleep one meter above water because of the ground predators," says the beekeeper. "Foxes and weasels swim out during the night to eat the starlings, but they can't climb up the reeds."

Lotte raises her arms, forms a cloud as Sister Sieglinde did in this very field when Lotte was a child. Sabine's fingers fly up, graze Lotte's, and their hands plummet together. Fly up again.

And in the plunge Lotte links her fingers through Sabine's. Asks, "Can Wilhelm stay at your house tonight?"

"Of course."

"Thank you. And part of tomorrow?"

"What should I be asking you?"

"Whatever you want to ask."

"Where will you be?"

"Südfall."

Sabine waits.

"My cousin Nils needs help with . . ."

"You promised to tell me if—"

"I am telling you."

Sabine shakes her head.

"We need to help my cousin on Südfall."

Tilli and Heike make their own clouds, pull Wilhelm into their radiance, and the three laugh and bump into grown-ups and one another. Tilli's cloud separates into fingers that shiver and fly and *she's a starling now who must hide in the night.* As Wilhelm wiggles his fingers, it comes to Kalle how—in this twilight flicker of wings and hands—the birds and humans belong to one migration.

It was like that when he and Lotte took their first baby to watch the sun turn black with birds. As they carried Hannelore through the fields, sun slanted from the right. Ahead of them, marshes. They spread some hay across the muddy ground. There they wait. He twirls a hollow stem between his fingers, blows into it to make the wispy hairs on Lotte's temples rise with his breath. She smiles. Clasps Hannelore to her breast till her eyes close. Together they bundle their sleeping baby and back away from her on their knees, soundlessly, into the deeper grass behind a stand of reeds, from where they can still watch her. There, they love one another, loosen each other's clothing just enough to stroke, to merge, half-covered if Hannelore were to wake up.

They can finish in two minutes.

Can take two hours.

All day and again as in their first year of loving. Hiding from parents and nuns and teachers and neighbors; only now it's their baby daughter they're hiding from. Sun, deeper and glowing, dips behind the reeds, hones their silhouettes, miniature trees in Japanese drawings, each leaf suggested. While Hannelore sleeps, a fine ribbon of milk on her throat; while her parents love one another in the deepest grass, screened by a stand of reeds.

Hannelore. She's here, Lotte thinks. *Hannelore is here. We are ready. Soon.*

The beekeeper says, "Starlings sleep squeezed next to one another."

"Feather to feather . . ." Heike says.

"All the starlings. That's why it gets so hot."

"How hot?" Wilhelm asks.

"Over one hundred degrees," Heike says.

"No, no," Tilli says. "You know what happens at one hundred degrees."

"Water boils?" Heike asks.

"Good. And at zero degrees?"

Heike nudges Tilli.

Tilli whispers to her.

Heike says, "Water freezes."

Wilhelm hums.

"Forty degrees Celsius," the beekeeper says, "that's how hot it gets in the center of the flock when the starlings sleep."

"Forty degrees is still very hot," Heike says.

"Like the hottest day of summer," says Tilli.

"The starlings come here because it's easy to catch insects with all that water around," says the beekeeper.

"Rain, too," Heike says. "Do they eat sleeping bugs?"

"Sleeping bugs and awake bugs," Tilli says.

"Where do they go from here?"

"As far north as Sweden and Norway," Tilli says.

"Finland, too?"

"Finland, too."

When we walk from the darkness into our house, my daughter shouts, "Wilhelm is here."

Tilli says, "I've already made up a bed for him on the bench by the *Kachelofen*."

Already? What do you know? I search Tilli's face, but her eyes flicker away.

"We'll be back middle of the day tomorrow," Lotte tells me.

I feel the tug of our friendship and know she feels it too, is just one slip of one word away from telling me. "Please, Lotte—"

But there's Kalle with a chair from the table. He sets its back against the bench. "Climb in, Wilhelm."

"No!" *Something's not right not true not right*—

"It's your favorite spot," Heike reminds Wilhelm.

"Climb in," his father says.

Wilhelm pretends to try. Slides off, limp arms and legs. "I can't."

"You do this all the time by yourself," Heike says.

"Carry me," he wails and lifts his arms to his mother. Hides his face in the dip between her neck and shoulder.

Heike tickles him behind his knees. "You're not a baby."

"Go home . . ."

Lotte's eyes are on Tilli.

Who nods. Says, "Tomorrow."

"Tomorrow," Lotte whispers to her.

"I'll stay here with you," Tilli promises Wilhelm.

"Me too." Heike pulls him from Lotte, swirls him around—cries of protest, then laughter—before she plops him onto the bench.

"Let's check what's happening here. Lie down." Kalle pulls up Wilhelm's shirt, plants a kiss on his belly.

Wilhelm giggles.

"I think we missed a spot here."

"And here," Wilhelm says and pulls his shirt higher, pokes a finger into his belly.

More kisses. "Tomorrow, you and I'll check your belly again."

When Lotte tucks Wilhelm in, his body eases.

I slip my shawl from my shoulders, cover him.

"We'll bring you a surprise," Kalle promises him. And when his son nods, something deep within Kalle opens toward him.

Tilli beams. "A surprise beyond anything you can imagine."

You Must Grip What You
Cannot Bear to Lose

Smells of fish and salt and rotting earth as Kalle and Lotte drag their rowboat across the tidal flats. Mist beads on their faces, on the backs of their hands, assumes the shimmer of all matter, and melds those colors as they shove the bow into the sea.

Kalle climbs in first and sits on the forward bench, his back to the sea, and grips the handles of the oars. Once Lotte jumps in and is on the center bench, he leans toward her and submerges the blades, leans back, working the oars hard. Then forward again.

"What if—" Lotte stops.

"What if what?"

"What if we cannot bring the children back here? What if their new family won't let them go?"

He rows, steadily. "All I want is for us to be together."

"You know that's what I want too. But what if this is the one chance we have to live with them?"

Wilhelm's absence reaches across the waters, weighs down their boat.

"So if we believe—truly believe," Kalle starts, ". . . why didn't we take Wilhelm along. Along to the others."

"Because we thought we could bring them back here."

"And now?"

"I think we have to live there . . . with them."

"No one has returned."

"We must want to be there."

"I do. But—"

"Doubting Thomas had to lay his hand into Jesus's open wound. I don't call that belief."

Belief is your inheritance. Doubt a sin.

"We have to get Wilhelm." Kalle turns the boat—rapid strokes with one blade—till they face where they've come from.

"Take him with us."

"Proof of our faith that we'll be a family again."

Noise outside the beekeeper's house. Tilli gets to the door first to let them in. We're relieved until Kalle says they've come for Wilhelm. To take him along. There's a wild exhilaration about them.

"No!" Tilli cries.

"He's asleep," I tell them.

But Kalle hurries toward his son whose body is warm from the tiles of the *Kachelofen*. As he picks him up, my shawl drops from him. "How light you are. When Hannelore was two and a half, she was already heavier. Soon—"

"Stay here," I implore them.

"Tilli will stay," Kalle says.

"No!" Tilli spins toward him. She's shaking. "It's not supposed to be like this!"

"Have some soup with us, Kalle . . . Lotte." The beekeeper's voice is urgent. "We made a pot of chicken soup with carrots and barley."

"We can't be late," Kalle says.

"Late for what?" the beekeeper asks.

Tilli holds her arms wide when Wilhelm leans away from

his father, pivots, and dives toward her. A game that usually makes them laugh because they're sure she'll catch him. But his father only holds him tighter. So tight that Wilhelm kicks and screams.

Tears in Lotte's voice. "I am so sorry, Tilli."

Tilli grips her wrist. "It's not what you promised me."

I embrace Lotte to keep her from getting away. "Tell me what's happening!"

"I'm just . . . cold."

"Another reason to stay with us."

Lotte's arms come around me, won't let go. Her body trembles.

"Something is terribly wrong," I whisper. "What is it? Tell me. At least take my shawl."

"I can't."

Tilli scoops the shawl from the floor, shoves it at Kalle. "Sabine says it's yours now."

Kalle extends his arms with his son to Tilli. Asks gently, "Would you like to wrap the shawl around him?"

But Tilli takes a step back. Another step and she's out the door without closing it.

She runs. Not in the direction of the dory as they may expect, but away from it. Around the back of Sabine's house. Then in a wide loop beyond Lotte's house, the house she helped prepare for the Jansen children, believing she, too, belonged to their family. That's how she stayed calm when they left without her and Wilhelm to get their children from Rungholt. But then they came for Wilhelm. Only Wilhelm.

Fury rips through her. Faster she moves. Faster across the dike in a low crouch so they won't see her approach from the side. *You must grip what you cannot bear to lose.* She has trained for this ever since her own girl was stolen. Tilli screams. Screams no to the hands peeling her baby from her chest. Screams no to her mother pinning her legs apart on the kitchen table. Screams no to her father standing on the dock while the ferry takes her away. Screams no to Lotte who is climbing into the dory, Wilhelm on her hip.

"No!"

Lotte turns. Yells, "Go back to Sabine. Please."

But Tilli already grips the stern. "Let me come with you."

"You can't—" Kalle grabs the handles of the oars.

But Tilli has lost enough—her own girl, her brother, her parents—and she won't lose Wilhelm and his family. "Let me push you off. Then I'll go back." She can tell Lotte does not believe her.

But Lotte does not object. Keeps her eyes locked on Tilli's.

"Now!" Tilli rams her palms against the stern—*oh I can be cunning so cunning*—rams her entire body forward till the boat glides into deeper water.

Then, she leaps.

The boat tilts, rocks as she tumbles in headfirst.

And Kalle yells, "*Dummes Mädchen!*" Stupid girl.

Blades parallel to the water, he steadies the dory with quick, shallow strokes, two on the right, two on the left, and again.

Lotte yanks Tilli onto the center bench next to her. "We're not coming back."

"I know."

"Never. Do you understand *never*?"

Tilli nods.

"What about Heike and the others?"

Heike. She hasn't considered losing Heike because the plan was for Lotte and Kalle to bring their children back home. But now Tilli will lose Heike and Sabine and everyone at the St. Margaret Home.

"You can still get out of this boat."

"I'm coming with you." *If I knew how to keep all of them together, I would.*

"We'll live on Rungholt with our children."

"And with me."

Lotte nods.

"But how? Drop into the sea?"

"We'll step on dry ground when the island rises."

The surface of the Nordsee is flat as the dory glides into mist, easier to maneuver with the new ballast.

"Figureheads," Kalle says.

"What?" Tilli asks.

"I'll carve figureheads."

"I'll work as a midwife," says Lotte.

"I'll help with your children," says Tilli.

"Good."

"I'll ask the shipbuilder about work in the harbor," Kalle says. "Ship repair. Even unloading cargo until I find something better."

"With our skills," Lotte says, "there'll be many jobs we can do."

"I'll carve toys for the children of Rungholt." He feels the familiar clarity that tells him he's making the right choice. *That's how you know. By that clarity.* "If only I could bring my tools . . ."

"You know we can't bring anything with us," Lotte says.

". . . wrap them in oilcloth and tie them to my body."

"You can't bring anything," Tilli says.

"I don't want to arrive there poor."

"We'll have everything we need," Tilli says.

When they arrive above Rungholt, Kalle stills the oars, steadies the boat in place.

"Soon now," Lotte says.

.   .   .

As they wait for slack tide, the mist thickens, conceals them from the world till they no longer know the direction they came from. Sea and sky are one color now, pearl-gray, without borders. Wilhelm shivers in *Mutti*'s arms. Above him gray shapes and no faces. He knows the shapes are Tilli and his parents. *But what if they're not?*

They don't dare move, afraid of losing their position. Lotte wills her children to see the boat. *Here, right above you. See us here, HanneloreMartinBärbel.*

But the surface remains unbroken.

See us waiting for you to show us how to go with you.

Wilhelm screams. Throws up his arms *let-me-out-let-me-* scrambles up up and the world teeters scrambles higher and away from the gray shapes from the screams—

"Get him!" *Mutti* screams. "I can't hold on to him!"

Tilli springs to her feet and reaches into the fog and into the tangle of scrawny arms and legs that is Wilhelm kicking, grabs him around the middle to keep him from leaping— Kalle's arms then, around Wilhelm, around them all, who stand with their hands on Wilhelm, linked by his terror. Water sloshes into the boat. Cold, so cold. Lotte spreads her legs, shoves the outer edges of her feet into the junction of bottom boards and sides to keep the boat from tipping. Wilhelm stiffens into an arch, kicks and claws, but Kalle turns him swiftly, his son's back against his chest, a firmer hold because Wilhelm can only kick away from him. One arm around Wilhelm, he drops to his knees and starts bailing.

"What if there are no miracles?" Lotte asks.

Kalle is disoriented. Queasy. Feels Tilli slip past him. He cannot see her—can only sense movement and knows it's not Lotte, knows how Lotte moves.

Lotte's voice: "What if all we have are our hopes puffed up into miracles?"

"No longer cowardice then to doubt?" he asks.

"Not cowardice, no."

He keeps bailing. "What, then?"

"Courage."

"Then doubt must be the true blessing."

On the forward bench, Tilli grips the handles of the oars. Feathers the blades to stabilize the dory.

"We were so sure, Kalle."

"We were."

The spell is dissipating. Laying bare their sorrow and loss. Hannelore and Martin and Bärbel have not been alive for one year and eight months.

But Wilhelm is. Alive. And what Kalle recognizes is that he cannot be without this one—

Sobbing, Vati *sobbing. Wilhelm squirms, finds wet skin, wet face* Vati's—

And with that touch, Kalle can grieve that he'll never hold his other children, sobbing while Wilhelm consoles him. Choosing Wilhelm. Daring to hope that this son will trust him.

"We must turn back," Lotte cries, "before the current reverses."

But already the boat is turning—

Tilli. Rowing. Flying.

"I'll take Wilhelm," Lotte says.

Kalle tilts toward her voice. Makes sure her arms enfold their son before he lets go.

Tilli. Relying on the strength of her body as she leans back to submerge the blades, and lets them catch hold of the water, pulling through hard before releasing them. And again. Away from the island and the fog that billows behind them; and though they can't make out land, their course doesn't matter as much as getting away. *Are we moving in circles?*

Rowing, Tilli keeps rowing.

Then Kalle rows.

Hours of this, taking turns while the other rests.

They are cold. They are tired. They are hungry.

"Sabine will dry us off."

"We'll sit by the *Kachelofen*."

"The beekeeper will heat his soup and slice black bread."

Lotte points to a halo of light burning through the fog.

They beach their dory. Kalle swings Wilhelm onto his shoulders. And they run, Tilli's fingers around Wilhelm's ankle, her other hand in Lotte's, tethering them to her—*mine, all mine, what's left all mine*—run through the dense white in the direction of the dike and the burning white that fans out—

—its shimmer so intense that it exhilarates Lotte, wounds her, and *forever Sister Sieglinde is pulling one orange apart, golden half moons, and you open your lips, extend your tongue to receive a sliver of gold—juicy and sweet—but you won't close your eyes as you must when you receive communion. And are not struck for seeing.*

Wilhelm has his hands across *Vati*'s forehead tight because he's bouncing on *Vati*'s shoulders. *Where do I begin and where does he?* Tilli's hand around his leg tight like a new sock. On Kalle's shoulders the sweet weight of his son. On his forehead those cold little hands. Wilhelm, counting on him to carry him home. Perhaps asking himself—*Where do I begin and where does Vati?* It is even before that question is only the suggestion of that question being born in Wilhelm's soul as he rushes on his father's legs through the marshland, toward the blinding halo that reveals the crest of the dike and the crowns of the trees, closer to Wilhelm now than to his father because Wilhelm is the one riding high. And enchanted.

Acknowledgments

Many thanks to my agent, Gail Hochman: Forty years, Sweetie, of growing up together in the publishing world!

I thank the dedicated and insightful editing team at Flatiron Books—Amy Einhorn, executive vice president and publisher; Caroline Bleeke, senior editor; and Conor Mintzer, assistant editor.

Thank you to my amazing readers, Mark Gompertz and Barbara Wright, and to my husband, Gordon Gagliano—always my first reader.

In my research I learned so much from the writers and visual artists who, over many decades, explored the landscape and myths of the Friesian Islands.

PLEASE NOTE: In order to provide reading groups with the most informed and thought-provoking questions possible, it is necessary to reveal important aspects of the plot of this novel—as well as the ending. If you have not finished reading *The Patron Saint of Pregnant Girls* by Ursula Hegi, we respectfully suggest that you may want to wait before reviewing this guide.

The Patron Saint of Pregnant Girls
DISCUSSION QUESTIONS

1. Discuss the different ways in which motherhood is depicted in this novel, particularly through the stories of Lotte, Tilli, and Sabine. How are their experiences similar and different?

2. After losing her three eldest children to the hundred-year wave, Lotte tells Kalle she would sacrifice their surviving son, Wilhelm, to get the other three back. Do you sympathize with this heartbreaking perspective? How is Lotte's and Kalle's grief portrayed over the course of the novel?

3. Discuss the ways in which many people of Nordstrand view the nuns: "that they don't act like real nuns, that they float in a floaty world with art as their God; that they are dreamers." Were you surprised by their characterization? What role do they play in the story?

4. The Old Women of Nordstrand are described as "its chroniclers, its conscience, its judges." What role do they play in this story?

5. Discuss this passage: "Legends, the Old Women know, are ancient gossip; yet not all gossip leads to legends. By itself gossip won't last, but legends feed on gossip." How would you describe the difference between legends and gossip?

6. Lotte reflects: "Because there are two sides to longing, hope and the danger of letting hope devour you." What does she mean? What do the different characters long for in these pages?

7. What does Rungholt represent for the characters in this novel, especially Lotte and Kalle?

8. Herr Ludwig tells Heike: "Music is your magic . . . your very own magic. We're all magicians in a way, divining what lies beneath the surface of the ordinary and the extraordinary. And the amazing." Using this definition, how are the other main characters "magicians"? How are you?

9. What role does the Zirkus play in this novel? What is the relationship between the town and the Zirkus? Did you have a favorite character from among the Zirkus people?

10. Although Sabine loves the beekeeper, she decides that it's safer for him to marry Heike, to give her security in case Sabine can no longer take care of her: "I won't consider him for myself because I've chosen him for my daughter, this decent man who'll honor his promises and his legal duties if he agrees to marry my daughter." What do you make of their arrangement? Do you think it's fair to each of the three?

11. The girls at the St. Margaret Home come to think of Lotte as their patron saint: "Sinner and savior in one. You can identify with her. Though you're not as craven a sinner. Or as selfless a savior. You have been longing for this saint, your own patron saint." What is Lotte's relationship to the girls, especially Tilli? Discuss the ways in which they help and harm one another.

12. Did you have a favorite character among the three women at the novel's center, Lotte, Tilli, and Sabine? What do you think the future holds for these characters?

Gordon Gagliano

URSULA HEGI is the author of more than a dozen
books, including *Stones from the River, Children and
Fire, Floating in My Mother's Palm,* and *Tearing the Silence.* A German-born writer, she immigrated to
the United States at eighteen. She has served as
juror for the National Book Award and the National
Book Critics Circle. Ursula lives with her family on
Long Island and has taught writing at Stony Brook
University, UC Irvine, and Barnard College.